# CHARLESTON

# CHARLESTON

Margaret Bradham Thornton

ecco

*An Imprint of* HarperCollins*Publishers*

CHARLESTON. Copyright © 2014 by Margaret Bradham Thornton. All rights reserved. Printed in the United States of America. No part of this book may be used or reproduced in any manner whatsoever without written permission except in the case of brief quotations embodied in critical articles and reviews. For information address HarperCollins Publishers, 195 Broadway, New York, NY 10007.

HarperCollins books may be purchased for educational, business, or sales promotional use. For information please e-mail the Special Markets Department at SPsales@harpercollins.com.

A hardcover edition of this book was published in 2014 by Ecco, an imprint of HarperCollins Publishers.

FIRST ECCO PAPERBACK EDITION PUBLISHED 2015.

Designed by Suet Yee Chong
Title page painting: Alfred Hutty, Magnolia Gardens (1920), courtesy of the Gibbs Museum of Art

Library of Congress Cataloging-in-Publication Data has been applied for.

ISBN 978-0-06-233253-0

15 16 17 18 19 OV/RRD 10 9 8 7 6 5 4 3 2

To John and our children,
John Randolph, Alexandra, Elliott, and Elisha

## ACKNOWLEDGMENTS

I would like to thank:

Dan Halpern and his remarkable team at Ecco for being further proof of Paul Bowles's view, "Things don't happen, it depends on who comes along."

Ann Patty, the editor every writer hopes to find.

William and Susan Kinsolving, Bettina von Hase, early readers.

John Eastman, who has always given me brilliant advice.

My parents, for passing on their love of the Lowcountry.

# CHARLESTON

# CHAPTER ONE

A SIMPLE GESTURE, A MAN'S HAND ON A WOMAN'S SHOULDER. It could as easily not have happened. Eliza often thought about how a series of unconnected events strung out over a number of years had brought about this chance encounter between Henry and herself. Had she not applied to the Courtauld for the fellowship, had she not fallen for Jamie when he described himself as "a man abandoned by space" at a London gallery, had they not gone to the wedding of his classmate from Eton—a wedding they almost missed because of a stupid argument—she might never have seen Henry again. A similar set of attractions and invitations had brought Henry to the same country house an hour west of London. Everything that had come before—so exact and perfectly timed—had forever changed the direction she was heading. Eliza used to think that Fate had abandoned her, but now she wondered if it had its arms wrapped so tightly around her that it would never let her go.

THE SPRING OF 1990 PROMISED TO BE A SEASON OF WED-dings. May was not half over, and Eliza and Jamie were already attending their third. After the ceremony, a flat gray sky threatened rain as they walked to the tent set up on the lawn for the wedding lunch. Jamie ducked inside to get two glasses of champagne while Eliza paused to examine the seating chart. She ran her finger down the list and found her table—number seven. She began to scan the list of names to see if she knew anyone. Then came the tap on her shoulder.

"Eliza."

She turned. Something galloped hard across her heart. The man standing in front of her seemed more real than anything around her.

"My God, Henry."

"I didn't mean to scare you." He reached out and touched her arm.

"God. Henry. You know, I thought I heard you. Your laugh. In the church. And then I thought I must be crazy." Henry looked the same—thin and angular with cheekbones that pushed beyond the rectangular frame of his face. She could tell by his tanned face and hands that he still spent a lot of time outdoors.

"I saw you come into the church." Henry leaned down and whispered, "Seriously late."

"What are you doing here?"

"I came over for the wedding."

"This wedding?"

"Mmmm."

"Why?"

"Caroline."

"How do you know Caroline?"

"My mother and her mother were distant cousins. She lived

with us for one summer. About . . ." Henry put his hands in his pockets and looked down at the ground before looking back up. "Six or seven years ago."

"That's wild. It's even wilder seeing you here."

"How are you? You look great." Henry squeezed her elbow. "I heard you were about to marry a lord and take up residence in some stately home outside of London."

"Charleston." Eliza shook her head. "The farther away you go, the more social standing and money they award you."

Henry stepped back to make room for an elderly couple who held on to each other as if they were lost. He folded his arms across his chest and looked at Eliza. "So you aren't married?" He spoke in a low voice.

"No."

"Engaged?"

"No."

"Are you sure?"

"Positive."

"So no lord?"

"No lord."

"No stately home?"

"Small flat in South Kensington."

Henry turned his head and looked at her obliquely. He was amused by something. "God, it's great to see you. What are you doing here?"

"Simon is a friend of my boyfriend's. They were at Eton together," she said.

"Boyfriend?" Henry tilted his head and raised his eyebrows.

"Boyfriend." Eliza nodded. "Jamie."

"Sounds serious."

Eliza smiled.

"Jamie," Henry repeated. "English?"

"Very." Eliza looked over her shoulder to see if she could spot Jamie. He was zigzagging through the sea of colorful hats and dark jackets, holding two flutes of champagne at shoulder height. "He's just coming, I'll introduce you." Jamie passed through an involved conversation between two matrons and appeared before them.

"Sorry, darling." He handed Eliza a glass. "I ran into Lady Caledon and couldn't get away."

"Jamie, I want to introduce you to an old friend from Charleston, Henry Heyward."

Jamie held out his hand. "Jamie Barings, very nice to meet you." He took a long sip of his champagne. "You've come all the way from Charleston? How do you know Simon and Caroline?"

"Caroline's mother was a distant cousin of my mother's," Henry said.

"Caroline lived with Henry's family in Charleston for a summer," Eliza added.

"Oh, I see. Caroline's such a lovely girl. I just met her a few months ago. Simon is absolutely besotted with her," Jamie said. "Charleston, well, you have such lovely weather in the Carolinas, not this filthy rain we've had all week. I keep trying to coax Eliza to take me down there, but she always finds some reason not to."

Eliza watched Henry to see what he thought of Jamie. She knew she shouldn't care, but she did. And she knew what he was thinking—that Jamie was too English and too mannered for her.

Jamie nodded hello to two bridesmaids and moved closer to Eliza to allow them to pass. Eliza sensed they were disappointed Jamie had not introduced them to Henry.

"So when was the last time you saw each other?" Jamie lifted his champagne flute first toward Henry and then toward Eliza before taking a last sip.

Henry tilted his head sideways, but he didn't take his eyes off of Eliza. "About ten years." He looked at Eliza for her acknowledgment.

"How long are you here?" The rain was coming down hard now, and Jamie raised his voice.

"I'm going back tonight. Catching the last flight. I asked Caroline to seat me somewhere close to the exit in case I have to leave early."

Jamie looked beyond Eliza at the guests taking their seats. "I think we should probably find our table. I'm just going to put this down," Jamie said, referring to his empty glass. "Can I take yours?" Eliza handed him her untouched glass. "I'll be right back."

Henry watched Jamie disappear. "He's crazy about you."

"Perhaps," Eliza said.

Henry waited, but Eliza offered nothing more. "So, do you ever come to Charleston? I used to see your mother some, but now I never do."

"I haven't been back in a while. You knew my mother remarried?"

"I did," he said. "Ben Hastings. They don't spend much time in Charleston now, do they?"

"Not really. They spend most of their time in Middleburg, but they come down some. Sara, Ben's daughter, goes to the College of Charleston."

"What about Christmas? Do you come back for Christmas?"

"To Middleburg. My mother has everyone there. Actually I'm coming to Charleston in a few weeks for Sara's coming-out party."

"Is Jamie coming?"

"I'm not sure."

"Eliza." He took her wrist. "Promise you'll call when you get to town."

Eliza looked at Henry to see if he understood what he was asking her to do.

"Promise."

A footman's voice asked everyone to please take their seats.

"Yes, okay."

Jamie returned. Henry let go of her wrist.

"Darling, we had better find our table."

# CHAPTER TWO

Eliza wasn't certain she had made the right decision. Several times she had decided it wouldn't be wise for her to return to Charleston, but when she called to tell her mother she had too much work and too many deadlines, her mother insisted how much her coming meant to Sara. In truth, work and deadlines were not the reason Eliza was reluctant to return home. She didn't know what spending time with Henry would do to her—and she wasn't certain she wanted to take the risk to find out—and yet there had always been something about Henry she had never been able to resist.

She was flying in on the afternoon of her stepsister's debutante party, cutting the edge as finely as she dared. Eliza looked out the airplane window, down at the landscape she knew so well. She liked seeing it from such a distance. So much of her time was spent looking at images on vertical surfaces at close range—paintings hung on walls or projected onto screens. She had been thinking about distance and location in painting for some time. She had gone to an exhibit at the Marlborough Gallery of a Spanish hyperrealist who had painted with such minute precision that she had overheard someone mistake one of his compositions for a photograph. He signed all of his work with a self-portrait, no larger than a dime, painted as if it were reflected on the convex head of a silver tack. And then there was the Englishman who had covered the floor of the ground gallery of the Tate Modern with a spiral, twenty meters in diameter, made of dried wooden sticks and pocket compasses of varying sizes and shapes. The title of the installation was *What Interests Me Is the Thing That Cannot Be Located.* The work of the Spaniard and the Englishman demanded vastly different distances to be understood.

When and where she might run into Henry was something Eliza had thought about from time to time for years. She imagined running into him at the National Gallery or on the Eurostar to Paris or at the British Airways check-in at JFK. It made no sense, but Eliza sometimes caught herself looking in the mirror and smoothing out her ponytail before she left for a journey. She even half expected that in the conversations with the collectors she had traveled to meet and whose paintings she had been hired to document, Henry's name might come up with the revelation of her Charleston background, but it never did.

She reached in the seat pocket in front of her for her folder on Bonnard. She opened it and looked at the image of Bonnard's *Déjeuner* one more time. A man and a woman sat at a table bearing a feast of fruit. Eliza still wasn't convinced, as Jamie had been, that this couple was not waiting for someone. Bonnard had, after all, painted an empty chair between them. Across the top of her draft essay on Bonnard she wrote, "What does it mean—the thing that cannot be located?" She would have two weeks in Charleston to figure this out.

Eliza returned her gaze to the window. Thousands of feet below, roads that curved and faded without apparent reason snaked through large green untouched forest. Unlike the ordered rectangles and quadrilaterals and polygons of the English country-side that fit together like irregular pieces of a jigsaw puzzle, every-thing here was sinuous, unordered, untamed. The only straight line she could see was the Southern Seaboard Railroad and the power lines that cut sharp tracks through large expanses of timber. Toward the coast, the solid forests gave way to winding rivers and irregular patches of marsh. Eliza guessed that the dark river that curled in lazy loops was the Ashley River—it reminded her of the white sugar icing her grandmother used to let her serpentine across the top of her lemon cakes. Eliza watched the plane's shadow flee in front of them across land that disappeared into marshes. She enjoyed the weightless feeling of the shadow's swift escape pre-cisely because running away from something or someone had never felt so easy.

As they approached Charleston, the waterways grew wider and the creeks and tributaries so numerous that it looked as if one big rainstorm would submerge the city. A local poet, long deceased, had referred to Charleston as a "sea-drinking city." As they descended, Eliza could see all the houses lined up along the marshes with long thin docks running to the deep water. She watched a motorboat making a tight circle to pick up a waterskier.

Eliza wondered where Jamie was now. Jamie had gotten angry with her for her ambivalence about his coming to Charleston. When the National Trust commission had come, he hastily arranged the trip without consulting her. He had always been so wonderful to her, and she hated that she made him unhappy. Was she looking for something that didn't exist? Did she even know what love was? Did she know the answer to the question she had asked herself before she left—could she live without Jamie? But was that even the right question to ask? She had lived without Henry. Maybe it was all as simple as she did not love Jamie enough.

The afternoon heat had not yet left the day when Eliza's flight arrived in Charleston. Eliza remained seated and reorganized her satchel while she waited for the other passengers to push past. She had told her mother not to send anyone, she would take a taxi. At the baggage claim, she looked at the people gathered around her, and she realized she could be in any city. There was not one familiar face—only the same redcap who had been there whenever she had flown home from college.

Eliza wrestled her bag off the luggage carousel and headed for the taxi rank. She paused for a moment to look at the palmetto trees outlined against the sky. Almost another three hours of daylight left, but the descending sun had already begun to pull the color out of the sky. The air was soft and heavy. It was as if someone had put an arm around her. A battered yellow station wagon appeared and a small black man hopped out. "Where are you going, young lady?"

"Downtown. Church Street."

"Alrighty, hop aboard."

He held the door for Eliza. They proceeded down the wide parklike retreat from the airport and then onto Interstate 26. The driver drummed his fingers on his steering wheel to the rhythm of Jr. Walker & the All Stars' "Road Runner." Eliza was relieved that Jamie had not come with her. She was tired, and she wanted to feel what it was like to come back to the place without having to translate or explain. Had Jamie come, he would not have been able to resist telling her that the roadway into Charleston was "oversigned" with billboards tempting tourists with promises of perfect beaches, comfortable hotel rooms, endless meals; that Charlestonians' reference to a colonnaded porch as a piazza was the equivalent of calling it an Italian square; and that Charlestonians' pronunciation of the

French street names was not only incorrect but also incomprehensible. He would, in his mock serious tone, begin discussing, as he did on every trip they had taken, the addition of a new chapter to his imaginary work *A Guide for the Perplexed*.

On the way into town, Eliza sat back and let herself be soothed by the clunk-clunking of the tires over the sections of concrete, past the acres of factories and worn-out land, until the tip of the Cooper River Bridge appeared above the railing. When the signs pointing to the turnoffs for King and Meeting streets loomed overhead, Eliza asked the driver to follow the sign to Mount Pleasant and then get off at the East Bay exit. "Whatever be your pleasure," he said as they dipped under the overpass and headed up the ramp toward the Cooper River Bridge, then down the East Bay exit and stopped at the light.

Nothing had changed. The massive three-storied Faber-Ward house, built in the 1830s and converted into a hotel for freed slaves during the Civil War, still stood haunted and empty—facing land that, for as long as Eliza could remember, was used by the Port Authority for stacking the containers of cargo ships. They continued on down East Bay Street past the Slave Market, which catered to the tourist trade, and crossed Broad Street. Soon the buildings on the east side gave way to a seawall and promenade, and the name changed from East Bay to East Battery. There was something soothing about coming back to a place where there was nothing new to see, where everything was known, where there were only confirmations and never any questions.

Eliza asked the driver to go all the way down East Battery past the towering antebellum houses and then loop back around White Point Gardens to Church Street. She wanted to take the long way home. She knew that once she left the taxi her journey would no longer feel free and effortless like the shadow of the plane she had been watching. As they turned onto Church Street and bumped slowly over the uneven brick paving of the streets, Eliza said, "It's the pale stone-colored house on the left."

THE PAST WAS A KIND OF WEATHER THAT PUSHED IN FROM the harbor and lingered long. Eliza stood on the sidewalk and looked up at the tall three-story stucco house that had been in her father's family for six generations. The Richardson-Poinsett house was a typical Charleston single house—two major rooms on each floor, the narrow side of the house facing the street and the length stretching back into a deep plot of land. As an only child, Eliza had had the entire third floor to herself. The Poinsett house, as it was now called, was distinguished with a double lot and a manicured lawn. In Charleston, houses were heritage and were sold only if they had to be. When Eliza's mother, widowed for nearly a decade, remarried eight years ago, she had moved with her husband to his farm in Middleburg, but the house and garden were maintained as if the family were still living there.

Instead of entering the front doorway to the piazza, she turned the handle of the heavy wrought-iron garden gate and pushed it open. The garden's lawn was surrounded by a wide border of densely planted China pinks and white and pale lavender heliotropes. Her mother had written that she had found two lead eighteenth-century plant labels and was going to fill the borders with these historic plants. Eliza walked to the back of the garden toward the kitchen house where she had kept a vegetable and fruit garden—figs, oranges, tomatoes, squash, lettuce. She had loved going each spring just after Easter with her mother to Cross Seed Company to pick out packets of seeds and small plants in cardboard containers.

Eliza set her bag down and lifted a tea olive branch, heavy with dark waxy leaves and small white flowers, to her face. She inhaled the sweet softness of the white blossoms. The scent made her feel more alive, and she broke off a small stem. She had wondered what it would feel like to be back. She didn't know if planning to stay for two weeks had been the right decision. She had worked hard to construct detours around parts of her memory that included Henry. She had work she needed to finish, and she had convinced herself that coming back to a place that didn't have any of the distractions of London would give her the freedom to complete everything. But she slightly suspected that she was daring herself to come back—to prove to herself that all that had happened between her and Henry didn't matter anymore. And besides, looking at her life in London from so far away might help her decide what to do next. Or maybe it was just as simple as missing her father and wanting to be as close to him as possible. She didn't believe in spirits or ghosts, but she always felt his presence in this house. She wished he could have known everything she had been doing these past years. The screen door of the back porch was unlatched.

"Hello? Mom? Sara?"

"Eliza." Her mother's voice was punctuated by the sharp taps of her high heels on the hardwood floor in the front hall. She came through the dining room with her arms open and hugged and kissed her daughter. She wore a simple silk champagne-colored evening gown. "Oh my, I do wish you had let us pick you up from the airport. How was your flight? You look exhausted." She called up to the third floor, "Sara, Eliza's here." She paused. "Oh dear, I hope she heard me. We're going off in a few minutes, we're late as it is. Ben phoned and said everything was in good order." Eliza's mother checked her watch. "The guests are going to arrive before we do. Sara!"

"Is Cornelia here?"

"No, dear, she only comes now on Mondays and Thursdays. She wanted to come and wait for you, but I told her you weren't getting in until quite late and everything would be rushed. Do you need any help deciding what you are going to wear?"

"I brought the dress we found on the King's Road when you visited."

"The black one?"

Eliza nodded.

"Oh, that will look lovely, but I do love you in color. It must be wrinkled in that case."

"No, I'm sure it's fine, I wrapped it in tissue paper. If it needs ironing, I can do it myself."

"Are you sure?"

"Absolutely."

"Oh dear, where is Sara?" She turned and looked up the stairs. "Sara!"

"I'll run up," Eliza said.

"You don't mind my rushing off?"

"No, not at all," Eliza said. "I'm desperate to take a hot bath." But what she really wanted was the house to be quiet again.

"I hope your room isn't too hot. I put a fan up there this morning. We'll see you tonight. Don't be too late. Oh, Eliza, it's so good to have you home."

Eliza was already halfway up the first flight of stairs when her mother called to her. "Eliza, I almost forgot. Henry came by and dropped off a note for you. It's in the tray on the hall table."

She heard her mother pass through the dining room into the kitchen. She turned and walked slowly back down the stairs. A small cream envelope with her name written in the center lay on the silver tray. Eliza recognized the distinctive rhythm of Henry's handwriting, somewhere between printing and script. He always started his letters from the bottom, never the top—so that each word seemed weighted to the line. She looked at the letter, turned it over several times, but did not open it, and then began walking up the stairs, testing herself.

Sara's room was across the hall from Eliza's on the third floor. She knocked on Sara's door. "Sara?"

"Eliza." Sara opened the door and greeted Eliza with a hug and a kiss. "Oh, Eliza, it's so sweet of you to come back for this. I'm so nervous. How do I look?" Sara held her arms out to the side of her white strapless ball gown and twisted left then right.

"Beautiful," Eliza said.

"Do I have on too much mascara?"

Eliza leaned toward Sara and looked closely. "No, you look great, just be sure you don't rub your eyes."

"What time is it?"

Eliza checked her watch. "Quarter past six."

Sara fanned her hands in front of her face. "I was supposed to be there by six for photographs. I know I am going to trip in these heels."

"Keep your eyes up, don't look down, that's the trick. And take them off to go down these stairs."

"Good idea," Sara said as she leaned down to take off her shoes. She gathered her dress in one hand, shoes in the other, and proceeded down the stairs.

Eliza heard her mother and Sara call good-bye and the front door slam shut. Eliza returned downstairs to retrieve her suitcase. She paused at the entrance to the front parlor. Everything was just as it had been when she left—the same pale wall colors, the same silk curtains, the same fabrics on chairs and sofas in the same positions. The air held a scent of lavender. She walked across the hall to the dining room. She liked seeing all of the familiar objects—the tall long-case clock that had belonged to her great-grandfather, the portraits of family members, her grandmother's silver service, her father's framed and ordered collection of early southern maps. She stopped to look at the eighteenth-century thermometer that hung on the wall. On a silver plate written in perfect script were various marks on the right-hand side of the scale. Across from 212 was WATER BOILS. She continued reading vertically down. SPIRITS BOIL 176 degrees, FEVER HEAT 112, BLOOD HEAT 98, SUM. HEAT 76, TEMPERATE 55, FREEZING 32. She had never considered, until now, why anyone would need to know at what temperature spirits boil.

Eliza carried her suitcase slowly up the two flights of stairs and opened the door to her room. It overlooked the garden, and the pale peach color of the walls made it feel as if the sun were always shining there. She walked to the window and looked down on the tops of the magnolia and live oaks in the garden below. The view always made her feel as if she were in the safest tree house in the world. She had chosen her flat in South Kensington because the bedroom looked out onto a beautiful and ancient sycamore and had reminded her of her bedroom back home. She wandered around her room, touching all the things she loved. The mirrored glass box where she kept all the treasures she and her father had found—shark teeth from the banks of Pinckney Island; an arrowhead from the Combahee River; shards of Indian pottery from an excavation site at Willtown Bluff; three Victorian glass marbles, a small bone cat that must have been from a little girl's bracelet, an old shoe buckle, all found in their garden—and two silver dollars her father had given her when she had lost her two front teeth.

Eliza opened her closet—her clothes were as she had left them—nothing had been touched. She had always been expected to return. She looked up at her bedroom ceiling, where her father had drawn a colored map in blues and greens of all of the waterways and rivers and islands around Charleston. She always wondered if he would have been happier as an artist rather than as an architect. She guessed the demands of supporting a family had pushed him toward architecture. She could still hear his voice telling her bedtime stories about his travels to places on the map. She had taken journeys that could not have been imagined by the map that lay above her. She remembered a line Jamie had quoted from a novel about a journey being defined as a gesture inscribed in space. And now she wondered about those words. Were journeys gestures, or were they something else?

Eliza sat on the edge of her bed and slid Henry's note from its envelope.

> Dear Eliza,
> I'll pick you up at seven.
> —Henry

How unlike the playful notes he had, over a decade ago, tucked into pockets of her jackets or jeans. He had referred to himself differently each time with such soubriquets as the "keeper of the flame" or "your most devoted and obedient servant." Now he was just Henry. What is he doing? she thought. Had her mother known Henry was coming?

Eliza suddenly wished that she had several hours to herself before she saw Henry. She kicked off her shoes and pushed herself up to draw a bath. She filled an empty glass with water and placed the tea olive blossom in it. She undressed and sank slowly in the hot bathwater. She listened through the raised windows to the breeze in the laurel oak that almost sounded like a slow kind of applause. She could hear the distant sounds of the city, the drawl of a carriage tour guide punctuated by the clips of the hoofs of a horse pulling a wagon, voices of a brigade of children—loud and shrill—passing by on bicycles. She reached down and checked her watch, which lay on top of her discarded clothes—6:40. She slipped lower into the hot water and considered where she was. When she had first met Jamie he asked her where home was, and she had paused before answering. "Charleston," she had said, possibly more in default than in affirmation. Eliza had thought from time to time about her pause. Would Charleston always be home to her even if she never returned? Would it always be home to her even if she didn't want it to be?

At 6:45 she pushed herself out of the bath and wrapped a towel around herself. She opened her suitcase and lifted the tissue paper she had wrapped around her dress to keep it from getting wrinkled. She laid her dress on her bed. She thought she could get by without running an iron over it. She hadn't given what to wear to this party much thought. She had fallen in love with the simple black dress with the tight waist and slashed neckline that she had found in a vintage clothing stall on the King's Road the last time her mother had come to visit. The stall keeper pronounced it a Pauline Trigère 1956, but Eliza didn't need to believe him to love the dress. She pulled her hair back in a tight ponytail and walked down to the first-floor parlor to check her appearance in the French gilt pier mirror that had belonged to her grandmother. She looked pale and tired. If only she could have had one day of rest before she saw Henry, before she saw anyone really. She knew she would be able to slip back into this world without missing a beat, but she would be noticed. One of the reasons she had never considered coming back to Charleston was that she had wanted to be in places where things did change. And maybe that was one of the reasons she had fallen for Jamie, nothing was ever the same with him. In fact, she used to joke that one of the guiding principles of his life was the "Baring Law of No Repetition." But Eliza knew, too, that one of the reasons she had not come back was Henry. The bells of St. Michael's began to ring, the long-case clock followed a beat later. God, he would be here any minute.

# CHAPTER THREE

AT 7:09 ELIZA HEARD THE IRON GARDEN GATE CREAK OPEN.

"Eliza?" Henry called through the screen door of the kitchen. He braced his hand against the architrave, as if to prevent himself from falling in. He wore a dilapidated white dinner jacket so warped that the front hem was at least three inches longer than the back.

"How did you know I didn't have a date?" Her words came as much as a surprise to her as to Henry.

"How about a kiss hello first?"

"Sorry," she said. "I didn't mean to sound like that."

Henry leaned forward and kissed her. "God, Eliza." She took a step back.

Henry moved away and leaned against the architrave. He held his hands behind his back. "It was very simple. I conspired with your mother. Actually I dropped by to see her and told her I had seen you at a wedding in England and that you said you were coming back for Sara's party and would she please put you with me for the evening."

"How did you know I wouldn't come with Jamie?"

"I took a chance. I was fearless. I met with your mother and spread my heart out as evidence in the case, and she conceded. So look, you know, you did promise me that you would call when you got to Charleston. I can absolve you of your guilt for not having called—you've been here"—Henry pushed the sleeve of his jacket up and checked his watch—"what? A couple of hours?—by coming with me. And I have saved you from the clutches of Edward McGee or one of those, shall we say, corpulent Bennett boys."

"My mother wouldn't have put me with any of them."

Henry put his hands in his pockets and shrugged. "Maybe not, but not many bachelors—eligible or otherwise—are left." He smiled at Eliza. "I'm one of the few. Furthermore and most importantly, I've come out of retirement for you. I don't go to debutante parties anymore. I haven't gone to one in—God"—he ran his left hand through his hair—"I don't know—since the last time you cooked for me."

"Henry, I've never cooked for you."

"Really, you sure? Not even breakfast after some party or . . ." He was trying to lead her down an avenue she did not want to visit.

"Okay, Eliza." Henry raised his hands in a gesture of surrender. "I'll stop. You may have forgotten me, but I can still read your looks. You know we could stay here if you . . ."

"I have to go."

"Yes, of course." He held his arm for her. "You can ditch me once we get there. You look great by the way. That doesn't look like a Charleston dress."

"It's not," she said as she pulled the kitchen door shut and turned the lock.

"Didn't think so."

"Looks like your same old white dinner jacket."

"It is."

When they reached the street, Henry asked, "Which way? Right or left?"

"Right is probably shorter," Eliza said.

"Then left it is," Henry said and moved Eliza to his left side so he would be between her and the street.

They walked down Church Street to White Point Gardens. Henry paused and surveyed the large rectangular park canopied by rows of live oak trees. "Let's walk around the park once before we go. I want to hear what you've been doing in London. Studying or working?"

"Henry, I should . . ."

"We'll walk quickly." He put his arm behind her to sweep her forward.

An ancient black Lincoln Continental motored by.

"Was that Edward McGee?" Eliza asked.

Henry nodded. "Dressed in black tie, but never without his 'traveler.'" Henry referred to the large plastic cup, filled most certainly with bourbon and ice, that Edward always had, after 5:00 P.M., balanced between the windshield and dashboard. "I hope you are beginning to appreciate what a savior I am."

"Is he still living in Ansonborough?"

"Everything is pretty much as it was when you left. Edward's still searching for distinction in imaginary causes, Larry's still looking after him, and when Larry goes on one of his drinking binges, Edward's lawn goes uncut for weeks, and some neighbor complains to the city, and then Edward takes up arms—nothing has changed. So, tell me, in London, studying or working?"

"Both actually."

"Both? That's a lot, isn't it?"

"I've just finished a fellowship at the Courtauld, and I've been working as an assistant to my adviser. He's writing a companion to the catalogue raisonné of Magritte."

"Man with the bowler hat and briefcase."

"In the clouds. That's the one."

"That's fantastic, that's impressive."

"Yeah, it's been great. When I first started, I was a bit of a glorified secretary. Gradually he started relying on me to do everything—typing up his notes, making corrections in the text, writing letters to collectors for permission to photograph their paintings."

"I bet you know where all Magritte's paintings are."

"Actually, I do."

"Fair to assume none are in Charleston?"

"Fair to assume."

"So what's next?"

"I need to finish work on Magritte by mid-June. My adviser has asked me to write an essay on Tennessee Williams and Pierre Bonnard for a book he is editing. That will take some time. But after that, I haven't decided. I have an offer to continue on at the Courtauld, but I've been thinking about applying to a Ph.D. program in art history in the States. I've also been doing some work for one of the contemporary art galleries in London—Jasper Marlowe. They offered me a full-time position, but I'm . . ."

Henry stopped to point out a flock of pelicans sitting in a row along a low horizontal branch of a live oak. "Look, Eliza, I've never seen that, have you?"

She stopped and looked away.

"Oh no," he said. "What have I done now?"

"Why don't I think you're listening to me?"

"I am, I promise, Eliza, I'm just thrilled to see you."

"What did I just say?"

"You've been telling me all about Magritte and an essay you're planning to write on Tennessee Williams and Pierre Bonnard, and after all that, what you're thinking about doing—continuing on at the Courtauld or applying to a Ph.D. program in the U.S., or accepting a full-time position at a contemporary art gallery in London." He hesitated, snapped his fingers, and pointed at Eliza. "Jasper Marlowe." Henry paused. "A little apology," he said. "Just a little bit. In honor of this remarkable retinue of pelicans."

"Sorry."

"Here, let's cut across to the bandstand, then we'll head directly to Sara's party. So, tell me, what's the relationship between Williams and Bonnard?"

"Williams saw a painting by Bonnard at an art fair in San Francisco in 1939, and he wrote a poem about it. But Jamie has worried me that I may have the wrong painting."

"Jamie? Your Jamie?"

"Yes." The sound of Jamie's name threw her off balance. "My Jamie."

"Interesting, so what do you think you will do?"

"You mean about the painting?"

"No—staying on at the Courtauld or—"

"Oh. I'm not sure, I've got to figure that out."

Henry was smiling at her.

"Henry, you know I just came for Sara's party. I'm going back in two weeks."

"I know, Eliza, I am . . . well, I'm just happy to see you. That's all. And since you haven't asked me one question about myself, I'll be brave, launch forth, and tell you. I am the publisher of *The Charleston Courier.*"

Eliza tilted her head sideways, as if she did not understand what he was saying.

Henry put his hand on his chest. "Really. Eliza, cross my heart."

"Really?"

"Really."

"Not sure I believe you."

"You should, you really should. See for yourself, proof is on the back page of the paper every day."

As they approached the large Greek Revival house owned by Sara's godfather, the faint sounds of a band could be heard. The Robert William Roper House was the grandest house along High Battery. With its south-facing double-height portico supported by massive Ionic columns that stretched almost twenty feet high, it was the most photographed house in Charleston. White tents had been set up in the back of the property on a well-tended rectangle of lawn. The older crowd had been invited for 6:30 P.M. The under-thirties for 8:00 P.M. It was now that time of dusk when the grass and foliage appeared greener, the men's white dinner jackets sharper, and the women's evening dresses more colorful than at any other time of day.

Eliza waved to Sara, who stood with her father and Eliza's mother. Eliza signaled to her mother and Ben they were going to bypass the receiving line. Ben winked and blew her a kiss. As they moved forward, they heard, "Well, I'll be damned. Eliza Poinsett. We all heard you had gone and married an English lord." The man who spoke was Edward McGee, looking just as disheveled as always. "Come here, sughah, and give a kiss. So what are you doing with this scoundrel?"

"How are you, Edward?" Eliza asked.

"I'm heading home," he said. "I'm handing it over to the young people. Eliza, it's great to see you, sughah. Don't stay away so long next time."

Edward stepped closer to Henry. He pulled his face into a long frown. "When is my article going to appear?"

"It's under consideration," Henry said.

"I'm looking forward to seeing it, you hear." Edward started to turn away but then stopped to add, "Let me know if they need a photograph." Edward stretched his neck and smoothed the front of his dress shirt down with the palm of his hand, as if preparing for that very moment.

Henry nodded. "I will certainly do that."

"You watch out for him." Edward looked at Eliza and pointed to Henry. "You take care of yourself, sughah."

Eliza turned to Henry. "What article?"

"He's written a long article, in fact, a very long article, on the difference between northerners and Yankees, northerners being the educators and Yankees being the carpetbaggers. Edward calls my office every week for the publication date."

"So you are the publisher."

Henry nodded.

"You aren't going to publish it, are you?"

"No, of course not. But now you see what I've saved you from. Let's go find a drink." He took her hand and serpentined their way through the clusters of people. Waiters and waitresses glided around the crowd with trays of ham biscuits, shrimp paste sandwiches, and mini crab cakes. Bartenders stood stationed behind tables covered in white tablecloths. White lawn chairs had been arranged in small groups for the weary.

The band was playing a repertoire of Nat King Cole songs and had just started "Mr. Cole Won't Rock and Roll" when a large top-heavy man, drink in hand, stepped alone out onto the empty dance floor. He started sliding across the floor, swiveling his feet, dipping and raising shoulders and elbows, marching knees up and down, as if he were trying to disassemble his skeleton to the beat of the song. Arms now down at his side, shuffling baby steps, as if wearing flippers, he tilted his head and smiled beatifically at someone on the edge of the dance floor. The bass player was laughing so hard he could hardly keep playing. Henry and Eliza watched until the song finished and the man stepped off the dance floor, mopped his brow, and headed straightaway to a bar.

"Who is that?" Eliza asked.

Henry shrugged his shoulders. "Don't know. But without question someone's long-forgotten second cousin. What would you like?" Henry asked. "How about a glass of champagne to celebrate your homecoming."

"A club soda would be great."

"Always the wild one, Eliza."

Eliza watched Henry disappear into the crowd. Do we always see with our memories? she wondered. If she had just met Henry for the first time tonight, who would she see? She remembered the first time they had met—twelve years ago—at a summer party at Fenwick Hall. She was seventeen and he was twenty. She had always known who he was, but Henry went to boarding school and always stayed at Oakhurst when he was home. Even back then he seemed to embody confidence and calm—as if he had everything under control and always would. Henry still had that poise.

Eliza looked across the crowd. She didn't recognize as many people as she thought she would. She had heard that a lot of new people had moved to Charleston and were buying the houses that had been in the same families for years. The property taxes and rising real estate prices had pushed many of those she had grown up with to the suburban areas west across the Ashley River or east across the Cooper River to Mount Pleasant.

Henry returned and handed her a silver plastic cup that was bright pink on the inside. "How does it feel to be back among us?"

"Nice," she said. "There is something so easy about it." Charleston was a club, a small society, and if you belonged once you always belonged. You didn't have to prove yourself or work hard at membership. It had been given to you at birth, and no matter where you lived, it would always be open to you. Eliza understood that she could always come home. "There are many people I don't recognize."

"Sure you do." Henry stood behind her and leaned down. "Over there in the blue dress is Mrs. Middleton—she'll be by, my guess"—Henry checked his watch—"in five, seven minutes max, to find out what you are doing here. A few years ago she turned to selling real estate. She knocks on the doors of newcomers and tells them she doesn't approve of northerners moving into the city, yet she can't resist selling them houses or going to their parties. Apparently she often recites the inventory of their furniture and pictures, both good and bad, to the members of her bridge club. She is speaking to Peter Marshall, a rather tricky art dealer from New York who opened a gallery down here a couple of years ago. He will be trying to find out how to join the board of the Gibbes, and she will be trying to get information on the value of someone else's painting." Henry put his hands on her upper arms and turned her. "Over there in the navy dress is Alexandra Lockwood, you remember her, she was in your class at Ashley Hall."

"A year behind." Eliza could tell that Alexandra had already become one of the young Charleston matrons who kept busy with the Junior League, church work, and children. In another ten years, her life would be indistinguishable from her mother's.

"She is talking to Cal Edwards, who is still unmarried and is still living with his mother. Isn't he your very distant cousin? Alexandra married a nice fellow from North Carolina or Tennessee, though not the match her mother would have wished for. He is a banker with First Federal in Spartanburg, but they are moving back here soon. He came to see me about a job at the paper, but we didn't have anything for him. To her left is Mrs. Izard who is still living in that large house on Rutledge Avenue and has turned her swimming pool into a turtle pond. Apparently turtles have become her passion. And your mother is talking to the mayor. He is probably explaining why the board of the Coastal Conservation League is wrong to oppose his plans for port expansion. He had that same look on his face when he came by my office last week to discuss his position. Just beyond them the tall man—heading to the bar—is Dr. Walker—who is still making consistent misdiagnoses. And of course you remember Charlie."

Charlie. God. She never thought he would make it past thirty. She remembered the night he won his bet that he could drive a car with no hands through the four blocks of the open-air Slave Market going fifty miles an hour. Any small miscalculation and he would have hit one of the supporting brick arches head-on.

"The last time I saw Charlie, I think he was in a Boston Whaler headed out to the jetties to fish for sharks with a baseball bat and a revolver. And come to think of it, I think you were with him," Eliza said.

"I might very well have been," Henry said. "But Charlie has reformed his ways. He's not nearly as wild as he used to be, in fact, he's not wild at all. He decided he wanted to be a doctor like his father after all, and now he's considered one of the best cardiologists in the Southeast."

"My mother had mentioned how well Charlie was doing. And she said he had married someone from Beaufort?"

"A rather quiet, Junior League type. Ginny is very sweet, always in pink and green. Couldn't be nicer though. They live up the street from us in Charlie's grandmother's house. They have twin boys— very bright six-year-olds who last November set their lawn on fire."

"How do you set a lawn on fire?"

"Apparently they had convinced the gardener to keep a large pile of leaves for an extra day so they could play Geronimo. Within an hour of the gardener leaving for the day, they set the pile on fire."

"Sounds like they take after Charlie."

"Clearly. And you know Drayton," Henry said, pushing his chin in the direction of a tall lean man with a drink in each hand. "He's

taken over his father's real estate business selling plantation properties. He's sold several to people who have made a lot of money
on Wall Street. He's gotten amazing prices for them. He's speaking
with Ralph and Nina Morton. They're from somewhere in Arkansas.
Ralph's made a fortune in fast-food franchises. They just bought the
Sword Gate House, and they, most likely, are now trying to find an
important plantation so they can mimic the weekend migrations of
Charlestonians out to their country houses. A few years ago Drayton
published a book on the plantations of the Cooper and Santee rivers. Now he's working on one on the plantations of the ACE Basin.
He's asked me to take some photos for it. Here, let's sit down."

Henry led Eliza to a cluster of unoccupied chairs. He pulled his
chair closer to hers. "Right over there, don't look now, is Charlotte
Pinckney. Her husband, Lucas, just ran off with the male curator of
the Nathaniel Russell House. Charlotte is talking to Mary Elizabeth
Frampton and Elliott Mikell. Mary Elizabeth is compiling a new
recipe collection, *Secret Charleston Family Receipts*. She's probably trying to charm Charlotte into parting with one. Her goal is
to include only secret recipes. Apparently she formed a Bible stud-
ies group for the sole purpose of finding passages to quote when
she solicits cherished family recipes. Mary Elizabeth got divorced a
couple of years ago. You remember her husband, Tradd, don't you?
Never worked a day in his life."

Eliza was surprised at how much she was enjoying Henry's gossip. She felt as if he were reminding her of characters in a much-
loved novel she had not read for some time. And Henry knew what
he was doing—he was staying on safe territory. In telling her about
everybody, he could be close and conspiratorial while avoiding any
mention of their past.

Henry lowered his voice, "I suppose you haven't acquired any
secret recipes?"

She shook her head.

"Still can't cook—still my Eliza." Henry took a sip of his drink. "So you haven't changed that much." He nodded his head toward Mrs. Langdon. "She is still terrorizing tourists she takes on her walking tours. See the woman she is talking to? That's Catherine Walsh." Eliza looked at the large woman with perfectly coiffed hair, wearing an aqua chiffon dress, a large diamond necklace, and an emerald-studded brooch in the shape of a peacock. "They moved down from Greenwich. Her husband was chief executive of a Fortune 500 company. They bought Lowndes Grove, up by Hampton Park. She lives rather grandly—butlers, laundresses, drivers, hot and cold running staff. She hired this majordomo—Ian or Roderick or something like that—who was grander than grand. She and her husband left him in charge when they went off to London for the season—Ascot, Wimbledon, you know—and when they came back unexpectedly, they found Ian and all of his friends lounging around dressed up in her clothes and jewelry. She is probably explaining to Mrs. Langdon why she decided to burn all of her frocks instead of giving them to charity."

"Henry, how do you know all of this? I don't remember you being such a gossip."

"I run a newspaper. Remember Louisa Eveleigh, my cousin? You may not. She's about ten years older than you."

"Vaguely, she had long dark brown hair and was rather wild as I remember."

"More loud than wild. She's our new society editor."

"*The Charleston Courier* has a society page?"

"By all means. Louisa founded it. Her husband got into some trouble four or five years ago. He was in the Trust Department at Citizens and Southern, he almost went to jail, they divorced, and Louisa had to get a job. She worked in a jewelry shop on King Street for a while, got bored, and came to me with this idea. It was hard to say no, given that our great-grandfather was the founder of the paper. She's been amazingly successful. You'd be surprised what people will do to get their name in the paper. Every Tuesday. It's called 'Doin' the Charleston'—Louisa's idea, not mine," he added with a raised brow. "You should have a look at it. In fact, I should get you a subscription to keep you up-to-date, so that the next time you come home, and"—Henry lifted his silver cup in a gesture of a toast—"I am pulling for a next time—you can save me from moon-lighting as the town gossip for you."

Henry took a sip of his drink. "And look who is approaching—right on time." As the rather large woman in a deep blue satin gown approached, Henry stood up. "Mrs. Middleton."

"Henry, my dear, how are you? I haven't seen you at one of these parties in, I don't know how long. It's a shame, you know, Virginia was just in town. If I had known you were going to be here, I would have made her stay and come."

"Mrs. Middleton, you remember Eliza."

"Oh my, Eliza, I wondered if that were you. Virginia was just saying how she hadn't seen you for such a long time. She reminded me of the time the two of you performed *Macbeth* in our back garden. My word, Virginia and I had a laugh about that. I was convinced one of you would go on to become a famous actress. Now tell me, I ran into your mother, and she said you were living in London."

"I am. I just came back for Sara's party."

"Now someone told me you were engaged to an English lord."

"No, just a rumor."

"Well, what a pity," Mrs. Middleton said, though she looked pleased with Eliza's answer. "Now where did I hear that? I think it was in your paper, Henry. Yes, I'm sure I read it in Louisa's column. Anyway," Mrs. Middleton continued without pausing, "I've just been speaking with Lydia Alston. I tried to talk to her about who should replace Charles Lowndes on the Symphony Board, but all Lydia can think about is Allington. She and Richard are beside themselves about Allington. After three years studying art history at George-town, he says he is changing his major from art history to criminal psychology. Apparently Allington took a course last year where they went on a field trip to one of the Washington prisons, and now all Allington wants to do is visit prisons. Can you imagine the type of people he meets in those places?"

As Mrs. Middleton continued, Eliza wondered if Mrs. Middle-ton's scattered monologue was a result of years and years of going to the same parties with the same people. She was shrewder than she appeared though. Eliza remembered Mrs. Middleton being cor-rectly suspicious twenty years ago when Eliza and Virginia had used her Jean Patou Joy Eau de Toilette as a substitute for the extract of vanilla called for in a batch of cookies they were making for the Ashley Hall bake sale.

"Eliza dear," Mrs. Middleton called her to attention. "Do you know anything about the University of Lyon? Lydia and Richard sent Allington there to study French as a way of trying to deflect his fascination with the underworld. It was Richard's view that dealing indirectly—not hitting anything on its head—was the way to go. He even arranged for a friend with a villa in Cap d'Antibes to have Allington for the weekend. Glorious villa, you know, but apparently Allington learned enough French to find his way to the prison outside of Marseille. Allington came back with a pierced ear, a strand of that glorious blond hair of his dyed black, and a tat-too across his derriere relating to, well, something, some nonsense. I told Lydia that maybe Allington was going through some poetic phase, you know like that French poet, oh what is his name, when Virginia was here we watched a movie about him played by Leo-nardo DiCaprio."

"Rimbaud," Eliza said.

"Who?" Mrs. Middleton looked confused.

"Arthur Rimbaud. The Fr—"

"Yes. Of course. Exactly." Mrs. Middleton snapped her fingers. Henry pretended to take a sip of his drink.

Mrs. Middleton resumed, "But Lydia told me there is more to it than that. That it is much deeper than some poetic phase. Apparently Richard's great concern was whether Allington had done all of this before or after his visit to Cap d'Antibes. It was shortly after Allington's return that Richard bought himself one of those metal detectors with the headsets. He now walks all over town with that thing on his head. I don't know what on earth he hopes to find. It's all too much for poor Richard. I don't know how Lydia is going to fulfill her duties as president of the Symphony—" She paused for a moment, as if she were studying something far away. "Do excuse me, I just want to have a word with Charlotte. I think they may be getting ready to put their house on the market, and I want to tell her I may have someone for it."

They watched Mrs. Middleton push her way through the guests toward Charlotte. Eliza turned to Henry. "In your paper?"

"I plead innocent. If it were in it, then Louisa put it in just to get me to stop pining for you all these years. But I'm almost certain it was not."

"Then why does everyone think I married a lord?"

"Because you know, Eliza, come on, everybody here has always loved you. You were the perfect girl—pretty, bright, charming, of course they all wanted you to marry some rich, titled aristocrat. It's Charleston's own version of kindness and support. It's what they think you deserve. And sounds like you have come pretty close—a Barings? If I recall there are a number of titles in that family and a bank, I might add."

"Nowhere close to Jamie, but he does work half of his time for his family's merchant bank. The other half he makes documentary films in remote third world countries." The mention of Jamie's name reminded Eliza how far away his world was from all that surrounded her now. She wondered how long it would take before he got restless in a place like Charleston.

"So he is an explorer?"

"No, filmmaker, but his last film was about an eighty-year-old explorer who was born in England but grew up in Kenya . . ."

A tall woman with gray hair pulled back in a tight bun and wearing a cream silk shift with a large African necklace of silver, turquoise, and orange beads came toward Eliza with open arms. "Oh, Eliza dear, you're back." Anne de Liesseline embraced Eliza. "Oh dear, it is so good to have you back. I'm just leaving"—she glanced behind her—"trying to avoid Mary Elizabeth, who is in relentless pursuit of my recipe for kumquat wine, which I am not inclined to give her. I promised my aunt Zenobia on her deathbed I would keep that recipe in the family. Mary Elizabeth is so desperate to get this recipe that she cornered me at church last Sunday and started quoting passages about sharing from the Bible—something from II Corinthians about whoever sows sparingly will reap sparingly and whoever sows generously will reap generously. I told her that my family's recipe couldn't hold a candle to Cecelia Langdon's. Cecelia has been serving it to all the tourists she tortures around this city. I thought I had managed to put Mary Elizabeth off, but apparently not. Must dash, but promise me you and Henry will come over Tuesday for a drink. Louisa Eveleigh—Henry's star columnist"—she winked and lifted her chin toward Henry—"is bringing her new beau. We have no idea what to expect, Henry, do we? The last one was some poor soul from one of the finest families of Camden—a manic-depressive who has tried to commit suicide three times. On his last attempt, he jumped off an overpass onto the interstate. Missed the eighteen-wheeler he was aiming for. Broke both legs but is surprisingly well. He might have tried something higher than an overpass. Really. I told Louisa that I felt dreadfully sorry for the poor fellow but, well, you know, he's surely not the one to pin her hopes on."

A waiter presented a tray of miniature crab cakes.

"Oh my, I think I will." Anne picked up a napkin and popped a crab cake into her mouth. "Thank goodness, she's your cousin, not mine. I think I'm related to almost everybody in this city either by blood or marriage or both—Lord, it's why so many of us are so crazy, but I think somehow I've managed to sidestep that side of the Eveleigh family. Eliza, your father and I—how I miss him, how we used to laugh—he could tell me how everyone was related to everyone else so that by the time he had finished with them, they looked like a voodoo doll with ancestral lines stuck in them. He had such a mind—he would never get lost. Oh dear. How he could make me laugh." Anne dabbed the corner of her mouth with her napkin. "Must run. Lots of love, do promise you'll come Tuesday evening."

Young women in strapless pastel dresses and young men in black tie began arriving. The band, which had been playing soft swing music, packed up their instruments and moved off the wooden platform at the back of the property. The second band, a geriatric but sprightly group of six black men dressed alike in tuxedos with hot pink lapels, began to set up. Three stood in a line to sing, while the other three adjusted and checked their instruments—keyboard, guitar, and drums.

"Let's watch this," Henry said. He rested his foot on the seat of a folding chair and leaned his forearm on his knee. "I bet they're going to be good." Henry shifted his head to the side to read the name in fuchsia glitter across the front of the drums. "Harold and the Exciters."

The singers stood at attention for a few minutes, almost as if in silent prayer, then the middle singer jerked his head up and counted loudly, "One, two, three," and they began "I Can't Help Myself."

"Not bad, not bad at all," Henry mused. He cracked ice in his

teeth as he watched. By the time Harold and the Exciters had finished their first song, the dance floor was filled with young couples,
by the time they had finished their second, most of the older crowd
had begun to leave. "Come on, let's see if you still remember how
to dance." And then more to himself than to Eliza, he said softly,
"Let's see if I still remember how to dance."

Henry was an accomplished dancer. Every child who grew up in
downtown Charleston was enrolled in fours years of Junior Cotillion
at the South Carolina Society Hall on Meeting Street. No one left
without knowing how to waltz and dance the foxtrot and the lindy.
But even among the Charleston crowd, Henry stood out. He made
Eliza laugh as he spun her away and pulled her back and passed her
hand behind his back or over his head. He danced with an ease and
nonchalance that made young men wish they could imitate him and
young women wish they could dance with him.

# CHAPTER FOUR

During the breaks between sets, Henry and Eliza drifted around the party, and Henry amused Eliza with stories about Charleston. As the night wore on, bow ties were loosened, makeup and perfume faded, and jackets abandoned to the summer heat. The caterers began to perform their end-of-evening decampment. Glasses and bottles were slotted away, tablecloths folded, and card tables collapsed into panes of metal. The band announced their last set. A few couples protested and clustered round them with final requests.

"Tired?" Henry asked. "Come on, let's go upstairs. We can go the back way." He took Eliza's hand and led her off the dance floor toward the house. A waiter passed by, hurrying toward the decampment with a tray of untouched drinks, and Henry leaned over and took one. Eliza followed Henry to the kitchen house, up a narrow flight of stairs, and through a back passageway that opened onto a large unlit library. He led her across the library to the door leading to the piazza. It was locked. "Here," he said and raised the sash of the wide window and steadied her as she scissor-kicked across the waist-high sill.

"Hold this." He handed her his drink as he followed, stepping over the sill. "I'd forgotten how much of this house I still remember. When my great-aunt used to own it, we'd come over for Sunday lunches. I spent most of the time playing hide-and-seek with my older cousins." Henry walked out onto the piazza toward the front of the house and stood with his back to Eliza and hooked his hands in his pockets. "I've always loved the view of the harbor from here." Henry flipped a switch to turn the lights off. "Now you can really see the water."

"Are you sure you should do that?" Eliza asked.

"No one down there will notice." Henry walked to the front of the piazza overlooking the harbor. "And now no one will be able to tell who is up here. We'll just be dark shadows on an unlit porch." A three-quarters moon spread a wide silver path from the battery wall to the horizon. "It's beautiful, isn't it?" Henry said. "It's like being on a ship. I've always felt as if I were somewhere else when I'm up here. It's too majestic, somehow, for Charleston."

Eliza sat on the wicker sofa. She took her shoes off and tucked her feet under her. Henry walked back and sat sidesaddle on the balustrading.

"You aren't wearing any socks," she observed.

"Couldn't find any—why I was late." Henry cracked the last cubes of ice in his teeth. "So tell me about Jamie."

"I don't know what to say."

"How did you meet?"

"We met one summer in East Hampton. His sister, Fleur, was in the graduate program with me at Columbia."

"After Princeton, you went there after Princeton." Henry confirmed what he already knew.

"Yes, I got a master's in English and then decided that the world did not need another essay on Jane Austen, or at least not from me, so I switched to art history and got a second master's. In between, I worked for a year at a gallery downtown. Anyway, Fleur invited me out for a weekend. Jamie had been working on a documentary in Chile, and he had come for a visit."

Eliza didn't tell Henry how Jamie had shown up when dinner was almost over because his plane from South America had landed late at JFK. He looked as if he had not slept for several days. He didn't say a word to anyone except to ask for an espresso. Nor did she tell Henry how, as she was leaving the next morning, Jamie had knocked on the window of her car. She rolled her window down, and he asked, "Are you Eliza?" She nodded, and he ran his hand over his unshaven jaw and walked back inside. He called her the next afternoon and asked her to dinner.

"And then?"

"And then what?"

"How did the two of you get together if you were in New York and he lived in London."

"I started seeing him when I moved to London."

"Is it serious?"

"Yes, I suppose so."

Henry slid off the railing. "What do you mean suppose?"

"God, Henry." Eliza held up her hand as if to shield herself. "I don't know, I guess I mean we've had our ups and downs."

"Sorry, I didn't mean to sound like such an inquisitor. But you are still seeing him?"

"I am."

"But you don't want to talk about . . ."

"No, not really."

Henry nodded slowly. "Okay."

Eliza listened to the intertwined currents of voices and music down below. Jamie had left London and headed to Scotland a few days before her flight to Charleston. If the weather held, he would be on a boat with a small film crew heading to St. Kilda. She doubted, as Jamie hoped, that distance or time would change anything between them.

"How about you?" Eliza asked.

"Me?" Henry leaned against a column. "What about me?"

"So what have you been doing since . . ."

"How much do you know about what happened?"

"Some, I don't know, not that much really. I heard things, but I never asked, I just . . ."

"Where do you want me to start? What if I tell you everything in reverse?"

"Start now and go backward?"

"I can start at the beginning or the middle or anywhere if you promise to stay until I finish."

She shrugged her shoulders. "I don't know where to tell you to start. My mother wrote me about your father. I'm sorry I never wrote you."

"Eliza, after what I did to you, I didn't expect to hear from you." Henry held the railing on each side of his body, as if to steady himself.

"What happened?"

"He had a massive heart attack. He went to work one morning, and we never saw him again." Henry looked down at the crowd and watched the band, which had been cajoled into one more set. "Dr. Walker said he was lucky to have lived as long as he did." He tapped the thin cocktail straw on top of the wooden balustrade and then moved his fingers back and forth across it. "After the funeral, I had to go to his office and sort out his affairs, and you know, I didn't even know where his office was. And I remember walking down the corridor, not certain I was in the right place but not wanting anyone to realize that I didn't know, and when I got to his office, I only knew it was his when I spotted a photograph taken after we had won a men's doubles tournament when I was fifteen. And I was undone by how arrogant and dismissive of everything I had been. And how hurtful it must have been to my father. It was a hell of a time to realize all that. I had to take over everything, so that's what I've been doing since then. Running the paper. I never expected to."

"I never imagined you working at the newspaper."

"I know, neither did I. When I was going through everything, I came across some copies of the newspaper from the 1920s and 1930s. It was a serious newspaper back then. You know it even won a Pulitzer in the 1920s. I'd had no idea. I've been gradually trying to turn it into more of a serious paper. More international news, and as more people move down here or have second homes, I think the desire for a better paper is there."

"And you do have that society page."

"We really mustn't forget that—it accounts for at least half of our increase in circulation," Henry laughed. "We've bought a few small southern newspapers. One in Mississippi, two in Georgia. Actually I'm going to look at one in New Orleans at the end of the week. The entire industry is going through a lot of consolidation." Henry came over and sat down next to Eliza on the sofa. "I feel as if you are floating away."

Eliza shifted her body sideways, closer to Henry. "I'm not. I'm right here. And your son?"

"Lawton."

"Is ten?"

"Lawton is nine."

"Does he look like you?"

"He does."

"And I bet you've already taught him to play tennis."

"I have. Actually he's not bad for his age."

The mention of Lawton made Eliza realize how many years had passed since they had last seen each other. The time she and Henry had been together could be folded three times into the time they had been apart. "Is your mother still on Legare Street?" she asked.

"She is."

"Where are you living?"

"We stay in the carriage house. I made the loft into two small bedrooms. When Lawton was born, I lived down at Oakhurst with my parents. I was working in Columbia for Judge Todd, but I came home to Oakhurst every weekend. Bessie—you remember Harold and Bessie—looked after him. When Lawton was three we moved back into town, into the carriage house behind my parents, so that he could be with other children. When I travel or have a business dinner that goes late, Lawton stays in my old room right across the hall from my mother. But most of the time it's just the two of us in the carriage house."

"Where does he go to school?"

"Charleston Day. Most mornings I walk him to school, and my mother collects him. In a few years he'll be able to ride his bike there and back."

Henry stood up again, walked to the edge of the piazza, braced his arms straight against the balustrade, and looked out over the crowd. He looked back at Eliza. "It's not so bad, this place, really. I never expected to be back here—or at least not so soon. I always thought that we would—well—that after law school I would go to New York and you would be there, too." Henry paused and sighed. "Anyway, you know, Eliza, as long as you've had the chance to get out of here and see it from the outside, then it's fine. Then you know what you're dealing with. Then you know you can take it or leave it." Henry stopped talking and listened to the band playing "You Send Me."

Eliza looked at the clusters of remaining guests as if she were trying to discern some pattern. "So why haven't you gotten married?"

"Again?" He closed his eyes for a moment and tucked his chin close to his chest.

"Yes, I guess again."

Henry looked at his watch. "It's almost one."

"You're avoiding me."

"I am, I absolutely am, but it's late. Much too late now to talk about anything serious." He looked down at the knots of people who remained on the lawn. "Come on. I'll take you home." He took her hand and helped her across the window transom and down the dark hallway to the back staircase.

"I can't see anything."

"Here, let me go first." Henry stepped in front of her. "Put one hand here." He placed her hand on the stair rail. "Now put your other hand on my shoulder." When she did as he instructed, her feeling of safety somersaulted away from her.

"Henry, I still can't see anything. I can't even see you."

"Don't worry, I know this place blind. Eleven steps down to the landing, then left, another twelve to the bottom." He counted slowly, "Here, eight, nine, ten, eleven, landing—end of the landing is just here—careful."

When they emerged from the house, the band was packing up. Henry held Eliza back in the shadows to let a cluster of three guests pass. "Wasn't that the Alstons and Sallie Izard?" Eliza asked.

Henry nodded. "I'm surprised they're still here."

"Shouldn't we have spoken to them?"

"Probably." He held her back for another group to pass. He took her hand and led her to Sara.

"We're trying to convince them to play one more set," Sara said in an overly optimistic voice.

"We're off, your party was lovely." Eliza kissed Sara good night.

"We're all going to Big John's afterward, you and Henry should come."

"Don't think I will make it, I'm five hours ahead of you," Eliza said.

"Well, if you change your mind . . ."

Eliza waved good-bye as they turned to leave.

"She is sweet," Henry said.

"She is. It's odd, having a stepsister I barely know, but then, when I was in tenth grade she was in first. She's leaving in a few days for the summer to travel around Italy with a group of girls from Ashley Hall."

They walked across the street and up the stairs to High Battery. Henry looked over the railing. "Tide's coming in," he said. The water beat a gentle rhythm against the seawall. They both heard the sound of air being forced through an opening.

"What was that?" Eliza asked.

"A dolphin." Henry leaned his forearms against the railing. "Exhaling. You really have been away for a long time." He turned to Eliza and put his finger to his lips and motioned for her to come closer. She looked where he pointed. They watched the gray curve arc across the top of the water and then disappear. They looked ahead some fifty feet and waited for it to reappear. When it had disappeared for the second time, Henry whispered, "I haven't seen one this close in a long time." They waited and watched and listened until the sound of the dolphin blowing disappeared. Henry straightened up, and they began walking north along the seawall. The lamps cast a soft yellow light. They walked to the end of the promenade without saying anything. Voices died out, a car door slammed, and an engine started as the last of the partygoers dispersed.

"Are you tired? Do you want to go home?" Henry asked.

Eliza thought about her plan to awaken early and finish checking the changes made to the first twenty pages of the Magritte manuscript, but she gave in to the luxurious feeling of everything being suspended. "No, I'm okay."

"Then let's cut across the playground to Adger's Wharf."

They walked past the concrete tennis court that doubled as a basketball court and on across the green playing fields toward the water's edge.

"Do you remember the woman who used to coach all the track teams?" Eliza asked.

"Of course."

"What was her name?"

"Hazel. Hazel Wilson. Miss Wilson to us." Henry reached down and picked up a worn tennis ball and threw it back toward the tennis court. "I remember when she cut me and Charlie from the track team because we missed one practice. Charlie was upset, and we went to see his father to see if he would intervene. Dr. Walker had no sympathy for us. He felt Miss Wilson had done the right thing and gave us a lecture on commitment. When he later learned that we were the two best runners on the team, he reversed his position and spoke to Miss Wilson, but she was adamant that we could not run."

As they reached Adger's Wharf, Eliza was surprised to see that only two of the old warehouses remained. In their place, rows of small townhouses had been built. When they reached the cobblestone street, Henry said, "Here, we can go this way," and led her along the sandy pathway onto the oyster shells. "Better?"

"Much." It was typical of Charleston never to upgrade the oyster shell paths, first used as a type of gravel in the 1700s, even when cement was invented a century later. The oyster shells had, over the years, been crushed to a fine grade. The sound of their footsteps on the shells reminded Eliza of the slow ticktock of the long-case clock in her front hall. When they reached Gillon Street, Henry said, "This is all new. You haven't seen it yet, have you?"

"No."

"It's one of the mayor's pet projects, this small park." The park was laid out as a long rectangle along the water's edge with benches punctuating the straight lines of paths.

"It's nice," she said.

"There's a dock at the end. We can walk down to that if you're not too tired and then head back." There were no city sounds, no voices or buses or cars, just the crunch of their footsteps on the shell path. It was six in the morning in London, and the early June day—with light that lasted from six in the morning to almost ten at night—would just be beginning.

They reached the wide dock that stretched out past the marsh into the water. The tide had not yet turned, and the rotten egg smell of the pluff mud was faint.

"Does the city use this for tour boats?"

"No, no boats," Henry said. "Fishing isn't even allowed. Just for people to enjoy. A lot of Charlestonians, especially the old ones, don't like it."

Henry found the swinging bench at the end of the dock. "Hop on."

He started them off with a push of his feet. "You have to sit closer or else we'll be out of balance." Eliza edged over a bit. Henry pushed the ground with his feet. "I bet you haven't been on a porch swing in a long time. They don't have these in England, do they?"

Eliza shook her head.

"I have to go down to Oakhurst early tomorrow morning to take some photographs for Drayton's book. Come with me."

Before Eliza could answer, they heard a voice call to them. "Hey, I am the Master of the Moon. Who are you?"

Henry scraped the soles of his shoes hard against the wooden planks to stop the swing. The voice called again. "Hey, I am the Master of the Moon. Who are you?" The voice was coming from a dark crumpled form in the corner of the dock. An old black man held a bottle in a brown paper bag in front of him. "I am the Master of the Moon. I said, who are you?"

Henry stood up and walked over to him. "I, my friend, am the Master of Time."

"Hey, man. That's good. That's all right. Hey, that's good. I like that—Master of Time—that's all right. Hey, man, you all right."

Henry leaned down. "Are you going to be all right, my friend?"

The old black man spoke in a loud, almost songlike voice. "The Master of the Moon thanks the Master of Time for his concern, but the Master of the Moon is in fine shape. He is enjoying this beautiful night with the moon and the stars and the peace all around. The Master of the Moon will take care of himself directly."

"Well then, my friend, enjoy the rest of the night."

"I sure will, and you take care of yourselves."

Henry returned to Eliza. "I'd better get you home."

*Home.* The word sounded unfamiliar. She listened to the sound of Henry's footsteps punctuate the receding lilt of the old man's voice as he echoed what he had said before. Where was home? she wondered.

They walked the seven blocks to Broad Street without saying anything. Their silence pulled their shared past in close around them.

When they reached Broad Street, Henry said, "We can walk down Church Street. I bet you've never walked down Church Street at"—he lifted his left arm and twisted his wrist so that his watch would catch the light of the street lamppost—"quarter to two in the morning."

They turned onto Church.

"He's still there. Plenge the Hatter," Henry said, referring to the Hat Man, the painted figure of a man whose body and face were composed of all different types of hats. "He just got repainted. I

liked him better the way he was, but he was so faded and the paint
was beginning to flake off—I guess he was in danger of disappearing. Too dark to see him now though."

It was comforting to be back in a place where the most that
could happen to a German haberdasher's sign from the 1870s was
a fresh coat of paint. "You know who I think that man was?" Eliza
said.

"What man? The old man on the dock? The Master of the
Moon?"

"I think he's Clarence who used to work for Mrs. Lockwood.
I think he was an alcoholic back then, but I think Mrs. Lockwood
would get him to polish her silver and brass and help her in her
garden when he was up to it. I could be wrong, but I'm pretty sure
that's who he is."

Where Church Street crossed Water Street, its original brick
paving remained, and Henry guided Eliza to the sidewalk.

"Well, here we are. Front or back door?"

"Front door is fine."

"So I'll pick you up tomorrow morning?" Henry turned Eliza
toward him. "Come on, Eliza, don't look at me that way, we both
know what we're doing."

"I know. You're right. We do."

"So I'll pick you up"—Henry looked at his watch—"in three
hours and seven minutes."

"Ouch, perhaps I should reconsider."

"No, don't. We can sleep on the dock later in the morning. On
the other hand, you could make it a little easier for both of us."

Eliza looked at him.

"If you would come home with me, we probably would have
another five, ten minutes of sleep."

Eliza smiled and shook her head.

"Ah, Eliza, five A.M. it is."

Eliza leaned against the closed door and listened as Henry walked down Church Street, whistling the last Sam Cooke melody the band had played. She listened to the sharp sounds of his heels striking the sidewalk until she could hear them no longer.

# CHAPTER FIVE

A T 4:50 THE CLOCK BEEPED AND FLASHED. ELIZA'S BODY, weighted by so little sleep, felt as if it were cast in a metal too heavy to move. Henry would be outside in ten minutes. Why was she doing this? If Henry wanted to be with her, he could see her later in the day. She looked at the clock again. The last time she was up at five in the morning was last August when she and Jamie had driven from London to St. Tropez. Jamie was not one for straight lines, and the idea of driving instead of flying to the south of France had been his idea. He had written down a list of cathedrals and châteaux they should see on the way. And as usual, they were late leaving London and missed their booking on the channel ferry and had to wait until a space opened on a later one. A fourteen-hour trip turned into twenty-one, so when they finally reached St. Tropez, it was 5:00 A.M., seven hours past their estimated arrival time.

Eliza felt the same heaviness Jamie had felt when, at a red light on the outskirts of St. Tropez, he had leaned his head on the steering wheel and asked her to wake him up when the light changed. Now she wanted to close her eyes for just one more minute, just for the space of a light to change, but she didn't.

She sat up on the edge of the bed to steady herself. She patted the walls until she found the bathroom door, reached inside, and flipped the light switch. She stood over the sink basin and looked in the mirror. God, she looked exhausted. She promised herself she was going to get more sleep and not drink so much coffee. She splashed water on her face, brushed her teeth, pulled her hair back. She slipped into a pair of ripped jeans she found at the back of her closet and grabbed a white tee shirt and flannel shirt from her chest of drawers. She was out the door into the cool morning air with two minutes to spare.

Henry was leaning, arms crossed, against his Jeep. "Good morning," he said and opened the door for her. He got back in the Jeep and reached over and stroked her cheek. "Eliza, my love, your face is creased. You must have just woken up."

She hid a yawn. "I'm assuming that's your polite way of telling me how tired I look."

Henry tilted his head and raised his eyebrows and shifted the Jeep into first gear. "An extra ten minutes might have been nice."

"It's midmorning in London. I feel great."

"You look great."

As they turned right onto Ashley Avenue, Henry slowed to pass an elderly man dressed in a full-length duster coat and aviator goggles walking unsteadily in the middle of the street. As he shifted back into second gear, he looked in his rearview mirror. "That was Mr. DuBose. I wonder why he is out so early. A few months ago he stopped Lawton and a few of his friends fishing on the Battery and instructed them to soak bread crumbs in bourbon and then to throw the alcohol-soaked bread to the seagulls and watch them fly into each other. Mr. DuBose must have spoken to a number of children because one of the mothers—Betsy Downing—they moved down from Chicago—heard about it and was horrified and called the police. Two officers went around and spoke to Mr. DuBose, and Charlotte had to promise to hire a nanny of sorts to keep him off the streets."

"I guess if you are not from here and haven't grown up with the DuBoses—well, you could get the wrong impression."

Henry checked his rearview mirror again. "I wonder if Charlotte knows he is out so early."

"Remind me again why we are out so early," Eliza yawned.

"It was my strategy to get you to spend the night with me or what was left of it. But seeing that it failed, I had no choice but to carry on. And I do want to take some early morning shots on the river."

"For Drayton's book?"

"Uh-huh." Henry hooked his arm over the seat and patted the seat behind them. "I brought some coffee. It's in a large dark green thermos."

"Here, I'll get it." Eliza lifted her body over the front seat as if performing a pike dive. On the floor behind her seat, she saw an old machete, a roll of red surveyor's marking tape, and a can of Deep Woods Off!, but no thermos of coffee. "I don't see it," she said.

"Maybe it rolled under the seat."

Eliza felt under her seat. "Found it."

Henry tapped the steering wheel with his hand. "Good. So tell me, how many men have brought you coffee at five in the morning?"

"Not telling." She twisted off the top and turned it over to use as a cup.

"Didn't think you would."

She steadied the cup between her legs and poured. "Coffee?" She offered the cup to Henry.

"You first."

Eliza held the cup in her hands and let the steam cover her face. She took a sip. "Not bad. You've gotten better."

"Ten years of practice."

She passed the cup to Henry.

He took a sip and passed it back. "You have the rest. Did you get any sleep?"

"A bit."

As they slid out of Charleston past the marina and the marshes, the morning was still dark and foggy. Eliza liked the feeling of being with Henry in a capsule bounded by darkness. They were overtaken by one pickup truck and one or two night travelers, but for most of the journey, they had the highway to themselves.

"You don't drive nearly as fast as you used to."

"No, I don't suppose I do," he said.

Far away the low whistle of a fast-moving freight train resonated in the soft heavy air. "Is that the night train coming from Yemassee?" Eliza asked, but before she finished her question, she knew the answer. "I remember when I was five or six, spending the night with my grandmother in the country and being all tucked up with her in her feather bed with a silk comforter and the window being open and feeling the cool air and the night crickets and hearing the sound of that train heading north across the marshes and feeling as if I were in the safest place in the world."

"I know—that whistle makes you feel as if everything is perfect and in its place."

"Back then it pretty much was."

Henry braked before the railroad crossing and checked for oncoming trains. He bumped slowly across the tracks. Eliza rolled her window down and listened to the frog chorus in the misty darkness.

Henry picked up speed as they drove down Parker's Ferry

through the five-mile canopy of ancient oak and gum trees and then on past the acres and acres of cypress and tupelo swamps before coming to the rise of Oakhurst Plantation. The air was cool and damp and fragrant with wild honeysuckle.

After years of being away, Eliza had accepted that these sights and sounds were no longer part of her life, but here they were. And now being alone with Henry—everything she had been so careful to construct detours around—all disregarded in the course of one morning.

A large gray-brown bird arced down across the front of the Jeep before disappearing in the woods.

"What was that?" she asked.

"Red-shouldered hawk." All this land, now on both sides of the road, was his. "Do you remember the blessing the priest ended Simon and Caroline's ceremony with?"

"I do," Eliza said. "Deep peace of the quiet earth to you, deep peace of the gentle night to you."

"When I heard those words, it made me think of being out here like this in the early morning hours."

Henry stopped in front of the massive gates of Oakhurst Plantation. Eliza looked beyond the brick peers and wrought-iron gates to the double row of ancient live oaks. Coming back to a place that was so familiar began to collapse time for her, and she felt as if she had never left.

"Slide over—you can drive through." Henry climbed out to open the heavy gates. He slid back into the driver's seat, and Eliza moved back to her side. "You don't have to run away."

The dark was lifting as they drove down the long oak allée to the main house. Several hundred feet away, three young deer froze and then disappeared into the mist of the forest. The two-and-a-half-story plantation house had been built in the early 1800s on a foundation of brick arches. A wide porch wrapped around it. It sat on a rise of land unusual for the Lowcountry that sloped down to the large rice field that buffered it from the river. The house had been spared being burned during the Civil War because the daughter of a governor of New York had married into the family that owned it.

"Lawton and I used to come down here every weekend, but now that he's older, he likes to stay in town and play sports with his friends. He started playing tennis with some of his friends at a small tennis academy at The Citadel. They have matches every Saturday."

Henry parked the Jeep to the left of a small canal that led past the rice field to the Edisto River. Eliza got out and walked along the bank toward the river while Henry got his camera and equipment from the backseat. He fished out a vest covered with zippered pockets and shook it out before putting it on.

"Eliza," he called. "What kind of shoes do you have?" He transferred rolls of film from a camera bag into his zippered pockets as he spoke.

"Moccasins," she said.

"You might want to take a pair of snake boots—we'll probably get out and walk. Come with me. And watch out for snakes." She followed him into the boathouse. "They are bad at this time of year." He pulled a pair of boots off a rack and shook them upside down and then looked inside. "Snake free," he said. "These should fit, here, try these."

She winced as she slipped her foot into one.

"Too small?"

"No, blisters from last night," she said and pulled her foot out.

Henry jogged back to his Jeep to get his machete. Eliza climbed into the small camouflaged aluminum boat and watched as Henry returned and placed the machete in the boat. He untied the boat, pushed it away from the dock, and jumped in. He yanked the electric motor to start. When they reached the river, he pointed the boat south toward Jehossee Island and pushed the motor full tilt.

They were going fast now across the smooth river. Eliza leaned to one side and skimmed the palm of her hand across the glossy gray surface. Here she was in a small boat headed south, and somewhere off the coast of Scotland, Jamie was headed west. The North Atlantic would be rough, and his large sailboat would have to fight every inch of its way west. Their destinations—the swamps of the South Edisto and the barren windswept rocks of an Outer Hebrides island—could not be more different, and yet both she and Jamie could get lost. But she wouldn't, because she was with Henry. Henry knew every inch of his world, and she felt safe with him. Jamie was always going to some new place, where he observed and reported, and he relied on others—on guides and sailing crews and pilots—to get him to his destination. In some ways Jamie documented what Henry lived.

As the boat skimmed past Willtown Bluff and the vast rice fields of Dodge Plantation, Henry leaned forward and cupped his hands around his mouth, "Just bought by some fellow from Florida who made a lot of money in the video rental business."

Eliza pulled hair from her face. "Why did the Dodges sell it?" She had met several grandsons of old Mr. Dodge at the Bachelor Ball many Christmases ago.

"Oh, you know, too many heirs, no real interest. Mr. Dodge died last year. Drayton said it went for a bundle." Henry sat back up and turned his attention to the river. Eliza could tell he wanted to get somewhere before the light changed too much. The Edisto was considered one of the more treacherous rivers in the Lowcountry because of the number of hidden sandbars and unpredictable currents, but Henry knew the river better than he knew most things, and he made wide curves around unseen shallow areas. The sun had already lit the undersides of clouds and appeared to be chasing them west.

Henry loaded his camera and began taking pictures of the rising sun. The sky was now blurred with soft pinks and lavenders and blues. Eliza had never seen such skies in England. The sky from the kitchen window of her flat looked hard and cold and far away. She thought that if she could ever reach one of those hard London skies, she would be able to lean against it—that there was nothing behind it except more hardness.

A pink cloud with a lavender underside stretched across the sky, as if a banner connecting the cypress trees. Henry spotted a blue heron standing along the bank, and he motioned to Eliza that he wanted to get as close to the bird as he could. He cut the motor and let the boat drift with the outgoing tide toward the riverbank, then moved to the middle of the small boat, braced his legs, and held out his hand to steady her as she crouched past him to the back of the boat. He twisted the lens off his camera and replaced it with a larger one. When they were within thirty feet, the heron stretched its neck and lifted off low across the river. Henry followed the bird as it tucked its neck into an S shape and disappeared over a stand of cypress trees.

They shifted positions again, and Henry restarted the motor. "I've been watching herons all my life. The way they look back at you. I can't tell if they're really smart or really dumb." He pointed ahead. "Jehossee Creek is just up there on the left."

The small aluminum boat sliced quietly through the still water of the creek that snaked back and forth between rice fields on both sides. Jehossee Island had been owned by several prominent Charleston families but now was part of the ACE Basin National Wildlife Refuge. It had once been one of the largest rice plantations, but it could only be reached by boat, and no attempt had ever been made to develop it. Eliza remembered seeing a black-and-white photograph of a Jehossee hunting party on display at the Charleston Museum—a double row of men, the front line kneeling and holding their guns across their knees. The men looked straight into the camera with a solemnity as if they had just come through a long campaign full of hard battles. Laid out on the ground in front of them were hundreds of ducks. At the men's side, next to a mule and cart, stood six black men.

When the creek narrowed to barely twice the boat's width, the rice fields gave way to swamps of cypress and tupelo and gum, whose thick bases rose from the shallow water and then tapered straight and tall. Their canopies reached wide with feathery leaves. Henry cut the motor and tilted it out of the water. He picked up an oar from the bottom of the boat and moved the boat forward by pushing the oar against the shallow bottom of the creek.

"We're going to pull up just there." He pointed to a narrow tip of land. "Put on those boots." Henry spoke in a low voice and kept his eyes fixed on the spot ahead. "When I tell you, move to the very front of the boat, hold on to that rope"—he flicked his eyes to the rope curled in a sloppy circle on the bow—"and jump out." Henry dug hard into the bottom of the creek and pushed the boat ahead. As the boat began to slide into the muddy bottom, he said, "Now."

Eliza jumped into several inches of soft mud.

"Good," Henry said, "don't let go." He picked up the machete and jumped. He took the rope from Eliza and pulled the boat up hard on the land. He wrapped the rope around a tree and knotted it with two strong pulls. "Just making sure it'll be here when we get back." He checked the camera that hung around his neck and patted his vest to check for rolls of film. "Okay, let's go. Follow directly behind me. Watch where you step. Keep your eyes on the ground."

"Where are we going?"

"Into the most beautiful cypress swamp you have ever seen. We can follow the dikes. They're not too bad in most places. Won't be any more difficult than Kensington High Street on the first day of Summer Sales."

"Just how far do you think you can go with that metaphor?"

"Not very." Henry looked back and laughed. Eliza stood back as he cleared an opening in the underbrush with his machete.

They walked across the top of an old rice bank that was now a tangle of roots and vines packed with dirt and mud. Henry turned around and checked on Eliza. He watched her wobble and almost lose her balance. He held his hand out to steady her. "Take your time. You'll get used to the footing. I'll slow down a bit."

Eliza didn't say anything, instead she concentrated on where she put each foot, careful to follow right behind Henry, careful not to fall in the dark water on either side of the dike, careful to watch out for snakes curled in the dark hollows of the cypress trees she passed. Henry held his hand up to halt and pointed to his ear. Far off they heard the staccato kuk-kuk-kuks of a woodpecker's call. He looked high up the tree and pointed over his shoulder. "Pileated woodpecker, his call follows the same rhythm as his pecking." Eliza looked where Henry pointed. She didn't see anything except layers and layers of leaves and branches. They continued to move forward.

The woodpecker called again.

Henry turned back to Eliza. "When I was little, no matter what anyone told me, I was certain every time I heard that sound, it was Indians. Lawton won't admit it, but I think that sound scares him, too."

The bird called once more, and then Eliza spotted a black bird the size of a crow with a red crest and a streak of white down the side of its neck as it flew away.

Eliza looked at the "knees" of the cypress trees, the gnomelike protuberances of root systems that randomly stuck up out of the water around the trunks and provided a wide foundation for the tree in the soft swamp bottom. What would the English artist who had laid his twenty-meter spiral out of desiccated sticks and pocket compasses choose to make from this swamp?

"If you need to steady yourself take hold of my shoulder. But watch out for the knees, that's where the copperheads and moccasins hide out—especially at this time of year." A few yards later, he stopped and pulled a crumpled piece of paper from his shirt pocket.

"I hope that's not your map," she said.

He smiled and shook his head as he uncrumpled the small piece of paper. "If it were, you'd be in more danger than you already are."

"You do know where we are, don't you?"

He nodded and waved the paper in the air as he turned forward to continue. "Notes from Drayton. I just wanted to make certain I remembered everything he wanted."

After a while Eliza had gotten the rhythm of walking so that she was able to look up and take in their surroundings. The air was cool with a faint trace of menthol. The canopy was so dense she could not see the sun. The little light that did make it through created eerie reflections of the tall trees in the still, brackish water of the swamp. Henry held his hand up, signaling for Eliza to be still. He focused his camera on two Great White Egrets, resting high in a tall cypress tree. In the still quiet of the swamp, the sound of his camera was amplified and sounded like the crack of small branches breaking in rushed succession. The large birds froze, then rose gracefully into the canopy for safety. Eliza judged their wingspan to be over five feet.

Soon they came to a large break in the dike. Henry surveyed the damage. "Let me see how deep it is," he said and walked behind her and broke a four-foot branch from a sweet bay magnolia across his knee. The long branch disappeared into the water. "It's probably a little too deep. It's not so bad at low tide but that won't be"—he checked his watch—"for a couple of hours. There's a bank not too far back that intersects this one."

They turned around, and fifty yards later, Henry took his machete and cut a large tangle of vines to open a path to another dike running perpendicular to the one they were on. Eliza followed him across the broken vines and branches. He walked ahead and continued slashing back the vines that had grown over the path so they could pass. Eliza was going to ask Henry how he didn't get lost, but he turned and pointed to a large alligator that lay on the bank ahead. She guessed it was at least eight or nine feet. Henry aimed his camera, took a shot, and then stepped in the water to get a better view. She was surprised the disturbance didn't startle the alligator. Henry crouched low and threw a stick into the water near it. With alarming speed, the alligator slipped into the water with a large splash and then resurfaced twenty feet away and turned toward them. Eliza grabbed Henry's arm.

"You're safe," he said. "She just wants to see what disturbed her. She'll leave us alone." Henry took a few more pictures of the alligator's head. Growing up, Eliza had always been told that the way to know the size of an alligator submerged in the water was to guess the distance in inches from its eyes to its snout. Eight inches meant the alligator was eight feet long, nine inches—nine feet long.

They continued on, and Henry took pictures of a stand of old cypress trees with bases four and five feet wide. At the base of the widest one, a single blue wild iris grew.

"We're not too far from dry land. Just up here is a clearing with the chimney of an old rice mill. If it's not too grown over, I'll show it to you." Eliza followed quietly behind Henry through the overgrown vegetation. He worked hard with his machete. "These multiflora roses are taking over this bank." He stood up straight and pointed with his machete. "Look, they've crowded out almost everything else." He resumed hacking away at the unruly, thorned bushes.

Eliza could have argued right there and then, as she had done with herself many times before, that after six, seven, eight, let alone ten years, she and Henry would have changed so much that there would be nothing between them. And despite all of her equations, why did it feel so thrilling to be following him into this swamp? She had left and been a part of other worlds—first New York and then London. Henry had never left. He had remained not because he wanted to, but because he had to, she understood that, but even so, ten years of such different worlds—wasn't that enough to shift things between them so that even if they tried, they would never be able to fit together anymore? Maybe she and Jamie never even had a chance. Maybe somehow in the back of her heart these equations between Henry and herself had remained unsolved.

"It's just up there." Henry pointed to a large brick chimney that stood by itself. It was almost completely covered by dense, tight-leafed fig vines. The ground rose slowly and became increasingly firm until they found themselves in an open area of high land. The rising heat made Eliza's lungs feel heavy—it was almost hard to breathe. Henry leaned down and picked up a feather from the ground. He showed it to her.

"Screech owl," he said. "Look." He ran his finger down one side of the feather's shaft. "It's why you never hear them. They don't have vanes on both sides of the shaft, only on one." He handed her the feather, and she ran her finger down the bare side.

"I didn't know that." She handed the feather back to him, and he tucked it into his back pocket.

They stood looking up at the two-and-a-half-storied structure. The bricks, not covered in vine, appeared large and irregular. The chimney's broad base tapered into a tall column. "Very few of these left standing. I keep meaning to get the curator of the Charleston Museum down here to document it. The threshing mill would have been here somewhere," Henry said, looking around where they were standing. With quick reflexes, he caught Eliza's arm as she reached to pull the fig vine away from the base. "Careful." He held her from moving forward.

She put her hand on her chest and stepped back. "You scared me."

"Sorry, but last time I was here"—he pointed to a recessed area of the structure—"there was a den of copperheads right there."

She took another step back. "How old do you think it is?"

"Don't really know, I'd guess early eighteen hundred, given the size and shape of the bricks. They match the ones at Oakhurst. Come on, we can get back this way. I've gotten everything I can get this morning. The sun's gotten too strong." He adjusted the strap on his camera. "There's one dike intact up there." He gestured with his chin. "It goes along the river, it shouldn't be too bad getting to our boat."

# CHAPTER SIX

It was nearly ten o'clock when they reached the boat. The morning sun had compressed and weighted the air. Henry shoved them off with an oar. Eliza slipped her boots off and started to put her moccasins back on but changed her mind. The water was quiet, and the world seemed as slow and as silent as Eliza had ever felt. She had been in a boat with Henry countless times, just the two of them on some river or waterway going from one point to another. But now it felt as if he were taking her away from a world in which she had been perfectly balanced to another—a secret world, where gravity had shifted and destabilized her sense of equilibrium.

At the opening into the river, Henry lowered the motor and ripped the cord fast. The sky was now a robin's egg blue dotted with cottony patches of clouds that were mirrored in the water. They slid silently past untouched marshes.

When they reached the boathouse, Henry tied the boat up and

helped Eliza onto land. She stood and raised her arms to stretch her back. "You can leave those in the boathouse," he said, referring to the boots she had borrowed. "We can get something to eat at the house."

He placed his camera equipment on the backseat of his Jeep. Eliza dug her toes into the sandy ground not covered in grass. Just below the hot surface, the sand was cool and dry and silky. In England, she could never walk barefoot, even in the summer. If she and Jamie were out in the country, she would have to find some sort of waterproof boot to wear. As Henry and Eliza walked toward the house, a dragonfly hovered in front of Eliza, as if it recognized her and wished to guide her up the sloped lawn to the house. God, she was tired.

"It's locked," Henry said as they approached the house. "I keep a key around the other side."

Eliza followed him to a large magnolia, where he reached up and took a key from a nail placed high on the trunk. She did not follow him up the steps to the house. He turned around. "Coming?"

"I just wanted to see what this dragonfly would do if I stood still." The dragonfly, its green body sparkling in the sun, hovered in place and then headed back toward the river. She held back a moment longer to slip on her moccasins.

The key didn't want to move in the lock. Henry pulled the front door tight toward him and jiggled the key. "This lock's always been difficult. I was out here a few days ago. I thought I'd fixed it. There," he said and pushed the door open for Eliza to enter. "You remember where everything is?"

Across the threshold, the wall of cold air stunned Eliza. She tilted her head back and held her arms out to the side and turned around. "Air-conditioning? When did you put in air-conditioning?"

"Mother put it in after Father died. She's never been able to take the heat very well. It's not bad, is it?"

"Feels great."

They entered a large wide hall that ran the length of the house and ended at a formal door with glass transoms that looked out over the river. The dark hardwood floors were covered with faded Persian carpets. Above the wainscot, the walls had been painted with scenes of the Lowcountry. Eliza walked ahead of Henry and examined the paintings of rice fields and swamps with nesting egrets. "I'd forgotten how beautiful these were. Anne de Liesseline painted them, didn't she?"

"Yes, just after she came back from New York—sometime in the mid-1950s. When I first moved out here, she came out one afternoon and talked a lot about her past. She explained that she'd been studying at the Parsons School of Design and had fallen in love with someone, but her father didn't approve, and the relationship ended—it's something no one ever talks about—but she was in bad shape, and according to Anne, I think my father asked her to paint this mural as a way of helping her. I don't think he had any idea it would turn out so well."

Eliza traced the trunk of a cypress tree with her finger.

"Come on, I'll make you breakfast." Henry led the way down a narrow hall to the kitchen. He pulled a package of coffee from a cupboard and set it on the counter, then opened the refrigerator. "Eggs, bacon, toast?"

"Anything would be great." Eliza looked over his shoulder. "Do you always keep so much food down here?"

"I was here earlier this week."

She sat at the table and watched Henry measure the coffee and crack the eggs.

"Would you mind if I had a look around?" she asked.

"Yeah do. Everything's the same. Nothing has changed."

Eliza walked to the front of the hall that overlooked the river. To the right was the large living room with a massive fireplace. She wandered through the living room and looked at the pictures set in silver frames on a table next to the sofa. Mostly photos of Mr. Heyward and his friends, dressed in camouflage pants and jackets for duck hunting, one of Mr. and Mrs. Heyward on horseback, two of large house parties. Eliza peered closer at the photos to see if she recognized any of the couples. Only one or two faces were vaguely familiar. She wandered through the French doors to the cypress-paneled library and was looking at a map of South Carolina dated 1731 when she heard Henry call her name.

"I thought I'd lost you for a moment. Hope you're hungry." She followed him back to the kitchen, where he presented her with scrambled eggs and bacon.

"Looks great, but it's way too much. Give me about half. I never eat breakfast."

"Okay, but it's more like lunch now."

They sat at a small kitchen table next to a window. "I was looking for that photograph of you and Cleve. I remember it being in the library," Eliza said.

"The one with the fish? It's in my room. I'll show it to you after we finish."

"That's okay. I just wondered where it was."

Henry laughed. "Eliza, you don't have to be afraid of me. You can go up by yourself. No ulterior motives."

"You must miss Cleve."

"I do," he said. "You know, I can't sit at this table without thinking of him. We spent so many summers here together. I think my parents first left me here for the summer when I was eight, but I'd been following him around since I was five. I had no desire to go with them to Maine. Cleve's job was to stay two feet behind me at all times. But it was the other way around. I was always one step behind him. He used to call me his shadow. Whenever he sensed I was sad or homesick for my mother, he'd say, 'Gracious Lawd, where'd dat no good shadow of mine gone.' And I would try to stay completely behind him so he couldn't see me when he turned. You know, I truly believed he didn't know where I was.

"Coffee." Henry snapped his fingers and jumped up to pour coffee in two mugs. He handed one to Eliza. "Now that I think about it, my parents must have really trusted Cleve. I certainly wouldn't leave Lawton down here with anybody. The only thing Cleve liked doing was fishing. I took you to visit him once. Remember?"

"I do. He lived in a small whitewashed house with his wife off of Jacksonboro Road. He had painted the door and all the window frames blue to keep the bad spirits out."

"Exactly. I even helped him one summer give everything a fresh coat of paint. Cleve was deeply superstitious."

"If I remember, he was quite tall and his wife was minute, she had an unusual name."

"Queen Esther, but everyone called her Daughter."

"And she had just fixed a large pot of collard greens and red rice, and she filled a lovely glazed bowl for us to take down to Oakhurst. I don't think we left one grain of rice."

"It's right there." Henry lifted his chin toward a sideboard where the olive glazed bowl sat.

"Oh my God, that's it." Eliza stood up to look at it. "It's lovely." She turned it around and then upside down to look for markings but found none. "You know, I think it's quite good."

"Cleve always said it was made by a slave potter. I tried to return it to him, but he told me to keep it, that it would bring me good luck. That was right before Cleve died."

"If I close my eyes and rub the rim, will my wishes come true?"

"Don't know," Henry smiled. "It's worth a shot. I'd always wanted to take you to his church to hear one of his sermons—the sermons of the Reverend Cleveland Washington of The Holiness Church of Deliverance in Ravenel, South Carolina. I don't think he ever missed a Sunday. He even preached the Sunday before he died. I swear he could recite ninety percent of the Bible."

Eliza wondered if Henry's bringing up a part of his life that had nothing to do with her was his way of trying to make her feel comfortable. Had he sensed how unnerved she had felt coming back to this house? Though she had sometimes dreamed about running into him, she had never allowed herself to imagine that they would get back together—and now here she was—with him—in his house.

Henry continued, "You know, I'd forgotten a lot of Cleve's lessons, but when I started bringing Lawton down here, it all started coming back. Cleve used to make me promise that whatever I did, I'd always 'jump for de sun.' I remember not knowing what he meant but promising anyway." Henry shook his head. "More coffee?"

"No, thanks, this is perfect."

"I think I learned everything I know about right and wrong either sitting in a boat or standing on a riverbank with Cleve. Monday through Saturday were devoted to fishing, and Sundays were saved for preaching. His favorite way of fishing was to tie lines on branches and in the morning come back to see if they were shaking. I can still hear his delight when he came across a shaking branch. Cleve had some little song he sang about frying up the catfish for his breakfast. Now that I think about it, it seems awfully cruel." Henry leaned back in his chair and played a beat on the table with closed fingers. "So you really were worried we were lost out there."

"Well, maybe, for a moment."

"Come on, Eliza, I know you."

She laughed. "Okay, yes, I was. It's just that you're the only person I know who would go into the deep swamp of an uninhabited island with a small scrap of paper as a map."

"It wasn't a map, it was a 'to do' list."

"Exactly."

"What's the worst that could have happened? We would have

walked around those old rice fields for a couple more hours. And then eventually, I would have figured out where we were, and it would have been the second time in less than twenty-four hours that I had acted as your savior, and you would be even more indebted to me than you already are. And besides"—he reached across the table for her plate—"you'll never be in danger of being lost with me—at least not out here." Eliza knew he was right. She had felt that when they were heading toward Jehossee Island. But that wasn't the danger that concerned her. She was fearful of being in a world from which she could no longer retreat. Was that the danger Henry had been referring to earlier?

"I've got it," he said when she tried to help. "By the way, I have to go to Savannah tomorrow. I've got a meeting that shouldn't last too long. Why don't you come. We could have a look around and then have dinner. There's a new restaurant down there that serves only locally grown organic—"

"Thanks, but I have to make some headway on work. I came here to finish some things, to avoid all the diversions of London."

He nodded. "Okay, but you are missing an opportunity for collard greens and red rice that rival Daughter's—just want you to be fully aware of the consequences of your decision. Oh, and that photograph of Cleve"—Henry pushed a plate forward in the air—"have a look upstairs."

"Up the stairs, turn left—last bedroom on the right?"

"That's it," he said, without looking up from placing a plate in the dishwasher.

THE UPSTAIRS WAS QUIET. ELIZA FELT AS IF NO ONE HAD walked down the hall for a very long time. She followed the collection of prints from *Indian Tribes of North America* that lined the walls. She knew she was daring herself to return to Henry's bed-

room. The last time she had been in this room was ten years ago—
the night before she left for New York to attend summer classes at
the Art Students League. It was the summer after her freshman
year of college. She and Henry had left a house party at Bulow
Plantation and driven to Oakhurst to be alone.

She pushed the door open. It was just as she remembered—a
large mahogany four-poster bed dressed in a navy and green tar-
tan, an English writing table positioned in front of the large window that looked out over the rice fields to the river. On the writing
desk, Eliza recognized the photograph she was looking for—an
eight-by-ten of Henry holding up a string of a dozen or more fish,
a tall thin black man standing by his side. Henry's two front teeth
were missing. Next to the photograph was another in a small silver
frame that startled her. It was a photograph of her sitting on the
side of a boat. Her hair was tied in a bandanna, and she wore a
white embroidered peasant blouse that fit loosely across her shoulders. She was laughing. Eliza remembered when the photograph
had been taken. It was the day she and Henry had sailed with
Weezie Vanderhorst and her older brother, Billy, out to the Morris
Island Lighthouse.

Before she headed back downstairs, Eliza looked around, as if
she had left something behind. As she started to walk down the
stairs, she heard Henry coming up three at a time.

"Oh, there you are," he said and stopped where he was. "Did
you find it?"

"Yes," she said.

"And did you see the photograph of you?"

She nodded.

"Do you remember that day? When we sailed to Morris Island?"

"I do, we sailed from the Yacht Club."

"It was rough, and we sailed fast. It took us all day."

"And we anchored close to the lighthouse and swam ashore. You and Billy climbed all the way to the top. Weezie and I were too scared."

"I was going through a closet a couple of years ago, looking for some keys I thought I'd lost, and I started checking every pocket of every jacket. In an old windbreaker at the back of my closet, I found a roll of film. I didn't know what it was or where it was from, but I developed it, and there was that beautiful photograph of you and a lot of the Morris Island Lighthouse and a really nice one of Weezie and Billy clowning around together. That film must have been sitting in my pocket for almost a decade. I keep meaning to give Mrs. Vanderhorst that photograph. Here, I'll get it." Henry sprinted up the remaining stairs, three at a time. Eliza turned and followed him. Henry opened the top drawer of his desk. "It's here somewhere." He bent over and looked at the back of the drawer. "Aha." He pulled out a packet and held it up. "Come look."

They sat together on the edge of the bed. Henry did not take his eyes off the photos as he flipped through them. "Here it is," he said and handed her the image. Billy was standing behind the wheel of the sailboat, holding up two fingers in the shape of a V, and Weezie had her arms and legs flung out, as if she were in the middle of a cartwheel.

Eliza looked at the photograph for a long time and then handed it back to Henry. She, Weezie, and Billy had done so many things together. As five- and six-year-olds they had chased pigeons in Hampton Park, as nine- and ten-year-olds they had pricked their thumbs with safety pins and sworn allegiance as blood brothers, and a few years later, they had tied strings with weights and chicken necks procured from Mr. Burbage's grocery store on the corner of Broad and Savage and had gone crabbing off the Battery. And for the next several years they had dragged discarded Christmas trees back to the Vanderhorst garden to build Christmas tree forts. "This was a few weeks before the accident. I need to see Mrs. Vanderhorst. I feel horrible I never came back to see her. Right after the funeral I used to drop by every week, and we would talk a lot about Billy and Weezie, but then when I went off to college and my mother moved to Middleburg—and I never— I'll go tomorrow."

"You could give her this. I keep meaning to do it." Henry opened his desk drawer and found an envelope.

"Does she still work at Century Antiques?"

"Don't know. My mother used to see her walking almost every evening, but she was just saying the other day that she hasn't seen her for a while." Henry put the photograph in the envelope and handed it back to Eliza. "Let's go down to the dock. You can leave that here and get it before we go back into town. You don't have to be home at any time, do you?"

They walked down the front lawn of the main house toward the river. The heat of the midmorning sun had already begun to silence the day. They crossed the bank separating the two large ponds. Henry pointed to a small alligator submerged below the surface of the water. At first Eliza thought that Henry was pointing to a stick or a piece of a small log, but then she made out the eyes and snout poking above the surface of the water. The little alligator floated toward them.

"Look at him. He thinks he has the whole pond to himself. Let's see how bold he is." Henry stood without moving as the little alligator swam within ten feet of the bank and stopped. When he took a large stride toward the edge of the pond, the alligator disappeared in a flash under the water.

They crossed the bank and turned toward the dock. Eliza lagged behind and stopped to peer down at the long expanse of mud the dock crossed. Frightened by Henry's passing shadow, the small fiddler crabs scurried to their holes. Eliza sat on her heels and watched them begin to peek back out, brandishing their oversized white claws as if it were possible to frighten the menacing giants who passed.

Henry walked to the end of the dock and was examining a small stretch of railing. "What's the matter?" she asked as she stood up and slipped off her shoes.

"Just some rotten wood." He looked up. "Be careful about splinters."

He pushed the section of railing back and forth to test it. "I need to replace these boards before they get too bad." He opened the doors of a wooden cabinet that had been built along the railing in the covered area of the dock. "Do you want to lie in or out of the sun?"

"In."

"You sure? Might be risky. You look like you've been in England a little too long for that."

"Sun would be great," she called back.

"Okay," he said. "But the sun can be pretty brutal if you haven't been in it."

The sun had already begun to warm the wooden floorboards of the dock. By midafternoon the boards would be too hot for bare feet.

Henry pulled cushions from the cabinet and positioned two next to one another in the sun. He sat with his elbows resting on his knees. Eliza joined him and lay on her stomach and looked through the cracks in the boards down at the water below. The sun felt like tiny needles of heat on her calves, and it made her skin feel tight.

Henry leaned forward. "Eliza, you did tear up your feet."

"I know."

"I would have thought in London you wore high heels all the time."

"I do, but I don't walk across a city."

"Look, over there." Henry pointed to a dark shape in a myrtle growing on the side of the riverbank. "An anhinga drying its wings."

Eliza raised her head to look at the dark bird that held its wings out as if hanging from a clothesline. "My father used to call them snakebirds."

"When they swim with only their neck above water, they do sort of look like snakes."

"You've spent a lot of time out here," she said and rested her cheek on her forearm.

"Yeah, I guess I have."

Eliza filled her lungs with the warm, rich country air. "Sun, smell of pluff mud, sound of the tide going out. What more could anyone ask for?"

"Well exactly, that's what I was trying to say to you last night."

"Henry, I wasn't being serious."

"I know, but I was."

Henry stretched out on his back with his knees bent and cushioned his head with the back of his hands. "God, I could go for a nap," he said and squinted up at the sky. He straightened one leg and then the other. He covered his eyes with his forearm and then turned his head to look at her. "So why Magritte?"

"'Why not?' as my adviser would always say to me as a way of always getting a positive response."

Henry laughed. "Why not? Exactly, why not?" He turned to face the sun. "You're going to regret having told me that. I am officially informing you that from now on—whenever you resist me on anything—that will be my new line of offense."

"We'll see." Eliza turned over on her back.

They watched a plane scratch a long line across the sky.

"Cleve used to tell me that the streams left by jets were souls disappearing into the sky on their way to heaven. He called them 'runn'n' clouds.' He told me that whenever I saw blue spaces in running clouds, it meant the souls were on their way to Jesus. I was probably a little younger than Lawton when he told me that." Henry looked at Eliza. "Did you ever think anything like that?" He continued without waiting for her to respond. "I believed every word. Now that I think about it, Cleve had me convinced that we could hear 'dem souls.' We would be fishing somewhere down the South Edisto, and he'd look up in the sky and say, 'There goes another one,' and I would ask him what he meant. 'Dem da souls,' he said, 'who is faithfully departed.' I don't think—in fact, I'm sure Cleve had never been on a plane. I don't think he'd ever been out of Charleston County—so those vapor trails—well, to him they were the souls making their way toward heaven. Cleve was full of colorful theories. I'm sure if my father had any idea of all the things Cleve filled my head with, he'd never have allowed me to stay with him all those summers."

Henry shook his head, as if he were trying to let go of something. "You know it's strange, but when I was at my father's funeral, I looked up at the sky, and I saw the trace of a jet and felt for a few minutes that Cleve was by my side. It was as if everything—all those years—had collapsed into one second."

He pulled his white tee shirt over his head and dropped it at his side. "I can't entice you to take your shirt off."

"Not a chance."

"Didn't think so." He laughed and lay back down and looked at her. "Do you think you can—I mean, can one—ever return to a place one's left?"

"What do you mean? I'm here."

"I mean, can you ever truly find the place you left?"

"Because the place is the same, but you are not?"

"Exactly, that's exactly what I was thinking."

"No, I guess not," Eliza said and covered her eyes with the bend of her elbow. She wanted to stop her mind from thinking, from going any further than the perimeter of her body. No past, no future, just here—the hot sun, the water lapping against the dock, the salty, rich smell of the pluff mud, and Henry by her side, as if nothing bad had ever happened.

She had drifted half asleep, when Henry asked, "So tell me, what did you mean by 'perhaps'?"

Eliza took a minute to find her bearings. "What are you talking about?"

"At Caroline and Simon's wedding when Jamie went to get you a drink, I said he is crazy about you, and you said, 'Perhaps.' What did you mean?"

She sat up and looked at Henry. "I'm not sure I know."

"Is it that, or is it that you don't want to tell me?"

"Probably a little bit of both."

Henry nodded his head. "Any chance of explaining to me why he didn't come to Charleston with you?"

"As soon as you tell me why you aren't married." Eliza shaded her eyes to look at her watch. "Ten thirty-four A.M.—neither too early nor too late for serious subjects. You're safe to tell me. Why didn't you stay with Issie?"

Henry got up and sat on the edge of one of the dock chairs. He took a deep breath and then looked straight at Eliza. "I didn't love her, not even close. I never did. We got together at one of those wild house parties at her grandmother's plantation where everyone drank way too much. I told her it was wrong, that it never should have happened." He pulled a splinter of wood from the floorboard. "I loved you. Issie went back up to Boston, and I never expected to hear from her again." Henry's voice turned quiet and soft. He leaned forward and rested his elbows on his knees. "At the beginning of the fall, she came down to Yale and told me she was pregnant, it was too late . . ."

"That's when you came to tell me," Eliza said.

The tide slapped and gulped against the side of the floating dock. Eliza sat down on the edge and watched the current
run across the arches of her feet. "You know, when you called
me and said you were coming to Princeton, I thought you just
wanted to see me." She shuddered as if trying to shake off something. "I remember it was in October—right before my midterm
exams." She lifted her feet a quarter of an inch and leaned forward
to see how thin she could make the layer of water run over her
arches. She watched the iced tea color of the river water disappear into perfect clearness as the layer got thinner. "I met you
at PJ's Pancake House across the street from Firestone Library,
and I remember, as you were telling me about what had happened
between you and Issie, watching the cream disappear into my coffee and feeling as if my skin were a thin layer of metal, and that
there was nothing inside of me except air. I remember getting up
and saying to you, 'I would never have done that to you,' and walking back across the street to the reading room on the first floor of
Firestone and sitting there all day. I felt as if my mind had disappeared. I couldn't process anything." She looked up at Henry, who
was standing over her. "I thought you were my best friend. I didn't
really understand what had happened."

"Oh, Eliza, I . . ." Henry moved toward her.

"Please go on. I interrupted you." She had only meant to listen,
but returning to the memory of that day had overwhelmed her.

"So we got married three months before Lawton was born,
and we divorced three months after. God, as I say this, it sounds
so mechanical, but actually that's the way it was. Do you want me
to keep going?" Henry looked down the river. "We got married to
make things right for Lawton, or as right as we could. We were
married in form only—we never were together. Issie never really
wanted Lawton. I think she was just looking for a sense of security
with me, and that wasn't going to happen. So she gave him up to

me, and with the help of my mother, I've been raising him ever since. But you knew some of this, right?"

"Some," she said.

Henry paused before continuing. "As soon as Lawton was born, Issie split to travel around Europe, I think she went to school for a bit in Paris, but she didn't stay there very long. I haven't seen her since she left, Lawton has never met her, last I heard she was living with a painter or an art dealer in Tangier. The more exotic, the better for Issie. Her grandmother died a year or two after Lawton was born, and the funeral was in Boston. Very few people from here went. I don't even know if Issie came back for it. Issie's father kept his mother's plantation on the Combahee River as well as her house in town, but both have been closed up for some time. Do you want to hear this? Do you want me to stop?"

"No, it's okay."

The approaching hum of a motorboat made Henry and Eliza turn to look down the river. They watched the boat make a slow curve and turn toward a sandbar. The driver turned the motor off and let the boat glide into the shallow water. Three adults, two small children, and a dog jumped out. They wandered around the edges, looking for things in the sand. They were far away and looked like stick people. The two children sat down and began to play in the sand.

"I thought about you all the time. How I'd screwed up everything. And I thought so many times about finding you and trying to explain everything, but then I guess I thought I didn't have the right. I didn't deserve another chance. The best I could do was to give Lawton everything I had. And I guess, too, I felt if you wanted to be with me, you'd come back." Henry looked back down the river, as if he were waiting for something to happen. He turned back to Eliza. "Why didn't you?"

"Why didn't I what?"

"Why didn't you come back?"

"I don't know. It's not that I didn't want to come back, it's just that I—I don't know—I had a lot going on in New York. Then London. And it's not as if Charleston were going anywhere. I'd get wedding invitations from friends, and I suppose I should have come down for them, but Charleston felt both too familiar and too far away in a lot of different ways. I felt I knew everybody and everything down here. And right after we broke up—I didn't want to run into you and Issie—or anybody really—but then later it was more that I never had a reason to come back."

Henry looked up into the sun and shook his head. "Eliza, I'm so very sorry. It was god-awful of me. I've thought all these years about what I would say to you, but now that I'm with you, I can't think of anything to say except that I'm really sorry. What I did was unforgivable. You have every reason to hate me. Whatever happened between Issie and me—whatever you want to call it—ended as soon as it began—a decade ago."

"I still didn't want to run into her. Or you."

"It shouldn't have happened. It would have never happened if we had been together."

She turned and looked at him. "You're not going to—"

"No, no, Eliza, that's not what I mean."

"It can't be repaired," she said.

"What can't?"

"Any of it."

Henry's voice calmed. "I know. I know that. It's just that I'm trying to explain it—to get you to understand it a little better. Life doesn't always go as planned. It's rare that it goes smoothly or without complications. It's messier than that. It's not like those night trains we used to listen to. Nothing is perfect, and nothing is ever quite in its place."

"If you cared so much, why didn't you come and see me or even write me a letter? One letter. Just one. You know, as devastated as I was, as much as I felt I hated you—for over two years—every time I checked my mail—I don't even know now why I'm telling you this—I thought there would be a letter from you."

"Eliza, I don't know what to say."

"Why didn't you write to me?"

Henry paused before he answered. "I should have. But I guess I was so certain that you were completely finished with me that it would have made things worse. I went to see your mother about a year after we broke up, and she told me it wasn't a good idea to get in touch with you. She was very clear that I should leave you alone. And so I did, and I know it sounds like a story, but I always thought about you, and I kept thinking that I would run into you at some point in Charleston. And enough time would pass so that things between us wouldn't be so raw, and things would heal over time— slowly and naturally. I knew if I tried to force—or push it—it would never work. Eliza, I'm fearful of telling you this because I may scare you off, but you know I am in love with you. I never stopped loving you." He stopped and looked down at her. "Look, I know I'm asking a lot, and I know my odds aren't great, but just give us one more chance. Really. What do you have to lose?"

"I have quite a lot to lose, Henry."

"Jamie?"

"Yes, Jamie, and a much sought after fellowship at the Courtauld and a whole other world over there that has nothing to do with anyone or anything down here."

Eliza lightly tapped the soles of her feet against the top of the water. Henry sat down beside her. "I remember once with Weezie, we'd been given lockets for our birthday with our birthstones. She had a garnet, and I had an aquamarine, and we were on her dock down on Wadmalaw Island, and we dared each other to hold our locket above a crack in the dock and let go and then try to catch it."

Eliza pulled her knees to her chest and rested her forehead on her knees and took a slow deep breath. "I have no idea why I'm remembering this now." She started to stand up. "Listen, would you mind if we went back into town? My mother and Ben are going back to Middleburg this week, and I should spend some time with them."

Henry didn't respond.

"You know, Henry, who's to say we would have stayed together way back when. We were so young."

Henry stood up and turned her toward him. "Eliza . . ."

She looked at him hard before she spoke. She didn't pull away. "I'm just tired—that's all. In the past thirty-six hours, I've had three hours of sleep." She turned and walked up the ramp and leaned down to pick up her moccasins. Eliza looked back at Henry. "Thanks for the tour and," she added, "not getting us lost." She squinted up at the sun and checked its position overhead. The afternoon was stretching long in the sun. "I should stop at the house to get the photograph for Mrs. Vanderhorst."

# CHAPTER SEVEN

ELIZA DIDN'T WAKE UP UNTIL AFTER LUNCHTIME THE NEXT day. There was a tight pain on the tops of her shoulders and the backs of her legs. She ducked her head under her pillow to escape the light. She listened to the staccato sounds of footsteps across the hardwood floors on the first floor. Her mother was saying something in a loud voice to Cornelia. Things never changed here—that was both the comfort and the danger. She could leave for another ten years and slip right back in. But London wasn't that way. In ten years there would be different people everywhere—new artists, new museum directors, new ideas, new collectors. When she returned in two weeks, *something*—she didn't know what—would have happened that people would be talking about. Eliza's thoughts were broken by voices from downstairs and the front door closing.

Eliza found Cornelia in the kitchen. When Cornelia saw her, she threw her hands up and gave her a big hug. "You had me thinking you weren't ever coming back. Miss Pamela just left, but she told me to tell you there's a party this evening she wants you to go to with her and Mr. Ben. She wrote it down, now what have I done with that piece of paper—seeing you has gotten me all stirred up. I'll find it directly."

They sat down at the kitchen table and had coffee. Cornelia told Eliza all about the aches and pains in her back and neck and knees, and Eliza knew it was Cornelia's way of explaining why she worked only two days a week now. As they sipped coffee together, Cornelia was filled with questions. Had Eliza ever met the queen? Did she go around wearing a crown? Had Eliza ever been to Buckingham Palace? Cornelia left the kitchen to look for the mislaid note, saying to herself that one day she sure would like to get over there and see for herself. Cornelia returned triumphant. Eliza's mother would be back at three. Richard and Lydia Alston were having a few people over for a light supper and wanted Eliza to come. Allington would be there, and Eliza's mother hoped Eliza could spend some time with him. Eliza had only the high heels she had worn to Sara's party. She thought she would walk up King Street to Bob Ellis shoes and look for a new pair of dressy sandals.

THE MIDDAY SUN WAS MOVING ACROSS THE TOPS OF ROOFS when Eliza set out. She checked her watch. She could buy shoes and still make it back in time to settle into a few solid hours of work before the Alstons' cocktail party. She avoided three young boys on skateboards, reckless and oblivious to her existence, who looped up and down the driveway slopes of the sidewalk. She walked up Church Street past the Eveleigh house. Legend had it that Francis Marion had broken his ankle by jumping off the second-floor balcony. It was a story Charlestonians never let go of, despite the incongruity with the facts. There were a number of such tales in Charleston—tales about pirates and ghosts and duels and embellished family histories. Charleston had its own mythology, its own rules, and sometimes its own language. We see with our memories, she reminded herself. Maybe that was one of the reasons why—without knowing it—she had left and had not come back. Maybe she had needed to be in a place where the past held no dominion.

Eliza crossed Water Street and passed in front of the window of the rare-book shop with the first editions of DuBose Heyward's *Mamba's Daughters* and William Faulkner's *Sanctuary* in the window. She continued walking north, past the First Baptist Church, and then across Tradd. She paused in front of Century Antiques. The yellow jasmine that surrounded the door architrave was unkempt and fragrant. A tall woman with short dark hair and glasses appeared from the back room. Eliza asked about Mrs. Vanderhorst. "No, dear, she only works on Tuesday and Thursday."

"Would you tell her Eliza Poinsett dropped by? I'll try to come by tomorrow."

Eliza walked on past 82 Church Street. A young woman dressed in a light blue shift was leaving with a large white shopping bag tied with a pink ribbon. She was followed by three little girls—Eliza guessed them to be between the ages of six and ten—all in matching white cotton dresses. A bell attached to the door jingled as it closed. Eliza remembered that same sound—no doubt it was the same bell—when her mother had brought her to 82 Church to pick out a new party dress.

Charleston felt quieter because she no longer recognized all the faces, and voices were meant for other people besides herself. It was as if she were invisible. All that happened in the city now bore no relation to her, had nothing to do with her. The mother cautioned her youngest daughter to be careful of the step down to the street. Her accent was southern, but the way she stretched out words defined her as not being from Charleston.

Eliza walked past the Nathaniel Heyward House and paused to

admire the symmetry and balance of its facade with its five open-
ings repeated on three floors. She had remembered going with
Henry to a reception in honor of his father after he had restored the
house and donated it to the city. She noticed a new plaque placed
just under the one designating it a National Historic Monument.
The new bronze plaque revealed that it was in the Nathaniel Heyward House that the citizens of Charleston had entertained George
Washington on his visit to their city in 1791. She crossed Church
Street and turned east down Elliott Street past Poinsett Tavern,
which had been built in the eighteenth century by an ancestor. She
had heard that it had been sold several years ago to someone from
New York. Its trim had been freshly painted, the brick repointed,
and a Preservation Society plaque added to its facade.

A horse-drawn carriage with a tour guide dressed in gray Civil
War trousers with a red sash was stopped in front of the small
building. "Elisha Poinsett was the builder of this tavern in 1732. His
descendant Joel Roberts Poinsett served as secretary of war from
1837 to 1841 under President Van Buren. As minister to Mexico in
1825, he introduced the poinsettia to the United States." The tour
guide slapped the reins on the rumps of the two large draft horses.
The leather harness creaked as they leaned forward. The voice of
the tour guide evaporated.

Eliza thought about what Henry had said about returns.
Charleston was a place that now—more than ever—looked more
backward than forward. People were defined by who their ancestors were—when and from where their families had come and for
how long they had stayed, what families they had married into, who
their first and second cousins were. Where you were from rated
more than where you were going. When someone not from Charleston bought a house South of Broad, the house was never referred to
as theirs, but as the house of the last Charlestonian who had owned
it. Charleston seemed to be protecting and cherishing something

that no longer mattered, or at least no longer mattered beyond its boundaries. Even the way they spoke—the absence of any drawl, the long closed-mouth vowels and dropped *r*'s that almost sounded English—defined them as being different from the rest of the South. And Charlestonians, especially the older generation, prided themselves on this difference. *Beer* sounded the same as *bear, pen* was indistinguishable from *pin, house* rhymed with *mousse,* and *eight* was in its own category. While some of the distinctive pronunciations had softened with her generation, when people first met Eliza and found out that she was from the South, they would always ask her, "What happened to your southern accent?" and she would have to explain that Charleston had its own distinct accent. It was an inflection that clung to the past. A number of the first inhabitants of Charleston were from upper-class English families who had come to Charleston to pursue fortunes. Eliza's mother was descended from the seventh son of an English earl who had come to Charleston as primogeniture insured he would inherit very little. Thoughts of England were never far from these early settlers. They imported furniture, silver, china, silks, and yards and yards of decorative plaster to adorn their ceilings and cornices. In the eighteenth and early part of the nineteenth century, they sent their sons back to England to be educated. Eliza didn't know if the vestiges of England that still remained in the language were by choice or circumstance. And yet there was something soothing and seductive about coming back home, as if Charleston were whispering to her, "Come back. Stay. Don't ever leave again."

Eliza reached the corner of Church and Broad streets and stopped in front of the Hat Man. She remembered Henry's words as they had walked past him last night, "He's still there." He wore a gray top hat with a thick yellow band around its base. His head was in the shape of a tall white hatbox, and his eyes were upturned bowlers, his mouth an upturned Stetson, his nose a tall sombrero, and his ears two flat straw hats turned on their side. His arms and legs were a combination of top hats of different sizes, and for feet, he had two sailor berets with black ribbon trailing in the front. He held a closed black umbrella and walking stick behind his back. The building on whose side he was painted was no longer a haberdashery but a boutique for china and gifts and lingerie. Eliza walked past the law offices with their shingles hanging with the family names of boys with whom she had gone to Cotillion, built Christmas tree forts, attended debutante parties, beach parties, and oyster roasts in the country. A few of the law offices had been converted to a smart antique shop, a stationery shop, a silver shop, but for the most part Broad Street looked the same. Everything was just in better shape.

Eliza stopped at the post office on the southwest corner of Meeting and Broad to check the times on the FedEx box. One and six P.M. She was still thinking about the work she had to finish in order to make Tuesday's one o'clock pickup as she crossed Broad Street and headed north on King past all of the small antique shops. Delano's was still in the same place, but Mr. Delano had died, and his wife had sold the business to a woman from Ohio who kept a parrot in the shop. Eliza's mother had told her that the antiques were no longer of the same quality as Mr. Delano's, nor was the new owner as reluctant as Mr. Delano to sell pieces. Eliza remembered that going in his shop was like going to someone's house for afternoon tea. There was rarely any discussion of selling and never of price. You came in, spoke, Mr. Delano quietly followed you around, sometimes telling you about pieces you stopped to admire. It was almost as if you were being interviewed. If Mr. Delano deemed you worthy of the piece of furniture, a typed note with a description of the piece and price would arrive in the mail several days later.

As she stood looking at a pair of Chippendale side chairs displayed in the window, she heard Henry calling her name. He had pulled over in his beaten-up white Jeep, window down, an arm hung over the side in the shape of a V. "Hop in," he said.

"I'm going uptown." She pointed north. "I have to buy shoes for tonight."

"I'll give you a ride."

"It's okay."

"No, I'd like to. Really." Henry checked the rearview mirror. "Jump in before the light changes."

Eliza looked behind Henry's Jeep at the cars stopped at a traffic light at the King and Beaufain streets crossing. She ran quickly around to the passenger side.

Henry turned and smiled at her. "It's great to see you."

"You saw me yesterday."

"I know, and it's great to see you again."

"I thought you said you had to drive down to Savannah today?"

"I did. I decided to postpone my trip until tomorrow."

"Why?"

"You."

"Me?"

"Yes. I didn't think yesterday went as well as it should have. I just wanted to make sure that you were okay and that you hadn't given up on me. I was going to call you, but I figured you might say, based on yesterday, that you didn't want to see me, so I thought I would just come and find you."

"By driving around?"

"No, actually I went by your house, and Cornelia said you had left to walk uptown to buy shoes. This is infinitely better, just running into you like this. Don't you think? Fate? Providence? Destiny? Divine Grace?"

Eliza didn't answer. She looked to her right at the window of the Preservation Society. It was filled with books on Charleston, recipe books, books on plantations, the Civil War, Francis Marion.

"Did you not see Mrs. Vanderhorst?" Henry asked, looking at the envelope Eliza held in her hand.

"She doesn't work on Mondays, but she'll be there tomorrow."

"Looks like you got a lot of sun yesterday."

"I did."

"Too much?"

"A little."

When the light turned green, Henry shifted into first and drove straight. "You could have turned down Queen," Eliza said. One block later Henry turned right onto Broad Street and continued on past Logan Street.

"We should have turned up Logan. Henry, why are we going this way? Where are we going?"

"Slight detour."

Henry drove past the tennis courts at Moultrie Playground and onto Lockwood Boulevard, the western boundary of the Charleston Peninsula.

"Come on, Henry, please? I really have to get shoes for tonight, and I have only three hours for work before I'm supposed to be at the Alstons' for an early supper."

"We'll know soon whether you trust me."

"We know I don't so—"

"But there is a chance?"

"No," Eliza stretched the word into two syllables.

"No?" Henry shook his head. "We'll have to fix that, then."

They passed the Charleston Marina.

"Remember Peyton Thornhill? He now runs the Marina shop," Henry said.

"You're ignoring me and changing the subject."

"I know, but it's not for much longer. I promise."

He turned the radio to FM 102.5, the station that played music from the 1960s. He reached over and turned the radio up. "Sam

Cooke—'A Change Is Gonna Come,'" he said. "See? Destiny. We're doing the right thing."

"Henry, it's a song about the Civil Rights Movement."

"True."

"James Island. Why are we going to James Island?"

"Just wait," Henry said.

When "A Change Is Gonna Come" was followed by "Ain't No Mountain High Enough," Henry turned the radio even louder and drummed his flat palm on the steering wheel. The highway dead-ended into Folly Road. Henry turned left toward Folly Beach. Eliza rolled her window down.

"You aren't going to attempt an escape?"

"No," she sighed. "Just conceding defeat and"—she leaned her head back—"I'm just reminding myself what it feels like to be southern again."

They crossed Folly Creek and sped across the marsh on the narrow causeway that connected the island to the mainland. The road narrowed to a single lane with a three-foot bicycle path on the margin. A band of seagulls rainbowed across the sky.

Eliza read a sign out loud. "'Welcome to Folly Beach at the edge of America.' Folly Beach? Why Folly Beach?"

"We're almost there."

The causeway turned into the two blocks of Main Street with a gas station, two surf shops, a liquor store, and a variety store that proudly displayed the plastic head of a shark with its jaws open. Main Street dead-ended at the pier.

"We're going to the pier?"

"No, but not a bad guess." Henry turned left, and they drove down the beachfront, where cottage after cottage had been built in the 1920s and 1930s.

At its very end, the island narrowed to a small strip barely wide enough for one road and a row of houses. Mothers with folding

chairs and towels and coolers were trailed by sun-drenched children back to the cars they had parked alongside the road. The road
narrowed to a thin sliver with water on both sides. They reached
the end and stopped at a gate with a sign that warned PRIVATE
PROPERTY—NO TRESPASSING.

Eliza had never been here. Henry stopped the Jeep in front of
the gate and leaned over her to open the glove compartment. He
fished for a key on a braided piece of leather. He opened the gate
and drove through.

"I bet you thought there wasn't anyplace we could go that we
hadn't been to before," Henry said.

"In Charleston?"

"In Charleston."

"We've been to Folly before."

"Yes, but not here."

"Is this yours?" Eliza asked.

Henry nodded.

"I didn't know you owned this."

"Nor did I until my father died. In the 1920s, my grandfather
bought a good bit of the northern tip of this island. He left most
of it to the Episcopal Church as a summer retreat for orphans, but
the church sold it, even though they weren't supposed to. When my
father died, I had to review everything. My father had been paying
taxes on a tract of land I didn't recognize. I went back to some of
the original documents and found that my grandfather had saved
fifty acres on the tip. My mother didn't even know about it. I asked
Clarence Frost, who had been my grandfather's and father's lawyer,
and he said he couldn't really remember, but there was something
about a distant cousin drowning out here. The current at this end
is treacherous. Mr. Frost is ninety-two so I don't know, but maybe
that's why my father never came out here or did anything about this

land. I do remember my father telling me about spending summers on Folly Beach when he was a child. He talked about a double row of dunes with palmetto trees. He said his favorite thing to do was to lie in a hammock at night and look up at the stars and listen to the sound of the waves." Henry braked.

Ahead the road was washed out for a good thirty feet.

"Can we make it through all that water?" Eliza asked.

"I think so, I went across it last week. Just depends on how soft the bottom is. Do you want to get out while I see if I can get through?"

"No, I'll stay."

"You sure?"

Eliza nodded.

"It's going to be rough. Put on your seat belt and hold on."

Henry yanked the Jeep into four-wheel drive and shifted into first and then second and pressed his foot down hard on the gas pedal. The Jeep hit the water and began to skid, and Henry kept his foot down and twisted and turned the steering wheel to keep moving forward. When the Jeep began to stick on the soft muddy bottom, he shifted into reverse and gunned the Jeep backward and then shifted into first and raced it forward and then back to reverse without ever letting the Jeep stop to sink into the soft bottom. Eliza braced herself against the dashboard and the car door. Henry rocked the Jeep backward and forward until it reared past the bad spot. He turned the steering wheel to the right, and the Jeep spun and skidded sideways, and its left rear side slammed hard into the trunk of a pine tree as they cleared the washed-out area.

"All in one piece?" Henry looked behind him in the rearview mirror.

"So is this how your Jeep has gotten so beaten up?"

"Pretty much. We can go out the back way on the way home. It can't be any worse than this. Hang on." Henry shifted into neutral. "I just want to check that I didn't bust the brake light."

He got back in the car. "All intact."

A quarter of a mile later they pulled up to a cleared area where a small wooden house, painted forest green, stood. It was raised several feet off the ground on pilings. It had a low-pitched red tin roof, which extended over a front porch that ran the length of the house. Huge palmetto trees stood in random clusters on the rough lawn.

"This cottage was about to fall down when I discovered it. I think my grandfather built it. He built a number of cottages down at the other end of Folly Beach just to keep people working during the Depression. It has beautiful cypress paneling inside. Here, I'll show you around."

Henry led Eliza up the front porch. It was bare except for a few pieces of driftwood and sand dollars. The house consisted of a large front room that was sparsely furnished, one bedroom and bath on one side at the back and a small kitchen on the other side.

"I'm sensing there's a limited range of physical activity that I can do with you," Henry said, then clapped his hands together. "So, well, what do you say about a walk?"

"Henry, come on, when are you going to tell me why we're really here?"

"I want to sort everything out with you. I figured the only way to do that was to kidnap you and take you to a place you couldn't tell me you had to leave. Plus, it really is beautiful down here at this time of the day. We have the entire beach to ourselves."

"God, Henry, is there more to say? Is it really going to help anything?"

"Maybe not, I just want to make certain we have the right ending before you disappear at the end of next week." He kicked off a pair of tennis shoes that were so old that the canvas had separated in several places from the rubber rims of the soles. "You can leave your shoes here."

They followed the boardwalk down to the beach. The breeze from the ocean rattled the tall sea oats that covered the dunes. The tide was low, and the sense of scale was distorted by the lack of any human figures. The broad beach stretched on forever.

"No one comes to this end much. There's no parking, plus it's known for treacherous rip currents. Look, right there." Henry pointed to an area of the surf where the waves were small and choppy, and the water had a sand-colored tint.

Eliza recognized the sandy water. She knew there must be a channel between two sandbars out there, and the waves, when they broke, flowed back through the channel. She also knew that the sandbars were constantly shifting with the tides and the rip currents were never in the same place.

"Let's walk north to the end," he said. "You can see Charleston and the Morris Island Lighthouse from there."

The beach sand was warm from the sun, and Eliza walked along the ruffled edge of the waves. She picked up a perfect sand dollar lying on the sand and then put it back down.

"Don't want to keep it?" Henry asked.

"No."

"Really?"

"I've stopped collecting."

"Doesn't seem possible, not even tempted?"

"No, not really. I don't know. It just feels—well, lighter."

When they got to the northern tip, they stopped and looked at the lighthouse that stood three hundred yards out in the water. The six wide stripes of alternating black and white were faded and peeling.

"There's hardly anything left of Morris Island. Look. It's low tide, and there's just a sliver of sand around its base," Henry said.

"We should go out there again. It's just as we left it. We could sail or take a canoe from here. Come to think about it"—he shifted sand over a shell with his toe—"sailing from the Yacht Club was probably not the smartest thing we ever tried."

They turned to walk back, but Henry stopped and looked at the lighthouse again. "I wonder how much longer it will be there. I took Lawton out there last summer. The door was open, and we climbed all the way to the top. It's in remarkably good shape. I had forgotten how beautiful its wrought-iron spiral staircase is. They've taken the old light out, so the top platform is bare. Just the same wrought-iron bars running every two feet or so, vertically and horizontally. So you can see all around you—three hundred and sixty degrees."

When they reached the path that led back to the house, Henry turned and pointed to the darkness gathering along the horizon.

"Cleve used to always tell me that was the shadow of the earth. And I guess I heard it so many times I believed him. I remember talking to my science teacher at Woodbury Forest about the possibility of such a thing. It makes no sense, but I really wanted to believe there was a way it was possible."

Eliza looked where he pointed. "I see," she said. "I've never noticed that before."

"It doesn't last very long."

Henry broke off a piece of a sea oat and chewed on the blade. "If we go around to the back of the island, we should be able to catch a couple of red drum."

"For?"

"Supper."

"Henry, I should get back to town. I can't waste another day."

"Waste? Waste? Oh, hard-hearted Eliza."

"Come on, Henry, you know I brought work to do, and so far I've done nothing except unpack my suitcase, and even that I haven't finished."

"I understand. I do. But it's just Monday. We haven't seen each other for ten years. And, Eliza, listen, I can't speak for you, but there's no place I would rather be than here with you right now. I promise I will leave you alone all day tomorrow." He held the palms of his hands out to her. "Promise," he laughed.

She shook her head and smiled. "You always do this to me."

"Do what?"

"Get me to do things I don't want to. But I should, at least, call my mother and tell her I'm not going to be able to make it to the Alstons' party. Is there a phone inside?"

"There's one in the kitchen. It should work."

Eliza called and the answering machine picked up. She waited for her mother's long message to finish.

When Eliza returned, Henry was sitting outside on the steps. He was turning a piece of driftwood slowly over in his hands. He looked up at her. "Did you get through?"

"Yes, fine, no one was home, so I left a message."

"I remember you liked fishing."

"I'm retired."

"Good Lord, Eliza, what have those English boys done to you? You can watch me, then. There's a nice spot to sit. You'll need your shoes."

He disappeared around the corner of the house and came back with a fishing rod, net, and small plastic box. He held the fishing rod up. "You're sure?"

"Sure. What are you going to use as bait?"

Henry rattled the box. "Lures."

They followed a small path from the back of the house that took them through the land that was too sandy and salty for much to grow on except for a few scrub pines. They emerged into a cleared area on the back of the island.

"Positive you don't want to give this a try?"

"I'll watch," she said.

Henry tied a fly on the end of his rod and walked out until he was waist deep in the water. He anchored himself and then pulled the line out from the rod with one hand and cast with the other. He let the line run with the current and then followed the line with the tip of his rod. When the line had stretched way past him, he pulled the line back in and cast again. The line caught the late afternoon sun and for a brief second hung in the air. On the seventh cast, Henry jerked his rod and began reeling in a fish. It fought hard, but Henry was patient. He twisted his rod one way and then the other, and when the fish started to run, he let it go, and when it paused, Henry started reeling again. He wore the fish down within five feet of himself and scooped it up with the aluminium net he had clipped onto his belt.

Henry brought the red drum ashore and cut a piece of vine from a tree and threaded it through its mouth and back through its gill. Its scales, iridescent in the water, were already beginning to dull and turn gray in the open air. Eliza watched without saying anything, and when Henry headed back to the water, she shifted her position several yards from the fish so she wouldn't have to watch it expire.

Henry returned within twenty minutes with another red drum a little smaller than the first. "This is probably enough, unless you are really hungry," he said. Eliza shook her head. He looked up at the sky. The late afternoon clouds had already begun to scatter. "They don't bite much after dusk anyway," he added.

They walked back to the house. Henry told her he was going to clean the fish and start the grill. "There should be some cold beers in the refrigerator. And if you could bring me a couple of plates. And some salt and pepper. There should be some candles on the kitchen table. Bring those and we can eat outside. There's enough of a breeze to keep the gnats away."

They ate the grilled fish and drank the cold beer and were quiet between themselves. Eliza pressed her fingers in the soft dripped wax at the base of a candle.

"You still do that."

"Do what?" she asked.

"Play with the wax."

"No, I don't."

"Yes, you do."

She knew he was right.

Henry stood up and took her plate and the two empty bottles. Eliza started to rise. He nodded. "I've got this, I'll be right back."

She sat back in her chair and looked out at the sky. It was becoming streaked with deep pastel colors of lavender, pink, and blue in patterns that looked like the small streams of water left by the waves that ran down to the ocean's edge. It was as if the sky were trying to run away from the evening.

Henry returned with a light-colored blanket that had a red and green stripe on it. He put his hand on her shoulder. "Let's go down to the water. We can sit on this."

"That looks like something from the West," she said.

"It does." He turned it over and examined it. "Must be from my uncle's ranch."

"Your mother's brother?"

"Yes, John. I can't remember if you ever met him. He's a bit of a recluse. He comes to Charleston maybe once every five or six years. He moved out to Wyoming straight from college and has been there ever since. Never married. Lawton must have brought it back last time he was out there."

"Don't you have to get back for Lawton?"

"No, he's spending the night with his best friend, Sam Logan."

"George Logan's son?"

"Exactly, from Columbia. Did you know him?"

"Not really. I was set up with him at some debutante party. Might have been Alexandra Lockwood's."

"Could be. He married Alexandra's older sister, India."

"He was a tennis player, wasn't he?"

"A very good one. Lawton and Sam play doubles together."

They walked in single file over the dunes. Henry spread the blanket on the sand and waited for Eliza. He walked to the edge of the ocean and watched for a while before walking back. "Tide's just turned," he said. "It's coming in." He sat down beside her. "Are you cold?" he asked.

She shook her head and unfolded her arms and straightened them behind her. She stretched back and looked up at the sky. All the colors were fading fast—soon it would be dark. "So what did you want to say to me?" She hugged her knees and turned her head toward him.

"A lot."

Henry pulled Eliza close and kissed her. She moved her hands over his shoulders and followed the ridges and dips of the muscles down his back to the old scar on his left hip. She still remembered the day years ago when he had snagged his skin on the corner of a boat's windshield, diving to retrieve a lost water ski. She had forgotten nothing of Henry's body, and he had forgotten nothing of hers. The ten-year gap, the distance of an ocean, had done nothing to who they were for each other. With Henry, there had always been a feeling of happiness that did not depend on what happened next.

"You have always been able to get me to do things I'm not sure I should be doing," she whispered to him.

"I still don't believe you," he whispered back and adjusted his arms around her. "I know you better than that" was the last thing he said to her before they drifted off to sleep.

A COLD WAVE RAN UP THEIR CALVES AND THEN RECEDED, and they both woke with a start. Henry shook his head. "Quick, here comes another one." He grabbed Eliza's arm and pulled her up. He reached down and took the corner of the blanket and stepped back quickly four paces, pulling her with him. The wave disappeared back down the beach.

"What time is it?" she asked.

Henry held his watch up to the sky. "Can't really see, but it's almost high tide, so it must be around two, maybe three."

"Did we fall asleep for that long?"

"I'd better get you home." Henry stood for a few minutes, looking out over the water. Eliza tried to see what he was watching, but all she could see was darkness that stretched the whole length of the beach with nothing to stop it.


HENRY DROVE SLOWLY OVER THE CAUSEWAY IN THE DARK-ness back to a sleeping Charleston. It was as if someone had put a blanket over the day. The windows were down, and the air was fresh and soft and full with the salt of the high tide. Eliza pulled her long hair back and twisted it in a knot. She pulled her knees up and rested her feet on the dashboard and tilted her head on her hand toward the open window. As they drove up and over the James Island Bridge, it was as if they would soon be flying over the tops of the houses and pine trees beyond the marsh. The streets were empty except for one or two cars they passed headed in the opposite direction.

Henry reached over and pushed the hair back from her face. "You haven't said a word to me."

"It's as if all of this doesn't really exist," she said, but what she was thinking was how strange and wonderful it felt to be alone with Henry. Somewhere, somehow, in all of the intense study and the hard work, she had lost some part of herself, and now it was coming back to her. It was as if something forgotten had been found. She closed her eyes for a moment to consider where she was. She felt as if she were looking at a detail of a painting that she knew well and finding the artist's choice of line and color more intense and purer than she had remembered. She thought about that afternoon she and Henry had jumped off the Ben Sawyer Bridge. She remembered being perfectly balanced on the outside of the railing and looking down and concentrating hard on the ridges in the water below and at Henry, who was treading water and looking up at her. And she remembered that before she jumped she looked behind her, and she never understood why. And now she suddenly felt that if she dared herself to look over her shoulder, she would see Jamie, and everything in front of her would disappear.

She looked across the marshes toward the Charleston peninsula and the row of large houses along Murray Boulevard. Only a few still had lights on.

"You know, I always dreaded the day my mother would call and tell me that you had married," Eliza said.

"You would have cared?"

"I wanted to believe I didn't, but I never let myself think so far."

Henry looked straight ahead and asked, "You still haven't told me why Jamie didn't come back with you."

Eliza braced herself. She could no longer avoid looking back. "I don't know—I just got—well, I just wanted to slow things down. And then I suppose I got overwhelmed with the whole idea of living in England for the rest of my life. There was something so final about it all."

"What happened?"

"I'm not sure really." She dipped her head to look into the side mirror. There was nothing but darkness behind them. "But the idea of being with Jamie started to feel so foreign." Eliza wondered if she were telling Henry too much, but she also understood that what had happened between them on Folly Beach had its own set of reasons and consequences.

"Jamie is wonderful, but he never stands still, and he never enters a doorway the same way. And the idea of living the rest of my life in England was so disorienting. Watching everything that was familiar to me disappear."

Henry slid off the overpass down the ramp for Lockwood Boulevard.

"I just finally told him I thought I should go to Charleston by myself—that I wasn't sure we were right together—that I would be away for two weeks and when I got back we would sort things out."

"How did he feel about that?"

"He told me I was making a mistake, that it wouldn't be good for us. He had been planning to go to St. Kilda in July to begin work on a documentary. The National Trust had just given him the go-ahead, so he decided to start on it straightaway and not wait. He's probably there now."

"But you decided to leave anyway."

Eliza paused and steadied herself. "I did." She looked out across the marshes. "I can't talk about this anymore."

He looked at her. She was still looking out the window.

Henry followed Lockwood Boulevard as it curved into Broad Street. Within a few hours the Moultrie tennis courts would be blooming with young matrons in white tennis skirts and instructors tossing tennis balls to children who hopped to different places on the courts in their game of Around the World. But for now the courts and playground were gray and ghosted with nothing but the damp morning air.

He continued down Broad Street past St. Michael's Church.

Eliza looked up at the clock on the steeple, but it was too dark to see the dial.

"Henry, no more diversions."

"I know," he said as he turned right onto East Battery. "I'm taking you home, I'm just going the long way. I remember driving home from Yale at Christmas and getting back here in the early hours of the morning. Before I went home, I used to drive around the city for five or ten minutes. Just enjoying the stillness of it. And coming from New Haven, where the snow had already started, the night air seemed so balmy, almost tropical. I used to love seeing the palmetto trees with the white Christmas lights strung in the fronds."

Henry turned down Atlantic and then onto Church. In front of Eliza's house, he twisted the key to turn the Jeep off. He turned to face Eliza. He reached for Mrs. Vanderhorst's envelope on the dashboard and handed it to her.

"I am truly going to Savannah tomorrow to see the editor of our paper down there. I'll call you when I get back. Anne called to remind me that she's having a few people over for drinks tomorrow, including my cousin Louisa and her new beau. What do you think of stopping by and then going to dinner?"

"How much risk is involved?"

"Very little."

"Hardly any at all?"

"Actually, now that I think about it—you'll be with me—so none."

Eliza laughed and leaned over and kissed Henry good night. "Okay."

As she was turning the lock of the piazza door, Henry beat the palm of his hand against the side of his Jeep door. "Hey, Eliza." She turned and looked over her shoulder. "I had fun tonight."

She paused before she pushed the door open. "Yeah, me too."

# CHAPTER EIGHT

Henry called the next day. "Sounds like I just woke you up."

"No, it's fine. I have to get up," Eliza yawned.

"How's your sunburn?"

"I'm clearly being punished for staying away so long."

"Oh no. Well, don't worry, I can think of ways to make amends."

"That's precisely"—she laughed—"why I should be worried. I thought you had to go to Savannah today."

"I did. I mean, I'm here. I'm calling you from the office. Mother wanted us to come by before we go to Anne's. I want you to meet Lawton. So I'll pick you up at—"

"That's okay, really. I remember what happened the last time you offered me a lift."

Eliza sifted through her suitcase for something to wear. She wondered why she had chosen not to finish unpacking. Was she keeping open the possibility she might leave earlier than she had planned? She checked her watch—ten thirty. She knocked on Sara's door to see if she wanted to have coffee with her. Eliza cracked the door, the curtains were drawn, and Sara, cocooned in her bed, was asleep. A standing fan purred in the corner. Eliza would walk up to Century Antiques to deliver the photograph to Mrs. Vanderhorst and then she would have the entire afternoon to correct, check, and double-check sixty pages of Magritte—her quota for Sunday and Monday—and to work on her essay and possibly even write her permission letters. She would delay sending her adviser her completed work by a day. She realized Henry hadn't told her what time she should be at his mother's house. She sat on the edge of her bed and called information for *The Charleston Courier.* "Mr. Heyward, please." Eliza realized it was the first time she had ever thought of Henry as anything other than Henry. She asked his secretary to transfer her to the Savannah office.

"Eliza, my love, you're calling me to tell me how much you miss me."

"Not exactly. You didn't tell me what time to be at your mother's."

"Six thirty. You sure you don't want me to pick you up?"

"Absolutely positive." Henry acted as if he knew exactly where they were going—like the other night when he led her through the darkness of the Roper House. But after all this time, how could he be so certain how she felt? Did he know her better than she knew herself? Eliza willed herself to concentrate on the present. With eight hours in front of her, she could visit Mrs. Vanderhorst and still make a serious dent in her pile of work.


WHEN ELIZA STEPPED INSIDE, MRS. VANDERHORST LOOKED up from the magazine on her lap, adjusted the glasses on her nose, then clapped her hands against the sides of her cheeks. "Eliza." She held out her arms. "My dear, what a delight. When Susan told me you had dropped by, I was so upset I had missed you." Mrs. Vander-horst held Eliza close and enveloped her with the soft scent of vio-lets. Mrs. Vanderhorst's dusting powder took Eliza back two decades and reminded her of a time when she and Weezie and Billy had helped themselves to the items laid out on Mrs. Vanderhorst's dress-ing table. Mrs. Vanderhorst still wore her hair—now all white—in a French twist. "You look wonderful. Now tell me all about yourself. Dear, do have a seat. Mary Anderson just sent us all of her mother's furniture." She adjusted a chair next to hers and patted it for Eliza. "I've just made some iced tea with mint from my garden. Let me get you a glass, it's awfully hot outside."

A middle-aged couple, marked as tourists by their permanently startled look and thick cushioned tennis shoes, wandered in and wandered out.

For the next hour, Mrs. Vanderhorst learned all about what Eliza had been doing. Just as Eliza was telling her what she might do next, a man with a camera hung around his neck entered and asked a question about a famille rose vase in the front room. Mrs. Vanderhorst stood up to assist him. Eliza reached into her bag and pulled out an envelope wrapped in white tissue paper.

"Oh dear, everyone wants a bargain." Mrs. Vanderhorst sat back down. She pushed a wisp of hair from her face.

"I brought you something." Eliza unwrapped the envelope and handed it to Mrs. Vanderhorst.

Mrs. Vanderhorst's hands trembled as she pulled the photo-graph out of the envelope. She sat looking at the photograph and then looked up and smiled at Eliza. "Oh, Eliza, I miss them so much."

"I hope it doesn't make you too sad. Henry Heyward found a roll of film he had forgotten to develop. It was a day we'd all sailed out to the Morris Island Lighthouse. Eleven years ago."

Mrs. Vanderhorst shook her head and smiled. "You know, a day doesn't go by that I don't think about Weezie and Billy. William never got over it. Somehow he felt responsible for it all. He never said anything, but I could see him thinking sometimes, and I knew what he was thinking—if only he hadn't taught them to sail and encouraged them to race in all those regattas. You know, there was nothing I could say to him. So we never talked about it. You and Weezie were such good friends. Good Lord." Mrs. Vanderhorst reached over and patted Eliza on the knee. "Do you remember when Billy decided to teach the two of you how to drive that old VW Beetle."

"Of course. It was a yellow convertible."

Mrs. Vanderhorst steadied her head with the palms of her hands. "I was on my way home, and I saw these two little heads, one blond, one brunette, sitting in the front seat and another blond head in the back, and I thought, Oh my goodness, who could that be? and then I realized it was you and Weezie with Billy in the back. I don't remember what I did, but I don't think I told William. Billy had no idea that what he did was wrong. When you pulled up in front of our house, Billy was so pleased with himself for having taught two thirteen-year-olds . . ."

"Almost fourteen."

"How to drive." Mrs. Vanderhorst looked down at the photograph again and then held it to her heart. "Thank you so much for this. I'll write to Henry. You know, he has done such a remarkable job with the paper. And I hear he is a wonderful father." Mrs. Vanderhorst looked across the room. "You know, Eliza, we all would be very happy if you came back to Charleston."

"I don't know what I could do here."

"Well," Mrs. Vanderhorst said, "there may be something you could help me with. That is, if you have the time." Mrs. Vanderhorst disappeared up a creaky set of narrow stairs and returned holding a framed canvas. "That nice man who runs the new art gallery was interested in seeing it, so I brought it into the shop."

"Here, let me help you." Eliza stood up and took the picture—a portrait of a young woman—from Mrs. Vanderhorst.

"Thank you, my dear."

Eliza took the portrait to the window and looked at it in the natural light. "It's lovely."

"It was passed down in William's family as a Henrietta Johnston." Mrs. Vanderhorst referred to the eighteenth-century artist who had come to Charleston with her husband when he had been sent from his post in Ireland by the Church of England to serve as minister of St. Philip's Church.

Eliza shifted the angle at which she held the pastel of the young woman dressed in a simple, pale green dress and yellow shawl that was characteristic of a colonial woman. The neckline formed a gentle V, and her neck and chest were unadorned. The sitter sat facing slightly away from the front of the portrait, about one-eighth of a turn. Her light brown hair was pulled back in a loose bun. Her most remarkable feature was her unnaturally large eyes, which looked straight ahead.

"I'm not that familiar with Johnston, but it does look like an eighteenth-century pastel. She has beautiful eyes." Eliza turned the portrait over.

"Sadly there is no signature. William always said that was Henrietta Johnston's style—those eyes. The Library Society and the Historical Society have a small collection relating to Henrietta Johnston, and then of course William's father gave a large collection of the Vanderhorst family papers to the Historical Society before his death."

"Do you mind if I put her over there?"

"Of course not, dear."

Eliza stood up and propped the painting in a chair across the room. She backed away, looking at the image from different distances. "Do you know anything about the sitter?"

"William thought that she might be one of the Guignard daughters who had married the son of Arnaud Bruneau, a wealthy French nobleman who had been granted three thousand acres on the Santee near the coast by the Lords Proprietors. William's grandmother on his mother's side was a Bruneau. At some point they suffered a great loss to their fortune, and the letters and records of that period became very sparse. William thought the change in circumstances may have had something to do with the Revolutionary War or possibly yellow fever. William had started the research in the archives of the Guignard family just before he died, and I thought I might carry it on, but I find those letters and diaries written in the 1700s and 1800s too difficult for my eyes."

Eliza knew what Mrs. Vanderhorst was asking her to do. "Do you by any chance have a measuring tape? I want to write down the dimensions."

Mrs. Vanderhorst stood up slowly and returned with a measuring tape, a pencil, and a photograph of the pastel. "This might be helpful." She handed the photograph to Eliza.

"May I keep this?"

"Yes, dear, that's for you. I also have Margaret Simons Middleton's biography on Johnston, which I can get for you."

"I think we have a copy at home, I think I remember seeing it in our library, but I'll let you know if we don't."

Eliza measured the drawing and wrote the dimensions on the back of the photograph. "I'll see if I can turn up anything more about her, but if nothing has turned up now, we should be"—Eliza read Mrs. Vanderhorst's expression—"well, we should just be aware of that."


ELIZA WAS MEANT TO RETURN TO LONDON A WEEK FROM THE coming Saturday. On her walk back home, she organized in her mind how she would fit the work for Mrs. Vanderhorst into the ten days she had left in Charleston. The two main historical archives, the Charleston Library Society and the South Carolina Historical Society, would be closed on the weekend, so that meant she had only eight days for research. She knew Mrs. Vanderhorst needed her help. She guessed that whatever Mr. Vanderhorst had left when he died was now depleted, and without children to help, Mrs. Vanderhorst needed the money that the sale of the painting could bring. She could probably build a career here authenticating works of art, but Eliza suspected the results would only bring disappointing news to families she had grown up with. The art of the eighteenth and nineteenth century was primarily portraits painted by a handful of artists—Theus, Benbridge, Sully, Johnston—and probably only a small subset remained. Many had most likely perished if not in one of the great fires of 1740 and 1838 then in the less-than-ideal conditions caused by the heat and humidity of Charleston summers. Eliza had been in most of these houses. When it came to attribution, what had been speculation, after a few generations, became conviction. She would do what she could for Mrs. Vanderhorst, but she would leave everything else alone. And she doubted she could find an answer for Mrs. Vanderhorst unless she delayed her return. When she arrived home, she gathered up the Magritte manuscript and for the next five hours sat at the dining room table, proofreading the pages to send back to London the following day.

At half past five, Eliza put her work aside. She had almost eighty pages ready to send. Her mind was no longer sharp. She walked down to the library at the back of the dining room to search for the Middleton biography of Johnston. In the eighteenth century, this small room, now lined with books, had been a "warming" room where servants kept food warm and waited until they were needed to serve. Eliza's father had designed the cypress bookcases to the ceiling with eighteenth-century detail. Eliza walked two fingers across the spines of the books and tilted her head to read the titles. The books, arranged alphabetically by subject matter, were as her father had left them. He had been the last person to open many of them. He would sit in the armchair in the corner next to the fireplace and read many evenings late into the night. The bookcase between the two windows facing the garden was devoted to books on South Carolina. She found his books on Alfred Hutty, Jeremiah Theus, Alice Ravenel Huger Smith, Elizabeth O'Neil Verner, but nothing on Henrietta Johnston. She turned back to the cases by the fireplace and looked through the biographies. She knew her father would have been pleased that she was searching through his books. There, between a fat biography of Victor Hugo and Ellmann's hefty biography of Joyce, was Middleton's *Henrietta Johnston of Charles Town, South Carolina, America's First Pastellist.* Eliza didn't allow herself to wonder what all these books told her about her father, for she knew if she had too many things to look for, she would get lost. She pulled the slim volume out and sat down in her father's armchair to read, but she found her mind slipping off the page. She closed the book and promised herself she would get up early tomorrow to start.

Eliza returned to her room, changed into a silk slip dress, and pulled a light shawl around her shoulders. Ten to six. She wasn't due at Henry's until six thirty, but she wanted to get away from her papers. She walked down to White Point Gardens and watched a group of four small boys playing on the cannons and mortars and cemented stacks of cannonballs. She, Weezie, and Billy had spent countless afternoons climbing the low branches of the live oak trees and playing games among the war monuments.

She did not know how Mrs. Vanderhorst had carried on without them. It was Henry who had told her. It was the summer before she and Weezie were headed to college, she to Princeton and Weezie to the University of Virginia to join Billy, who was a sophomore.

As a graduation present, Eliza's mother had taken her on a ten-day trip to Florence and Rome. When Henry called, Eliza had been in her room at the Excelsior Hotel folding a floral skirt to pack in her suitcase—for some reason she remembered the exact color and pattern of her skirt. Billy and Weezie had been sailing Billy's J/24 in the last regatta of the summer. They were winning the race, and when a late afternoon squall came up, they didn't turn back in time. Their boat was hit by lightning. Eliza and her mother returned early, and Henry met them at the airport, and they drove to see Mr. and Mrs. Vanderhorst.

LIVING IN CITIES LIKE NEW YORK AND LONDON HAD GIVEN Eliza a freedom and anonymity from her past. Nothing in those cities pulled her back. It was the exploration of the present—not the recovery of the past—that gave her joy. But she understood that the deep roots she had in Charleston were both a privilege and a curse, and she wondered if any other place could be home.

Eliza checked her watch—6:10. The sky was blue at the horizon and faded into a pale blue gray at the ceiling of the sky. She turned and walked west across the park under the canopies of the live oaks. As she turned up Legare Street, she saw Cal Edwards, standing in the middle of the street positioning a tall ladder against the side of his house. She called hello.

He crossed the street to kiss her on the cheek. "I thought I saw you at the party the other evening."

"If I didn't know better, I'd say you look as if you're planning to paint your house," Eliza said.

"I am. I asked Ross Barnwell to give me an estimate, and it was—as I told Ross—highway robbery, so I told Mother I would do it myself."

"Have you ever done this before?"

"No, but half the painters on Ross's crews are three sheets to the wind by eleven A.M., so I figured, how hard can it be?"

He moved the base of the ladder from the uneven slate paving stones of the sidewalk to the smooth asphalt of the street. He tested the stability of the ladder with a shake. "Well," he said, "here goes," and started to climb the ladder with his paintbrush and gallon of paint.

"Cal, I feel I should wish you good luck."

He stopped his climb, turned, and saluted with his paintbrush. "Perhaps *bon voyage*. This may take me a while."

A horse-drawn carriage had stopped in front of the Heyward house as Eliza approached. The tour guide was in the middle of telling the story about the ghost on the third floor of 14 Legare who occasionally appears to duel with the ghost in the house across the street. The tourists were straining upward to examine the third-floor window. As Eliza rang the doorbell, Isaiah, the Heywards' elderly butler, dressed in a white coat and black trousers, opened the front door. The tour guide gave a click of his tongue and a slap of the reins. The horse leaned into its harness and pulled away.

"Miss Eliza," Isaiah said. "I'll tell Mrs. Heyward you are here."

"Is Henry here?"

"He called and said he would be here directly."

Eliza followed Isaiah into the front parlor. She looked around the pale yellow room. It was a comfortable mix of Charleston pieces that had been passed down in the Heyward family and English pieces Mrs. Heyward had brought down from New York. Eliza was studying a portrait of Mr. Heyward's grandmother when she heard dog feet clatter down the stairs and then Mrs. Heyward's voice.

"Eliza, I'm so happy to see you." Mrs. Heyward's blond cocker spaniel leaped ahead and jumped up to Eliza. "Rascal, down, sit down." She kissed Eliza on both cheeks. "Eliza, you look wonderful."

Eliza sat next to Mrs. Heyward on the maize-colored silk dam-ask sofa.

The house was still so pretty and elegant with high ceilings, large symmetrically placed windows, and delicately carved neoclas-sical cornices and door architraves. The great houses such as this were built in the late 1700s and early 1800s from fortunes made from rice and indigo production. Owners had instructed architects to copy what they had seen in England, though what was built in the colonies was simpler and on a much less grand scale.

Rascal jumped up on the back of the sofa where Eliza was sit-ting and started licking her ear.

"Rascal, get down." Mrs. Heyward scooped the small frantic dog in her arms. "He is making a complete fool of himself." She turned to Eliza. "Now, dear, tell me all about you."

Eliza was in the middle of explaining her fellowship at the Courtauld when Henry burst through the front door and rushed into the parlor. "Sorry I'm late," he said. The sleeves of his white shirt were rolled up and crumpled.

"Eliza has just been telling me all about her interesting work at—"

Henry interrupted by asking his mother, "Is Lawton here?"

"He was just having his supper with Cora in the kitchen."

"Eliza hasn't met him yet. I'll get him." Henry disappeared and returned with Lawton one step behind him. He was thin and suntanned with sandy brown, sun-streaked hair. He wore a white tee shirt and a pair of white tennis shorts. He held out his hand to Eliza.

"Have you been playing tennis?" Eliza asked Lawton.

Lawton folded his hands across his chest and looked down.

"One or two-handed backhand?"

"One."

"Then your favorite must be Sampras?"

Lawton shrugged his shoulders, and Henry winked at Eliza. "I'm trying to get Lawton to sail with me in the Yacht Club Regatta, but all he wants to do is play tennis."

"Well, I think I'd rather play tennis than go sailing, too. I was never very good at sailing," Eliza said. "I could never figure out which way the wind was blowing."

Henry turned to Lawton and brushed the top of his head with his hand. "We'll let you get back to your supper."

As they walked back to the kitchen, Eliza heard Henry asking Lawton about the book he was reading and telling him to spend the night in the main house. "Just not sure what time we're going to get back, but it'll probably be after nine, so you should sleep here."

Henry returned and then almost immediately disappeared to change, and Mrs. Heyward entertained Eliza with stories about the time she had lived as a young girl with her family in England. "I had the most beautiful chestnut mare, and when my father told us we would be moving back, I was so upset. I went down to the barn and put my arms around her and sobbed. I cried myself to sleep with my horse. My word, I was a silly girl. You see, I was awfully young and I—"

Henry reappeared. "Mother, are you sure you don't want to come with us over to Anne's?"

"No, thank you. I have some things I need to take care of here. And I'm happy not to run into that crazy cousin of yours. I'm sure I'll hear all about it tomorrow—Anne is coming over for lunch."

As Henry and Eliza walked across the street to the large Italianate brick house, Henry caught hold of her arm and held her back to allow two young boys on bicycles to pass. "Don't worry. Lawton will come around."

But she was worried. She also had felt Lawton's resistance.

The boys held on to leashes that were connected to a pair of overexcited Brittany spaniels. The boys laughed and shouted to one another as they raced down Legare Street.

"So how are you?" Henry said and smiled, as if he had heard something funny.

"Okay."

"Let's improve that, then." Henry reached for her hand as they crossed the street. He rang the doorbell, listened for a few minutes, and then knocked hard with his fist. He opened the massive mahogany door. "Anne?"

"Henry, Eliza," Anne greeted them from the second floor, and with elaborate arm gestures, as if she were conducting a piece of romantic music, beckoned them to join her. "I'm so pleased you came." They climbed the wide staircase, and as they entered the formal rooms of the second floor, Anne said to Henry, "Louisa should be here any minute with her new beau." Anne turned to Eliza and shielded her mouth with the back of her palm. "Don't say anything you don't want to read about in the papers." She offered them a glass of wine and then disappeared to the back kitchen to get the cocktail napkins she had forgotten. A mixture of eighteenth- and nineteenth-century portraits hung among Anne's large bright abstract paintings.

Henry walked up behind Eliza and spoke so only she could hear him. "If you could steal anything in this room, what would it be?" He put his drink down and put his hands around her upper arms. He turned her slowly around the room. "The Lartigue family candlesticks," he suggested, then turned her ninety degrees, "the Ramsay of James Oglethorpe," and then another ninety degrees, "the portrait of Mary Golightly, the Thomas Elfe secretary, or one of Anne's canvases." He turned her toward him. "Then there's always me."

"Hmm, not sure," she mused.

"Wrong answer." He let go of her arms and held his forehead.

"You missed your cue. What am I going to do with you? You're always missing your lines."

Louisa arrived with Charles Stevens, and the conversation became animated and quickly wandered to what house had just sold and for how much, who might be getting divorced, and complaints about the mayor and the rising property taxes. Eliza's eye caught on a colorful painting of the back of three nuns looking out over open water. "Is this yours?" she asked Anne.

Anne nodded. "I did that several years ago, I was experimenting with using bright colors for things that are normally black, like nuns' habits. I'm doing portraits right now. I'm painting Sallie Izard. She wanted to be painted as a mermaid. You know," Anne added, "she collects turtles. She turned that glorious swimming pool into a turtle pond. We just have a few more sittings. When it's finished, you must come and see it. Goodness." Anne patted the side of her cheek. "I forgot the shrimp. Here follow me."

When they returned, Henry was standing next to the fireplace, and Louisa, next to him, was speaking quietly. When Eliza and Anne entered the room, Louisa stopped talking, and Henry took a small step back.

"Where's Charles?" Anne asked.

"He's just run to the car. He thought he might have left the lights on," Louisa said in a merrier voice than such a message warranted.

Anne offered a tray of boiled shrimp with one hand and cocktail napkins with the other. "Do try them, Richard Alston brought them round yesterday. Oh dear, the door, here, Henry, can you pass these around, I'll be right back." She shifted the tray into Henry's arms.

Anne returned with Charlie and Ginny Walker. "Eliza, I heard you were in town." Charlie kissed her hello. "You look great. This is my wife, Ginny."

Henry appeared without the shrimp. "Eliza and I were just talking about you. I told her what a great heart doctor you've become, and she said the last time she saw you, we were heading out to the jetties to do a little shark fishing."

"I thought it was Virginia Middleton's coming-out party," Charlie said. "I was set up with you. I think I might have had way too much to drink and asked you to drive my car home."

"I remember that now. I don't remember your drinking so much, but I do remember your doing a rendition of a 1950s driving manual as you drove me home."

"Exactly, precisely because I had had so much to drink. You may have thought it was funny, but it was my only hope of getting you home without crashing into something." Charlie's voice dropped into a calm monotone, "'Insert metal key into the ignition. Turn clockwise until a loud noise is heard. Check both the rear and side view mirrors for oncoming traffic or miscellaneous pedestrians. Having established that there are no vehicles or pedestrians, procedures for backing out should begin.'"

Ginny pointed with her thumb to her husband. "He still does it."

Charlie checked his watch. "We should go, we're meeting my father for dinner at the Yacht Club. How long are you in town?" he asked Eliza.

"Just for another week and a half."

"Well, that's not long enough. But when you come back let us know, we'll get you down to Fenwick Hall for the weekend."

He patted Henry on the shoulder and said to Eliza but looked at Henry, "Make sure he takes care of himself."

When Charlie and Ginny left, Eliza turned to Henry and asked, "Would you mind taking me home?"

"What's wrong?"

"Nothing. I'm just tired."

"You sure?"

"Yes. I forgot to mention that I saw Mrs. Vanderhorst today.

Your photograph of Weezie and Billy meant a lot to her. She said she was going to write you. She wants me to help her with an attribution for a portrait she owns. I want to get up early and call a friend of mine who works at the National Portrait Gallery to see if they have anything that would help me."

"So no dinner?"

"No. Thanks. The jet lag has really hit me."

"It seems so abrupt."

"Sorry, I don't mean to be abrupt. I'm just anxious. I have a lot to do."

When they were out on the street, Eliza asked Henry what Louisa had been telling him by the fireplace.

"I don't remember. We talked about a lot of things. Probably something about the paper."

# CHAPTER NINE

Eliza rose early the next morning and spread her papers out in a line on her bedroom floor—the Magritte manuscript, divided into thirty-page sections with sheets of blue paper, her list of permissions needed, the color photocopy of Bonnard's *Déjeuner*, Tennessee Williams's poem "Garden Scene," her notes, and her draft essay. Her adviser was doing her a favor to include her essay in his book. He had asked well-established art critics and museum curators and one or two poets to contribute pieces. Having an essay in such a collection would be incredibly helpful in applying for grants or Ph.D. programs. She knew it was her adviser's way of thanking her for the long hours she had spent on his book about Magritte. She picked up Williams's poem and read it slowly several times. An unnamed narrator addresses a woman named Aida who leans on a windowsill, waiting and dreaming. A table is set for supper and a cat with "eyes of pale green crystal" watches. The narrator asks her twice, "Aida, when will you speak?" The narrator confesses that against his will, he has failed to arrive at the appointed time for supper and instead waits crouched in the garden, listening to the sounds of the supper party.

Eliza looked at the image of the Bonnard painting. She had read in Williams's published diaries that he had gone to the Golden Gate Exhibition in 1939. She had checked the Tate's copy of the Bonnard catalogue raisonné, and this painting was listed as having been exhibited there. A few days before she left London, she had been looking at this poem and the image of Bonnard's painting at the kitchen table in her flat when Jamie had come over to say good-bye before he left for Scotland. He had forgotten to eat breakfast and was helping himself to a stale baguette and piece of cheese he had found in her refrigerator. "It's not the right painting," he had said as he looked casually over her shoulder.

"What do you mean? Of course it is. It's listed in the catalogue raisonné as having been exhibited at the Golden Gate Exhibition in 1939."

Jamie shrugged. "But there is no woman leaning on the windowsill, there is no cat, and the couple in this picture are eating lunch." Jamie pointed to the women with his finger. "They're not waiting for anybody."

"Just because they are eating lunch doesn't mean they're not waiting. They still could be waiting. Look, there's an empty chair just to the right of the center of the painting." Eliza put up a protest, but she knew Jamie was right. Jamie allowed himself to be led by intuition, and he had a rare ability never to second-guess himself.

Eliza reread Williams's poem and wrote a list of the prominent images—a garden "hung with lanterns like fabulous flowers," a dress in the color of "thin sunlight reflected," a cat with eyes of "pale green crystals," and compared the images to the Bonnard painting. Jamie was right—very little matched, but she disagreed with Jamie about the sense of waiting. This couple could be waiting for someone. Yet there was no getting around the fact that Williams described a woman standing outside a house, leaning with both elbows on the windowsill, looking inside. Eliza reread her essay and considered the question she had written across the top about "the thing that could not be located." She wanted to find a way to include this idea in her essay. But she would still have to find the right painting. She would have to return to the Tate and consult their four-volume *Catalogue Raisonné of Pierre Bonnard*. Any picture painted prior to the 1939 Exhibition was a possibility. She would start at 1939 and work backward. Eliza collected her essay along with the photocopy of the Bonnard picture and laid them to the side. Why was she having such a difficult time writing these permissions letters for the Magritte book? She divided the Magritte manuscript into pages she had corrected and those she had not. She got to work and corrected twenty more. She had just started the letter to the head of archives at the Tate, asking for access to their Bonnard archives, when the phone rang. It was Jamie. He was calling from a satellite phone from St. Kilda.

"Eliza darling, I can barely hear you."

"Jamie? Jamie? Can you hear me now?"

"I'm here with the crew. On St. Kilda's. It's fantastic. The weather has been great. We are going to stay an extra week. Eliza? Hello? Hello? Eliza, I can't hear you, but maybe you can hear me. I know I said I wouldn't call, but I miss you. I wrote . . ." The phone broke off. She sat by the phone for another thirty minutes in case Jamie called again. When the phone didn't ring, Eliza felt relieved, but she also felt disloyal. Whatever was happening between her and Henry—it felt wrong to be where she was without Jamie knowing.

Eliza spent the rest of the morning finishing her letter to the Tate and writing the remaining letters to other institutions, asking for permission to reproduce certain images. She tucked her finished one hundred pages of Magritte into a FedEx box. She had an hour to make the first pickup.

Instead of walking up Meeting Street to the post office, Eliza detoured east along the harbor's edge because she wanted to see Henry. He had mentioned he might be sailing with Lawton in the Yacht Club Regatta. The harbor was filled with small sailboats that moved like a cluster of butterflies blown about in a strong breeze. A few had yellow or blue sails, but most were white. The sails leaned and dipped and pivoted together in a gentle kind of chaos. Eliza didn't know what class of boat Henry and Lawton sailed. The tide was almost high and slapped the wall hard as it came in. She continued walking along the Battery toward the Yacht Club. As she neared, she noticed a cluster of fathers with binoculars lining the Battery railing. She turned into the Yacht Club and walked down the long drive to the wide dock. She saw parents chatting with other parents waiting for their children to finish their races. She recognized Louisa, who was arranging a group of children for a photograph, demonstrating how they should hold their ribbons. A man with several cameras hung around his neck stood nearby. Eliza waited for the photo to be shot and then touched Louisa's shoulder.

"Eliza, hey. Are you sailing?"

"No, I was looking for Henry. Have you seen him?"

"No, but I just got here." Louisa called to the photographer, "Tim, wait, I want to take a few more." She turned back to Eliza. "If I see him, I'll tell him. Will you be around?"

"It's okay, I've got to get to the post office by one."

Eliza walked past the playground, across Tradd Street, past the pastel-colored townhouses of Rainbow Row. As she reached Elliott Street, she heard her name being called. She turned and saw Henry running up East Bay Street. He waved as he sprinted toward her.

"I'm glad I caught you." Henry leaned toward her with his arm held against the wall of a row house. He took several deep breaths.

"Louisa said you were looking for me." He pushed his hair crusted with salt away from his face. "Where are you headed?"

"Post office." Eliza raised the FedEx box and stamped envelopes in her hands.

"Okay, good. You must have gotten a lot of work done." Henry was breathing hard.

"I did." Eliza leaned her back against the wall of the house. "Three hundred pages left. Sorry about last night. It was . . . I was . . ."

Henry pulled Eliza toward him. His shirt, strong with the smell of salt, was damp and clung to his chest. "You don't need to say anything."

"No, I do. I've just got to stop looking for ghosts everywhere. It's just that a part of this life down here doesn't seem real—at least for me—sometimes I feel as if it's going to vanish when I turn around. And the only thing that I know is real and that I will always have is my work. And then I'm with you, and I feel as if everything is going to be okay."

"Everything is. It's going to be better than okay."

"How did you and Lawton do?"

"Lawton and I came in a respectable sixth. " Henry checked his watch. "Hey, listen. I should go help Lawton put the boat up. I'm taking him to the dinner and awards ceremony tonight. Want to come?"

"I told my mother I would have dinner with her and Ben and Sara. They're taking Sara to the airport in the morning and then heading back to Middleburg. Ben's in a panic. His farm manager is threatening to quit, and he needs to get back to see if he can persuade him to stay."

"Your mother is going, too?"

"She offered to stay here with me, but I told her she should go—she can help Ben with the drive. Anyway, I know she wants to be with him. But tomorrow night is good."

"Yeah, of course." Henry started walking, then skipping backward. "So, Eliza, am I right that you just asked me out?"

She pulled her packages close to her chest and nodded her head once. "I did."

"Major progress," he said and raised his hand in the air as he twisted forward and sprinted back to the Yacht Club.

THE FOLLOWING MORNING ELIZA HELPED SARA WITH HER last-minute packing and scribbled a hurried list of the places she should try to visit in Italy. Eliza kissed her mother and Ben goodbye and promised she would try to make it up to Middleburg, but they all knew she wouldn't.

Eliza was rereading what she had written on Williams's attraction to Bonnard's painting when Henry called. She had almost finished a first draft. She thought that by discussing these two artists' shared pursuit of what was physiologically and psychologically real in emotion and image, she had figured out a way to work in the quote about the "the thing that could not be located." She wondered if the sense of mystery was partly what had fascinated Williams so much with Bonnard's work—possibly more so than the theatrical composition of his paintings.

"How's the quota coming?"

"Quota?" Eliza was confused.

"Magritte page count."

"Oh, good, fine, another fifty pages finished."

"Great, so two hundred and fifty more to go. And everyone got off okay?"

"They did. Sara, assuming she made her connection, should be boarding an overnight flight to Rome, and Mom and Ben should be arriving in Middleburg anytime now." Eliza knew that she would feel their absence when she returned home later that evening. Her mother was so happy with Ben, and he adored the way she fussed over him. All that her mother had ever wanted from life was to be happily married to a man who adored her. After her father's death, Eliza had remembered her mother telling a close friend that she was too young to be a widow. Eliza didn't know why this came to her now. At the time it had upset her, and she had stayed angry at her mother for weeks.

"So why don't you come by at six thirty—I'll show you around, and then we can go to Jasmine's. It's a new restaurant on upper Rutledge. My call is coming at five, it shouldn't last more than an hour and a half. To be safe, maybe we should say seven instead. You can park in one of the reserved spaces just out front. I'll tell the security guard to expect you. We're in the same place—on the corner of upper King and Mary—just a couple of blocks up from Reed Brothers."

IT WAS STILL LIGHT OUTSIDE WHEN ELIZA ARRIVED A FEW minutes late. The night watchman on duty in the lobby of *The Charleston Courier* saw Eliza coming, got up from his chair, and unlocked the door for her. "You must be Miss Poinsett. Mr. Heyward said to go right on up."

When the elevator pinged open, Eliza walked past a deserted reception desk, down a corridor into a large room filled with a grid of cubicles. Around the periphery were offices with glass walls. A few people scattered in cubicles were bent over computer keyboards or on the telephone. Eliza stopped at one of the open cubicles. The inhabitant, a young man on the phone, beat his pencil on the edge of his desk, as if playing the drums, and twisted his chair back and forth in rhythm with the beat. Eliza stopped, and he looked up. "Yeah, one sec," he said to the person on the other end of the phone.

"Is Henry Heyward's office on this floor?"

"Gotta go. Call you back." He jumped up from his chair. "Here, let me show you." He led Eliza thirty feet down the corridor and pointed to the office in the corner, close enough so that he might be seen by the owner of the paper. Eliza thanked him. Henry was sitting in a chair in front of his desk. He rested his elbows on his knees, his tie was loosened and dangling. Across from him sat Elliott Mikell and a young associate of his law firm. They listened and took notes while Henry spoke into a speakerphone placed on a coffee table. Eliza watched for a few minutes until Henry looked up. He directed his voice toward the speaker on the phone. "Could we hold off for a minute, I'll be right back."

He opened his door and leaned into the hall. "Hi, I'm glad you're here. I'm going to be another thirty minutes on this call. Do you mind waiting? Do you want to come in?" Henry looked at her so completely that the balance of everything changed.

"I'll just wait out here."

"You sure?"

She nodded. "Positive. I'm sure I can find something to read." Eliza wandered around and found a few back issues of a glossy magazine titled *Charleston*. She took a seat in a cubicle that was at an oblique angle to Henry's office. She watched him push his sleeves up past his elbows and resume his pose. He stared intently at the phone placed in the middle of the coffee table. The two lawyers sat slouched with their copies of a document on their laps. They listened to the voice on the phone and methodically flipped pages. After a while, Henry spoke. Eliza couldn't hear what he was saying, but she could see how intense he looked. Eliza returned to her copy of *Charleston* with the picture of azaleas surrounding one of the lakes at Ashley Gardens. At least a third of the magazine had been devoted to memorials to Charles Lowndes, who had inherited and run Ashley Gardens Plantation for over sixty years and who had died last winter at the age of ninety-seven. Eliza flipped past photos of women who had grown up in Charleston, raised their children, and now had traded their Junior League and Garden Club member- ships for the hobby of selling real estate. She got up and found a small stack of *Lowcountry Life*. She skimmed the contents: "How to Make the Perfect Venison Roast," "Quail Hunting at Bloom Hill Plantation," "Hip Dysplasia in Sporting Dogs." Didn't anyone read about art in this town? Eliza gave up and settled on an article about how to chart hurricanes. When she finished, she glanced up and saw Henry toss his document on the table, put one foot on the edge of the coffee table, and push back in his chair. He seemed to be lis- tening to something far off. He removed his foot and leaned toward the phone and responded. Elliott Mikell and his associate nodded their heads in agreement. Eliza flipped briefly past an article on the raising of a Civil War submarine off the coast of Sullivan's Island. She had just turned to an article on saltwater fly-fishing when she heard the door to Henry's office crack open.

Henry was thanking the two men for staying. Elliott Mikell spoke in a voice too quiet to understand, though Eliza did hear Henry respond, "Yes, I'm sure you're right." Henry came over to where she was. "I'm just going to show them out. I'll be right back."

Eliza returned to her reading until she heard his long stride approaching. Henry peered at her magazine. "Saltwater fly-fishing. Eliza, you amaze me."

"It was either that or how to garnish the perfect crab casserole."

Henry tilted his chin down. "I've just got to get a few things, and then we can go. Come on in."

Henry stacked some papers on his desk and pressed the palm of his hand against his forehead for a second before looking in a file for another document. He searched through his in-tray and pulled some papers out. He handed her a letter from Edward McGee. "Might amuse you," he said.

She read the letter that referenced a second essay Edward

would be sending to the paper as soon as his first was published. Edward described the article, titled "The Effects of Northern Aggression on Free Will and the Southern Educational System," as an excerpt from his forthcoming book. Edward ended with a call for Henry to uphold the tradition of his ancestors, to act honorably, and to publish his article written by one of the few true Charlestonians left. Eliza shook her head and handed the letter back. "Forthcoming book?"

"I know. Every time I see him—like at Sara's party—he asks me about the publication date. I haven't had the heart to tell him there'll be no publication date. I was hoping he'd forget about it. The last time I ran into him he told me he was working on another article. I couldn't bring myself to ask him what the subject was. I guess I know now." Henry waved the letter before tossing it back onto his desk. He pulled his suit jacket from the back of his chair, patted the pocket to check for his keys.

"Okay, ready to go." As Henry turned to lock the door of his office he said, "Listen, I have to go to New Orleans tomorrow. Just for two days. Want to come? I am looking for that magic phrase to get the answer I want." He snapped his fingers. "Why not."

"I can't."

"Oh, Eliza, wrong answer. You could work on the plane. Or, while I'm out at my meeting, you could stay at the hotel and work."

"I have an appointment to look through the archives at the Library Society. That portrait that Mrs. Vanderhorst wants me to help her with—she thinks it's by Henrietta Johnston, and she wants me to see if I can document it. It's important to her. I think she may need to sell it. A week and a half is no time to do this kind of research, but I want to get as much done as I can before I leave."

"What is the painting?"

"It's a pastel portrait of a young woman that has been passed down through Mr. Vanderhorst's family."

"You sure you couldn't postpone your appointment for a few days?"

"I want to try and get this done. Mrs. Vanderhorst seems quite anxious about it. I suspect she's worrying about money. She's all alone now. She doesn't have anyone who can help her or look after her—well, it would help her out financially quite a bit if I could make the attribution."

"I understand." The elevator door opened, and Henry leaned in front of her and held the door open. "Did you know that the library was founded in 1748 by gentlemen who sought to 'save their descendants from sinking into savagery'?" Henry pressed the button for the ground floor.

"Did not, but I guess that's useful to know. Do you think, Henry, that it worked?"

"Well"—he laughed—"given how quickly you were rifling through those magazines unable, I presume, to find anything that interested you, not well enough."

As they left the building, they said good night to the night watchman. "I'm just parked in the back. Let's go in my Jeep, and I'll bring you back here."

Before he turned the key in the ignition, he looked at Eliza. "So what if we shift to Plan B?"

"Plan B?"

"Plan B is that you postpone your trip back to London. No, wait, hear me out. You have plans to leave in a little over a week, I have to go to New Orleans, so why don't you stay a bit longer. I've been—if I must say it myself—exceedingly good about leaving you alone to work—and we can see each other at night. I know you're thinking of many reasons why this is a bad idea, but before you say no—just think about it. Okay?"

"But, Henry . . ."

"Just think about it."

"Okay. So where is this restaurant?" Eliza asked.

"Corner of Spring and Rutledge. Just up from Ashley Hall. Because it's not such a good location, it's always easy to get a table, and there are rarely any tourists. And the food's not bad either."

They parked in a lot next to Jasmine's. On what had once been a common wall between Jasmine's and another building long since demolished was a freshly painted billboard-size picture of a woman with a 1950s hairdo and waitress uniform, smiling down over a steaming bowl of okra soup. The word JASMINE was ribboned overhead. "That's new"—Henry said, lifting his chin toward the painting—"they must be doing all right."

The people sitting at the tables looked up as they entered. Henry nodded to two of the tables as they walked past. When they were seated, Eliza leaned forward to Henry and said, "I don't recognize anyone here."

Henry leaned closer and whispered, "I'm not surprised—neither do I. Except," he said, stretching out the word, "the couple sitting across from the rather large man at the table at the very front. He's moved down from New York and opened an art gallery on Broad Street that mainly deals in southern art. And at the other table just behind is Joseph Allison, he's a cardiovascular surgeon at the Medical University. Two out of"—Henry looked around the restaurant—"twelve tables. I can safely say I just failed you as the social impresario of Charleston."

The waitress came with the menu. Eliza ordered shrimp-and-grits and fried green tomatoes—things she couldn't get in England. Henry ordered the grilled fish.

They had begun to talk about her work on Magritte, and Eliza was describing a phrase Magritte used to describe his paintings, "thoughts rendered visible," when a tall man, a blond woman over-dressed in a pink linen suit, and behind them, a man in a navy blazer and bow tie passed by their table. Henry nodded to them. Eliza asked Henry, "Who was that?"

"Jonathan Pierce, the new head of Historic Charleston, and Ralph and Nina Morton. I pointed them out to you at Sara's party. They are the ones who just bought the Sword Gate House."

"You know, you're in danger of reclaiming your title."

"Sorry I didn't introduce you, but I didn't want to talk to Ralph. He came to my office a few days ago and asked me if we would be interested in selling the paper—rather extraordinary really. Hasn't been in Charleston long enough to know it has always been in my family, or maybe he knows that and doesn't think it matters. Apparently his wife has always wanted a house in Charleston. She's originally from a small town in Arkansas."

"Why did the Childses sell the Sword Gate House?"

"Professor Childs died last year, right before Christmas. He was almost ninety. Mrs. Childs died eight years ago, the same year as my father."

"Is Joe still there?"

"Yes, but he has to move out. As you know, he's lived there all his life. No one thought when Mr. Childs died last year that he would not leave any provisions in his will for Joe. It seems the brilliant historian was unable to come to grips with his mentally impaired son. He left the house to Historic Charleston, and they didn't waste any time selling it."

Henry paused as the waitress placed a plate piled high with shrimp-and-grits and fried green tomatoes in front of Eliza, grilled fish and spinach in front of Henry.

Eliza took a bite of a fried green tomato. "These are really good. Want one?"

"No, thanks, happy with what I have."

"So what is Joe going to do?"

"I don't know. I spoke to a few board members and told them they should find a small apartment for Joe even if it's only something at the Sergeant Jasper. I think Ross Barnwell is going to try to find a simple job for Joe on one of his work crews. So hopefully he'll be okay."

Henry shifted to telling Eliza about the paper in New Orleans that he was interested in. He had been down there several times in the last few months, and he entertained Eliza with stories about the eccentric family he was dealing with, the music and squalor of the French Quarter, and the ancestor worship of the Garden District, "almost as bad as Charleston."

The waitress came and cleared their plates and asked if they wanted dessert or coffee.

"I'll have coffee," Eliza said.

"Just water for me."

The waitress returned with Eliza's coffee and refilled Henry's water glass.

As Eliza stirred milk in her coffee, she shivered.

"What is it?" Henry asked.

"I don't know—nothing."

"Eliza, come on, I know you. Is it what I just told you?"

"No, it's not, but I don't want to say."

"Say."

She hesitated. "For a moment I felt as if I were sitting at PJ's with you ten years ago when you told me about you and Issie. I was stirring cream into my coffee."

"Oh, Eliza."

She looked up. "Do you ever think where we would be if that summer hadn't happened?"

"No, no, I don't. I can't. Lawton makes those questions impossible to ask." Henry watched her pour a packet of sugar in her coffee. "How about you? Do you ever think about it?"

Eliza looked past Henry and answered, "At some point I did, but it helped being so far away from Charleston. There was nothing to remind me of you. And I got good at avoiding situations that acted like mnemonics."

The waitress passed by, and Henry asked for the check.

"What did you tell Lawton?"

"I told him the truth as best I could," he said. "I didn't know what else to do. I told him that his mother was very young when she had him and was very depressed and felt that to be okay she had to move away and that she went to a faraway place that wasn't safe for babies or small children. She knew I would take great care of him, and she believed little boys should always be with their fathers."

"Has he ever asked about seeing her?"

"No, he doesn't want to talk about it. But I know that sometimes what bothers him the most is what he doesn't want to talk about. We'll be in the car, and he'll be unusually quiet, and then he will ask me a question that I know he has been thinking about for a while, and I will answer it, and then he'll not want to speak further. It's as if it is all he can take in at that moment. I just let him set the pace he's comfortable with, but I'm always willing to answer any question he has. I hope it's the right way to deal with it."

"Do you think that partly explains why he feels threatened by me?"

"No, I don't, at least not directly. He knows how I feel about you. He was upset with me yesterday when I left him with our boat at the Yacht Club to find you. He's fearful, I guess, of losing a part of me. It'll all work out, but it will take time."

The waitress returned with the check, and Henry stopped speaking until she moved away.

Henry paid the bill, and they stood up to leave. "Want to get a drink somewhere?"

"Where were you thinking?"

"How about Big John's?" Henry referred to the red windowless bar one block north of the Slave Market. It was always filled with a mixture of South of Broad teenagers with fake IDs, a few eccentric old Charlestonians, and a few down-and-outs who lived in wrecked buildings not far away.

"I probably should get home."

Henry closed his eyes and nodded. He opened his eyes and shook his head, as if he were trying to untangle something. "I don't know what I was going to say. But, listen, at least promise me you'll cheer for Lawton and me on Sunday. We're in the finals of the Charleston Tennis Club Parent-Child Tournament. We've been trying to get a finals played for over a month."

"You still play a lot?"

"No, not really, I play with Lawton, but that's about it."


THEY DROVE BACK TO *THE CHARLESTON COURIER*, AND HENRY walked Eliza to her car. He turned and leaned against her car door. "Eliza, it's just . . ."

"Henry, if I stay, it's because of you. That's got to be enough right now?"

"Yes, yes, of course."

He opened her car door, kissed her good night, and said he wasn't getting back from New Orleans until late Saturday night. He would call her Sunday morning.

# CHAPTER TEN

Eliza fished out her old bicycle from underneath the house. It still had its wicker basket attached with leather straps that were now in danger of cracking apart. A fine coat of dust had transformed the green paint into pale gray. The tires were flat and crusty. Judging by its condition, she figured her bike had not been moved since she had left it there over ten years ago. A sad sight, but she felt a sense of disloyalty abandoning it, so she disappeared back underneath the house and pulled out a red bicycle pump. Her old combination lock was wrapped around the seat, and as she pumped the air into the tires she tried to remember the order of the four numbers. She was surprised when the tires held the air.

She went back inside to collect her papers and notes. The phone rang, but when she answered it, there was no one on the other end. She thought it might be Jamie, and she waited for him to call back, but the phone didn't ring again. She tried her best to avoid thinking about how Jamie's voice had made her feel when he had called two days ago.

It wasn't until she had crossed Broad Street and was pedaling up King Street to the Library Society that the numbers 2739 popped into her head—not that anyone would think about stealing her old bicycle. She walked her bike behind 164 King Street, the turn-of-the-century Beaux Arts building that now housed the Library Society. As she spun the bike lock open, she heard the church bells of St. Michael's marking the hour of nine. She grabbed her papers from the basket and hurried up the steps.

An elderly woman sitting at the front desk looked at Eliza and asked her if she were a member. "I think so," Eliza said. "At least I was about ten years ago. Eliza Poinsett."

The woman's face softened. "Are you Pamela's daughter?"

"Yes, I am," Eliza said.

"I thought you looked a little like her when you came in. I'm Julia Hutson. Come right on in. We have to be so careful. So many tourists come in and try to pretend they're members. They just want to use the restrooms," she said and twisted her mouth in disapproval. "Now, is there anything I can get you?"

"Yes, thank you," Eliza said. "I'm here to look at the Henrietta Johnston papers."

"Oh dear." She cupped her palm against her cheek. "There was someone here two weeks ago looking at them. I'm concerned they may have been returned to the archives."

"Mrs. Vanderhorst called and spoke to the director. He said the boxes would be left on the reserve shelf for me. I believe they're part of the Margaret Simons Middleton collection."

"Thank goodness, I'm afraid I wouldn't know where to look for those papers. I just volunteer twice a week. Now, let's see."

Mrs. Hutson turned to the cabinets behind the desk. She opened the wooden doors and raised her chin to look through the bottom of her glasses. "Ah, here we are," she said, "Henrietta John-ston—on reserve for Miss Poinsett." She readjusted her glasses and read from a pale blue file card taped onto the first box, "It says there are nine boxes here and another nine downstairs."

Eliza lifted the heavy cardboard box off the front desk and looked behind her at two long library tables. "May I sit at one of those?"

"Of course, dear. But there is a very nice table at the back that may be a little quieter for you." Mrs. Hutson led Eliza back through the stacks to a large table at the rear of the building. "Now, let me know if you need anything."

Eliza organized her papers across the large wooden table. She lifted the top off the box and set it aside. Mrs. Hutson reappeared and handed Eliza a pair of white gloves. "I forgot to give you these. It is library policy for the archive material."

For the next three hours, Eliza went through each manila folder, page by page, but discovered no surprises or miscataloged items. Most of what she found had already been included in Mar-garet Middleton's book on Johnston. She'd finished seven of the nine boxes when she heard a voice she thought she recognized. She peered through the stacks but couldn't see anything, so she moved closer around the side. Edward McGee, dressed in a rum-pled seersucker suit and polka-dotted bow tie, was informing Mrs. Hutson about the imminent publication of his book. Eliza heard him ask if she could check to see if any other books on the same subject matter—specifically the difference between northerners and Yankees—had been recently published. When Mrs. Hutson assured him his would be the first, he asked to see the records of book-lending in the periods directly preceding and following the war. Mrs. Hutson asked him politely which war. He spoke with impatience, "The War of Northern Aggression, of course."

Eliza tiptoed back to her table to avoid being spotted by

Edward. When she heard Edward leave, she emerged. "I'm just going out for lunch. May I leave all my papers here?"

"Of course, dear, but you know we close from one to two."

Eliza walked up King Street. She thought she might have a sandwich at the lunch counter at Woolworth's. She crossed Beaufain past the old Art Deco Riviera Movie Theatre, which had become a Ralph Lauren store, past Mr. Kassis's Shoe Shop, now the Audubon shop. The shiny storefronts of Laura Ashley and Talbots and Banana Republic had replaced the dingy windows of antiques shops that Eliza remembered as always being crammed with displays of silver, colored bottles, china plates, and Confederate army pistols and belt buckles. Eliza arrived at the long storefront where Woolworth's had been. There was no trace that it had ever been there. A Gap store stood in its place with large posters of tanned models in white tee shirts and faded jeans. She stepped inside and asked the young man who wore a headphone with an attached mike and who swayed to the loud rock-and-roll music as if he was in a music video, "When did Woolworth's close down?" He didn't know the answer or even that Woolworth's had been there, but he did say that the Gap had been open for about six months. Eliza wandered farther up the street. She crossed Wentworth and stopped in the Old Colony Bakery, where a large loaf of bread in the shape of a four-foot alligator stretched the length of the window. She ordered a sandwich and then wandered into the garden of the Congregational Church and found a bench. The heat had quieted the city.

At two o'clock, Eliza returned to the library. By four, she had finished looking through the nine boxes marked HENRIETTA JOHNSTON. She returned the boxes to Mrs. Hutson and asked for the next nine. Mrs. Hutson said they could be brought up the following day, so Eliza spent the rest of the afternoon researching the names and dates of eighteenth-century newspapers that had been published in Charleston and then reading through any that had been preserved on microfiche. She was looking for any articles about Henrietta Johnston's husband becoming the minister of St. Philip's or any advertisements for portrait painting.

By five o'clock, her eyes ached. She rubbed the back of her neck and returned the roles of microfiche to Mrs. Hutson. She rode her bicycle down King and turned on Broad. She got off her bicycle before she passed St. Michael's and walked the rest of the way home down Meeting Street. In the garden of the house next to the First Scots Presbyterian Church, she watched a small boy and girl squatting down with a magnifying glass. They were trying to burn a hole in a leaf by tilting the magnifying glass toward the late afternoon sun.

When she arrived home there was a letter from Jamie. She had not told Jamie about Henry. She picked up his letter and took it with her and sat in the garden, listening to the sounds of the late afternoon sprinklers. It was postmarked from Scotland the day before she had left for Charleston.

*My dearest Eliza,*

*I know we agreed to have a break and not contact each other for these two weeks, but I felt badly that I left so abruptly. We head off tomorrow and, if the weather holds, may stay an extra week. No one on the crew has a pressing commitment, so we are going to try to get everything we need on this trip.*

*Aunt Annabel sends her love. She has put me in the same guest cottage with the bedroom and fireplace you loved so much. I remember the last time we were here together. We went on a walk, and you rescued the blind kitten, and you gave it medicine, and when I marvelled at how easily you could handle it, you told me sometimes things are so familiar they come back to you. I long for the familiar feeling of having you in my arms when I go to sleep.*

*We have another invitation to spend a week with Ian
and Diana in St. Tropez this August. It made me think of
our marathon drive last summer—you so sweetly stayed
up all night to talk to me and play music so I wouldn't fall
asleep, and you made me laugh when you could tell I was
getting tired. I told Ian I would check with you when you
got back.*

*I know things between us haven't been great, and I've
put too much pressure on you, but I love you, and I miss
you, and I'll do whatever it takes to get us back.*

*I will try to call you to let you know if we are going to
stay an extra week.*

*All my love, Jamie*

Had she moved so far away from where she and Jamie were
when she left that she no longer recognized where they had been?
Jamie was sweet and kind, and she loved that about him. She
remembered the little skinny black kitten they had found crouched
in the tall grass in one of the fields not far from his aunt's house.
She remembered how she had cradled its small head in her left
hand and opened its eyes for the drops she squeezed with her
right. And when she handed the small bundle to the caretaker's
wife, who was happy to have the kitten as a mouser for the grain
room in the barn, she also remembered feeling as if she were
handing over a part of herself. Now she felt as if she were getting
a part of her life back. But she had to return to London. She could
not delay any later than the end of the month. She called Jamie's
flat in London and left a message that she would be returning at
the end of June.

Eliza heard the kitchen door slam shut. Cornelia was leaving.
Eliza called to her.

"Good Lord, you gave me a fright. I can't tell you the last time I've seen somebody sitting in this garden. What's got you so sad?"

"I'm not. It's nothing." Eliza wiped her face. "If you're headed home, I'll give you a ride."

They sped out of Charleston taking the same route she and Henry had traveled less than a week before. Maybe it had taken her this long to return because she had feared the memory of a relationship in which there had been a history of almost any and everything—a laugh, a hand on her lower back, the way Henry sometimes looked at her. With Jamie, there had never been any danger of echoes.

Eliza dropped Cornelia off at her house, and Cornelia asked her to wait. She returned with a plastic bag of ripe tomatoes.

"Oh, Cornelia, thank you, but this is too many. I'll take just a few."

"Well, what about Henry?"

"He's away, he's coming back late Saturday night."


HENRY CALLED EARLY SUNDAY MORNING. "ARE YOU STILL ON for this tennis match?"

"I can't," Eliza said. "Helen Halsey at the Gibbes said she could meet with me this morning to show me their file on Henrietta Johnston. She has a record of all the documented Johnstons. She's leaving this afternoon for the next two weeks, and this was the only time she could meet me."

"Okay, then how about meeting us for lunch at one."

Five hours later, Eliza pulled up to what looked like an old railway car that had been set back on an asphalt parking lot behind the County Library on Calhoun Street.

"Bill's Grill," Eliza said, reading the large red letters that ran the length of the chrome and black railway car. "I don't remember this being here," she said to Henry, who had pulled into the parking lot ahead of her.

"It wasn't," Henry said

"Lawton, I bet this is your favorite restaurant," Eliza said.

"They have great cherry Cokes," Lawton said, as he passed through the door Henry held open. Lawton carried a stack of books in his arms. A few college students huddled in booths with the remains of breakfast on the table. Lawton wanted to sit at the counter on the red vinyl-covered stools.

"So how'd the match go?" Eliza asked.

"Painful. We lost."

"Oh no, who did you play?"

"Dan and Jay Downing." Henry explained, "I think I mentioned them to you—Betsy Downing was the one who reported Mr. DuBose. They bought the Simmons house on Tradd Street. Dan runs some sort of hedge fund. I think he mainly invests in distressed debt."

"They must be good," Eliza said.

"They cheated," Lawton said as he twisted back and forth on his stool.

"Yeah, they did," Henry said. "It was pretty pathetic. On match point, Lawton hit a winner three inches in, and Jay called it out, and Dan let the call stand. All during the match Dan was rifling Lawton with balls. Hey, Lawton." Henry leaned over and touched the bill of Lawton's tennis cap. "Hats off inside."

"They sound pretty horrible," Eliza said.

"They are. I doubt Dan was ever any good at sports when he was a kid, and now he takes these tournaments way too seriously. I think when they moved down to Charleston, they made a real play to join everything and got rebuffed pretty quickly. Dan got black-balled at the Yacht Club, and his wife didn't make it into the Garden Club. I'm not sure the Downings would've ever made it into any of the clubs, no matter how long they waited, but Charleston has a way of making monsters out of some of the people who move down here."

Lawton spun 360 degrees on his stool.

"Lawton, take it down three notches."

"We could have won if you had hit the ball harder at Jay. You always tell me to 'jump for the sun.'"

"Yeah, but if I had hit hard at Jay, then I would be just like Dan, wouldn't I?" Henry winked at his son.

"I guess."

"How y'all doing?" the waitress asked as she began wiping the counter in front of them. She laid down paper place mats and cutlery bundled in white paper napkins.

Eliza reached over and picked up Lawton's pile of books. "Have you read all of these?"

Lawton nodded.

"So which one did you like the best?" Eliza shuffled through the pile and looked at Lawton, who didn't answer. *"The Book of Dogs.* Are you thinking about getting a dog?"

Henry leaned back. "Possibly next summer for Lawton's tenth birthday."

"That's exciting." She picked up the book and opened it. "What is the name of the dog that looks like a mop. A professor at Princeton who taught the introductory course on music had two, and they would always come to his lectures. It's not a shar-pei, oh, what is it, it's an unusual name . . ."

"Komondor," Lawton said.

"Komondor? Are they in this book?" Eliza started to flip through, and Lawton reached over and took the book and found the page and handed it back.

"Look, here it is. Hungarian livestock guardian dog. That's

interesting—I didn't know that. So what other interesting books do you have? Let's see—pirates or ghosts." She picked *Blackbeard: Eighteenth-Century Pirate of the Carolina Coast.* "His real name was Edward . . . ?"

"Teach," Lawton said.

"That's right, and he was called the gentleman pirate, wasn't he?"

"No, that was Stede Bonnet."

"Then which one was hung on the Battery?"

"Stede Bonnet. Blackbeard was shot in Virginia."

"I'd say you definitely know your pirates." Eliza exchanged the book for the one on ghost stories. "Is the story of the gray man in here?"

"You mean the ghost who always appears to warn people before a hurricane?"

"Yes, exactly, that's the one."

Lawton leaned toward Eliza. "It's in the back."

Eliza turned to the back pages. "'The Gray Man of Pawley's Island.' So you must be pretty brave, if these stories don't scare you."

Lawton started to spin his stool again, and Henry looked at him. Lawton grabbed the counter with both hands to stop himself.

A waitress slapped down three menus before moving to the next table.

"And the last book?" Eliza asked as she handed Lawton back his book of ghost stories.

"Is about World War II airplanes."

"Lawton likes to draw them," Henry said.

Eliza was going to say that she used to draw animals—horses and dogs mainly—when she was Lawton's age, but she was tired of trying. Lawton was hard work. She picked up the menu.

"Hey, Lawton, when we drop these books off, we should remember to choose a book for your summer project," Henry said.

The waitress circled back, and she looked at Lawton and asked, "The usual?"

"Yeah." He smiled.

She looked at Eliza. "I'll have an egg white omelet with—"

The waitress cut her off. "We don't do those."

"You just separate the egg yolk and cook the egg whites."

The waitress looked at Eliza as if she were speaking a foreign tongue. Henry leaned over. "Eliza, you are in the South." He turned to the waitress and said, "She'll have a plain omelet very dry with toast instead of hash browns, and I'll have a tuna sandwich on wheat. She'll have iced tea, I'll have water." He smiled at the waitress and handed the menus back to her.

"I'm guessing it would have been a waste of breath to ask for unsweetened ice tea?"

"Time to enjoy being southern again," Henry said, amused. "By the way," he said as he snapped his fingers, "before I forget, I ran into Anne this morning, and she wants to take you to see her portrait of Sallie—"

"Want to play 'Overnight to Many Distant Cities'?" Lawton interrupted and began to twist side to side on his stool again.

"I don't know how to," Eliza said.

"It's okay. I'll just play with my dad," Lawton said.

"It's more fun with three, Lawton, tell Eliza the rules."

"You first think of a city, and then you say one thing you are going to pack in your suitcase, and then the next person has to repeat what you said and then add something else. If you forget what someone says, then you have to drop out. And you keep going around until only one person is left."

"I see," said Eliza. She looked at Lawton. "I can choose any city I want?"

"Sure," he said.

"Let's see." Eliza looked at the ceiling. "Okay, I've packed my suitcase for Istanbul, and I've packed my Gurkha knife." Eliza's mention of a Gurkha knife broke through one thin layer of resistance.

"I've packed my suitcase for Istanbul, and I packed my Gurkha knife and my tennis racquet. Your turn," Lawton said, swiveling his stool to face Henry.

"I've packed my suitcase for Istanbul, and I packed my Gurkha knife, my tennis racquet, and my surfboard." Lawton won the game of Istanbul, Venice, and Vienna and was battling with Henry for London with his string of cowboy boots, camel saddle, snow globe, rabbit's foot, yo-yo, violin, water pistol, peacock, soccer ball, skateboard, drawing pencil, jelly beans, sand dollar, Coca-Cola, pocketknife, whistle—when their food arrived.

"Be careful, sweetheart," the waitress said in a thick Georgia accent. "The fries are real hot."

"So tell me, how is your research on Henrietta Johnston going? Have you come any closer to identifying the sitter in Mrs. Vanderhorst's picture?" Henry asked.

"I haven't found anything to help me identify the sitter yet, but I've learned some fascinating bits about Johnston. Her first husband, who was the son of an English lord, died ten years after they were married. Her second husband was an Anglican clergyman who was sent by the Society for the Propagation of the Gospel in Foreign Parts to Charleston to serve as minister of St. Philip's. He found the people of Charleston 'headstrong' and 'gidday' and wrote back to England that they were the most 'seditious people in the whole world.' Henrietta drew portraits in crayons, or pastels as we would call them now, to supplement his income. At some point, she went back to England to plead with the church authorities for more income for her husband. Her ship was captured by pirates, but eventually she was released."

At the mention of pirates, Lawton put his cheeseburger down and turned to Eliza. "What happened to the pirates?"

"I don't know, I guess they took what they wanted and sailed away. I wish I could find an account she'd written about the pirates." Eliza reached over and took a French fry from Lawton's plate. "I bet you could identify them for me. There are so many parts of Johnston's life that I wish I could find more about. For example, Henrietta and her husband adopted a young Yemassee Indian boy and sent him to boarding school with their two sons back in England. I keep hoping I'll come across a drawing of him—he was named Prince George, but I guess there's a reasonable chance she never drew him, because she couldn't afford to use her art supplies on sitters who couldn't pay."

"I am surprised there isn't more at the Library Society," Henry said.

"They have quite a bit in their archives—eighteen boxes, in fact. They have all the papers of Margaret Simons Middleton, who wrote the only book on Johnston, in the mid-1960s. They have a brief file on Johnston, but all I found were two letters, one with a reference to her husband's ill health, the other a mention of their need for money, but no mention of portraits being painted. I've gone through all the microfiche they have of the newspapers published in the 1700s in Charleston. I was hoping I might find an ad for portraits, but the earliest paper they have on record is 1778. I didn't know that Charleston had so many different publications—most didn't last longer than a couple of years, or at least that's all the Library Society has."

"My father collected copies of old Charleston newspapers. He had them framed in his office. I should have shown them to you the other night. His favorite copy was one called *The Daily Evening Gazette and Charleston Tea-Table Companion*. I don't think it lasted more than a few months."

The waitress returned and refilled Henry's water glass and asked Lawton if he wanted another Coke.

"So what's next?" Henry asked.

"I have a few more boxes to go through. What I've looked at is not well catalogued, so maybe something will turn up."

"What about the Historical Society? They may have something."

"As soon as I finish at the Library Society, I'm going over there. They have all the Guignard and Vanderhorst family papers. I'm hoping to find some mention in a letter or will. I spoke to Claire Coker, who was in my class at Ashley Hall—she's now the head librarian. She said she thought someone had already gone through the archives recently. Claire thinks it may have been someone working for that art dealer from New York, Peter Marshall. She was going to try to find out. It doesn't really matter, I still have to go through everything myself."

"And if you don't find anything?" Lawton asked.

"Well, I haven't thought quite that far, but then I guess I'll look at all of the portraits by Johnston that I can locate to compare them to Mrs. Vanderhorst's portrait."

"How was your meeting with Helen?" Henry asked.

"Good, she showed me her files. She said that the Gibbes has three portraits, and she'll arrange to get them out of storage for me. She wants me to bring Mrs. Vanderhorst's portrait to compare it and to examine it under a black light. When she gets back she said she'd check with several of the owners of Johnstons to see if I can contact them."

"You know who has a portrait?" Henry said. "Randolph Porter. I think it's considered to be quite a good one. Do you know him?"

"No, I don't."

"I'm sure you've seen him. He has an enormous Irish wolfhound that he walks every morning and afternoon. Randolph used to teach classics at Sewanee. He retired here four or five years ago.

I met him when Lawton and I used to play tennis at Moultrie. On his walks around the lake, he always stopped and said encouraging things to Lawton. He bought DeRosset Simons's old house on Beaufain Street. Randolph grew up in Spartanburg, but his family is originally from here. His grandmother was a Prioleau. I'll call him for you. My guess is he'll be very helpful if he can."

When they left the diner, Henry sent Lawton on ahead with his stack of books to return to the library. Henry walked Eliza to her car. When she turned the key in the ignition, Henry leaned down with his arms braced straight against the roof. "So, Eliza, does this mean you aren't leaving at the end of this week?"

"I'm thinking about staying until the end of June."

"That's great—that gives me"—he tapped his fingers—"exactly twenty more days to seduce you."

"I think you've already done that."

Henry laughed and tapped the top of her car as he pushed away and turned to join Lawton at the library.

# CHAPTER ELEVEN

For the next two weeks, Eliza spent the mornings completing all of the work she had brought with her from London. She mailed the remaining pages of Magritte back to her adviser and did as much as she could on her Williams-Bonnard essay without being able to consult the Bonnard catalogue raisonné. In the afternoons, she worked at the South Carolina Historical Society located in the Fireproof Building on the corner of Meeting and Chalmers streets. She methodically examined the Guignard family papers before turning to the Vanderhorst papers. She read deeds and wills and letters until her eyes ached from the hours she spent deciphering the eighteenth- and early-nineteenth-century script. She found nothing that referenced Henrietta Johnston or any portrait. So little of Johnston's life was known, and yet by any standard she had left behind more than most. The soil of the South was filled with unnamed and unknown women who had not gotten a fair chance from life—women like Cornelia, who had never been given much hope for a better life.

Eliza admired these women's quiet dignity as they made do with what they had. She found their strength comforting.

Each day, she met Henry after work, and they walked to restaurants downtown or drove over to Folly Beach to the cottage where Henry grilled fish. They took Lawton to a few movies and early suppers at Bill's Grill. For those two weeks, the days stretched out with so much luxury that Eliza felt as if there were spaces between each second. She tried not to think too much about where she was for fear it would all disappear.

A FEW DAYS BEFORE LAWTON WAS LEAVING FOR TENNIS CAMP, he and Henry appeared late one afternoon with a shoe box, a bag of disorganized art supplies, and a two-by-three-foot poster board. Lawton hugged a large book with the title *Owls*.

"We need your help," Henry said.

Eliza placed the shoe box on the kitchen table and sat down and pulled out a chair for Lawton. She patted the seat. "Here, Lawton, sit here." She helped him put his large book on the table. She took off the top of the shoe box. Inside she saw a baseball and an unfinished papier-mâché object.

"Okay, Lawton, what do we have here?" Eliza listened as Lawton described his summer project. He had to choose one animal that lived in South Carolina and make a presentation to his class when they all returned in September. Eliza looked back in the box and lifted out the papier-mâché object that resembled a cross between a garden gnome and an unidentifiable species of rodent. "And this must be the beginnings of your owl?"

Lawton nodded. "Dad did most of it."

Eliza looked at Henry, who was leaning against the wall with one shoulder. He uncrossed his arms to press his hand over his mouth to cover a smile.

"And the baseball?" Eliza turned back to Lawton.

"That's how big its eye would be if a screech owl were our size. See." Lawton picked the baseball up and held it in front of his eye. "Dad said they can't move their eyes, just their necks. Like this." Lawton demonstrated by turning his neck left, then right as far as he could. "But they can make a full circle."

"I didn't know that," Eliza said, and she looked back in the box. She picked up a feather. "And this?"

"It's a screech owl feather. My dad found it for me."

Eliza remembered the morning Henry had found this feather. "It's beautiful." Eliza reached back in the box and picked up one more feather. "How about this one?"

"Oh, that's just from our garden. I think it's a dove feather. It's just there to show the difference. See"—Lawton touched the bare side of the owl feather—"it only has vanes on one side."

"It's freezing in here," Henry said.

"I know, it is, isn't it? Cornelia was here this morning, boiling a pot of shrimp, and I think she must have turned the air-conditioning up."

Henry stood up and looked behind the door at the control. "No wonder," he said and adjusted the dial. "It's set just above arctic chill. How does seventy-two degrees sound? Hey, but now," Henry said, reaching into the box for the object that looked like nothing more than some strips of newspaper badly orchestrated into a lop-sided ball. "Lawton and I are hoping you can help us with our sad little friend."

Eliza held her hands out to receive the object. She turned it around and over. "Okay, well, it is a little sad, but we can work with this. Do you have any pictures we could look at?"

"Oh, yes." Lawton opened his book to the double-page spread on screech owls.

Henry held the back of the chair. "Hey, listen, I think I'm going to go home for a bit if the two of you are sure this project will not suffer without my presence. I need to get some things done. I'm meeting tomorrow morning with the president at Citizens and Southern about getting some financing lined up for the paper in New Orleans if we go ahead, and the head of the Coastal Conservation League is coming to see me in the afternoon. He sent me a package on the controversy surrounding the Port Authorities' request to deepen the harbor. There's an informal hearing on it next week, and the League wants the support of the paper."

"Do you know what you're going to do?"

"Not yet. There's no easy answer. I understand both sides. Charleston depends on the port for jobs and has to stay competitive. The conservation groups fight hard against anything that has negative environmental effects, and Charlestonians don't want any more tourists."

For the next two hours, Eliza and Lawton discussed screech owls. Lawton told her how he and his dad had rescued one. It had been hit by a car and had a broken wing, and they took it to the wildlife sanctuary at Charles Towne Landing. "I named him Screechie. Sometimes my dad takes me to visit him. You can come next time if you want to."

"I'd like that." Maybe this wasn't going to be as difficult as she had feared. Eliza knew Lawton needed time to adjust to her presence. But she needed time, too. She and Henry had made it through the tough parts, and now there was a luxury in enjoying where they were and not rushing to where they wanted to be. She asked Lawton how the dog search was going, and he told her about all the breeds he liked—Australian shepherds, German shepherds, bullmastiffs, Labradors, golden retrievers, Nova Scotia duck tolling retrievers, springer spaniels, and collies.

By the time Henry returned, Lawton had almost finished painting an eight-inch papier-mâché model of a screech owl with big ears and big eyes. A poster organized with drawings and handwritten screech owl facts lay propped against the kitchen cabinets. Eliza could tell that Henry had taught Lawton how to write by the way he formed his letters. At the bottom of the poster, Eliza had helped Lawton draw a panorama of the marshes and forests where screech owls lived.

Henry looked closely at the landscape, which was filled with deer, wild turkeys, raccoons, opossums, alligators, herons. "Wow, this is great."

"We were inspired by Anne's mural at Oakhurst. Lawton decided where all the animals should go."

"This must be Screechie." Henry pointed to a small orange bird perched on a branch of a live oak. He examined the papier-mâché model Lawton was painting. "Hey, Lawton, it looks just like Screechie."

HENRY DROVE LAWTON TO COLUMBIA FOR TENNIS CAMP AND stopped to call Eliza as he was driving back to Charleston. "How do you feel about me staying with you? There are very few things we haven't done in this town, but being together in your bedroom is one of them. And if you say yes, I'll bring you a present."

"Okay, but if I don't like the present, can I change my mind?"

"Sure"—he laughed—"but you won't."

"RECOGNIZE THESE?" HENRY ASKED AND HANDED ELIZA a package of light blue airmail envelopes bound with a blue ribbon. He sat back down on the edge of her bed and untied the ribbon.

"Oh God, yes, I do, those are my letters. I guess I'd forgotten I had written you. I wrote you almost every day."

"I used to love to come back home and find a letter from you.

So"—he flipped through the uniform stack of envelopes and picked out a few—"here is what you were doing on"—he unfolded the thin blue paper—"a little over ten years ago, on June eleventh, 1980." Eliza reached to grab her letter, but Henry, in one swift action lifted the letter from her reach with his left hand and grabbed her wrist with his right. He laughed, "Wait, they're sweet.

> *"Dear Henry,*
>
> *I am writing this with a flashlight because it was a choice of light or air-conditioning. Remember that great apartment I found to sublet for the summer? Well, one thing the sub-lessor failed to mention was that only one electrical appliance can run at a time, and the choice between the air-conditioning unit in the window or light is easy tonight. I should have been suspicious of a copy editor from* The New Yorker *named Diana Wingfield, the combination of a huntress and a wilted southern belle should have tipped me off . . ."*

Eliza reached again for her letter, and Henry raised his hand and stood up so she could not reach it. "Just one more, one more, that's all I ask. On June fourteenth,

> *"Dear Henry,*
>
> *I have signed up for a life drawing course every Monday evening at the Art Students League. The artist who taught my drawing class at Princeton recommended it, but the instructor here is not nearly as good as he was. The class is a funny mix, a few really gifted artists and then an assortment, including one very wiry girl from Brooklyn who works for a graphic designer and whose favorite expression is c'est la vie, pronounced as if rhyming with 'zest la sky.' I don't have the*

*heart to correct her, and even if I did, I suspect it would not
put a dent in her confidence."*

"Why did you keep them?" she asked him before they fell
asleep.

"What?" he said.

"My letters."

"You're the one who's given up collecting, not me."


THE FOLLOWING EVENING, HENRY RETURNED TO ELIZA'S
after work, and as he was wrestling his tie loose, he asked her, "So
when are you going to cook dinner for me?"

"When would you like me to cook dinner for you?"

He laughed, "You've finally learned to play along." He unbuttoned his top shirt button. "Hey, Eliza, I have to go back to New
Orleans for a few days to speak with the owners of the paper. The
family who are selling want to meet with me to get my personal
commitment about some of the things that are important to them.
It's all spelled out in the contract, but I think it'd be reassuring
to them to hear our commitment directly from me. The Porcher
family has owned the paper for four generations, but Mr. Porcher
is eighty-one, and his two daughters are both married to doc-
tors, and no one is interested in taking over the paper. He is quite
unsentimental in that regard, but it is very important to him that
no one loses their job."

"Can you do that?"

"We'll have to, but we'd probably want to keep everyone, even
if it weren't part of the contract. *The New Orleans Gazette* is well
run, and the people there are very loyal. It's not as if it's a turn-
around situation where you have to make drastic cuts just to keep it

viable." Henry unbuttoned his sleeves and rolled them up. "Listen, why don't you come with me."

"I need to finish this research before I go back to London. I booked my flight for a week from today."

"Back to London? When did you decide that? What about Plan B?"

"Henry, you know I have to go back. I've delayed as long as I possibly can. My adviser is expecting me to work with him at the beginning of next week on the final proofs of the Magritte book. I need to go to the Tate and double-check that I have the right image for the Tennessee Williams poem. I can't finish the essay until I do that. I've got to deal with my flat." She squeezed the tips of her fingers together. "And I have to see Jamie."

"I haven't asked you when you were going because I didn't want my question to become a catalyst. There was always this slim chance you might just forget about London." He reached out and held her forearm. "How long will you be gone?"

"I'll be there three or four weeks."

"Eliza, stay with me."

"I've really got to go."

"What if I come with you?"

"I really should do this on my own."

"I just don't want to lose you again."

"You aren't, you won't. Remember what you said—we both know what we're doing."


ON THE WAY TO THE AIRPORT ELIZA TOLD HENRY, "YOU know, I always thought I might run into you. Not at a wedding, but for some odd reason I always thought—this is going to sound strange—I would see you strolling around a museum, or waiting at a train station, or running to catch a flight at an airport. And I never did, of course. And then I started thinking I would see you after I got married. And I'd have children with me, and they'd be beautifully dressed, and I'd be nicely dressed, too. You know, you see parents traveling with their children tending to their needs—buying them small treats—and watching them while they wait for planes." She shook her head. "I can't believe I'm telling you all this. I'd dress nicely just in case I ran into you—isn't that crazy? I guess, given how far apart we lived and how unconnected our worlds were—it was my only chance."

"Come here. Eliza, I will wait for you in any airport if you promise me you will come back. You don't even have to dress up."

Henry walked with her down to the gate. They watched a small child walk the palm of his hands across the long glass window, looking for planes. "Almost forgot," he said. He pulled an envelope from the back pocket of his jeans. "This is for you. But you can't open it before you land. Open it the minute the wheels of your plane touch the ground in England."

Eliza held her hand out. "Promise," he said before handing it to her. She nodded. She looked at the envelope and then tucked it into her satchel. Her flight was called to board. Henry kissed Eliza goodbye. She turned to present her passport and ticket. She turned back once more and looked for Henry, but he was gone.

# CHAPTER TWELVE

Wᴀᴇɴ Eʟɪᴢᴀ ᴄʟᴏsᴇᴅ ʜᴇʀ ᴇʏᴇs, sʜᴇ ᴋɴᴇᴡ ᴛʜᴀᴛ ʙᴀᴄᴋ at Folly Beach, the tide was low, and the sand was gray and hard and stretched forever away from the dunes. Before she fell asleep, she imagined a flock of birds that looked like a necklace of jagged shark teeth thrown up into the sky.

Tʜᴇ ꜰʟɪɢʜᴛ ᴀᴛᴛᴇɴᴅᴀɴᴛ ᴊᴏsᴛʟᴇᴅ Eʟɪᴢᴀ's ᴀʀᴍ. "Wᴇ'ʟʟ ʙᴇ landing in twenty minutes. You'll need to bring your seat up." Eliza collected herself and sat forward. She sorted out the navy blanket that was tangled around her legs. She couldn't see anything outside the window except for gray softness. She kept watch until they broke through the cover of clouds, and she could see the ground— rich green patches divided by hedgerows with an order and precision that didn't exist in America. As they approached Gatwick, Eliza looked down on the uniform rows of terraced Victorian houses, laid out many years ago with respect for simple geometry. She used to look down at all the order, and it would make her feel as if everything was in its place, but now it made her miss all that she had just left—the miles and miles of pine forests and sandy roads, the swamps of tupelo and cypress, the expanses of marsh, the way the water met the sky, and the live oaks with their wide canopies anchoring everything. It was in her heart and underneath her skin, and she could no longer pretend it wasn't.

The plane sliced down onto the runway. She reached into her bag and pulled out the envelope Henry had given her. She turned it over twice before prying it open without ripping the flap. Tucked inside was a slim accordion of paper. A small cast-iron figure of a man, no bigger than a thimble, fell from the envelope onto her lap. She held the figure in her hand. He looked as if he belonged to a childhood board game. A train conductor, perhaps? As best she could in the cramped airplane seat, she laid the eight joined images of a light blue hazy sky and a dark ocean across her lap. Eliza understood. They were photographs Henry had taken from the top of the Morris Island Lighthouse—looking north, northeast, east, southeast, south, southwest, west, northwest. She joined the two ends of the photographs together to form a cylinder. She opened her hand and looked at the cast iron figure. Of course. She saw now. He was the lighthouse keeper. On the back of this 360-degree panorama, Henry had written, "My dear Eliza, FHIN(2) O(3) TU(3) WY love, Henry." Eliza puzzled over the coded message. She double-checked inside the envelope to make certain there was nothing more. She folded the images and tucked the little man safely inside a fold and placed the envelope with its contents back in her bag.

Eliza pulled the note out and looked at the pictures again as she was hurtling toward London in the back of a taxi. She looked for a long time at Henry's handwriting, as if by staring at "love, Henry," she would find something more, but she didn't know what she hoped to find. Maybe she just wanted to hear his voice. But those words were all she needed to steady herself. She wrote the letters of the coded message in different orders on the back of her boarding pass but still could not find their meaning. A block away from her flat, she tucked the note and photographs into the pocket of her jacket.

Eliza paid the taxi and carried her bag up the two flights of stairs to her flat. She pushed the door open against a mountain of mail. She loved this one-bedroom flat all done up in yellow. It was quiet and cozy. Even on the most miserable gray rainy days, the yellow color of the sitting room made her feel as if the room were warmed by an afternoon sun. Stretched out on the yellow sofa, she had spent hours reading in that room. The bedroom at the back had a large window that looked into the leafy canopy of an ancient sycamore. But it was no longer home—just a place she had loved in London. She looked in the refrigerator to see if she had anything, though she knew she didn't. She checked the cupboards to see if she had any coffee.

Eliza ducked out around the corner past Christie's South Kensington to a small store to buy milk and orange juice and coffee and a newspaper. She crossed the street to the French patisserie and bought a croissant. She returned home and made coffee and sat at the counter in her shoe box kitchen and sifted through her mail. She skimmed *The International Herald Tribune* and pulled the croissant apart into small pieces.

She had sat here many mornings before, but now it felt sharp and disturbing because of what would follow. She had to call Jamie, she should have called him many times before now. He didn't know anything about Henry. She would be giving Jamie up forever, but she knew the longer she waited, the worse it would be.

Eliza took a long bath and thought about what she would say to Jamie. Jamie had always been good with words. She remembered when she had just moved to London, he had invited her to a show of his photographs titled "Jamie Barings—When Truth Made a Run for It—More or Less." At the crowded show he had found her and asked her to take pity on him as a "man abandoned by space" and to have dinner with him.

She had never told Jamie anything about her former relationship with Henry, and now she wished she had, because it might make it easier for him to understand. She thought about all the Saturday and Sunday mornings Jamie would make coffee and return with the papers and warm baguettes. She put the phone in front of her and punched the number of Jamie's flat. His younger brother answered and said that Jamie had gone to his office. Eliza had hoped to see him at his flat, but maybe his office, vacant on a Saturday morning, was a better place. She hailed a taxi. When she arrived, the main entry doors were unlocked, but the reception desk was deserted. She walked to the back, where Jamie's office was hidden around a corner. She could hear his voice. He was on the phone. She knocked and opened his door. He was leaning back in his chair, chewing the end of his pencil, his feet on top of his desk. He saw Eliza, and his feet hit the floor with a thud. "Oh my God. Call you back." He jumped up and put his arms around her and kissed her. "My God, Eliza, why didn't you call me to pick you up? You look great. You're so tanned. I've missed you so much. I was just about to head down to Christopher's for the weekend. Caroline and Simon are—"

"Jamie, stop." Eliza put her hands up, as if she were pushing against a wall. "Jamie, I've got to tell you something." She held on to the back of a chair but did not sit down. "I've been seeing Henry."

"Henry?" Jamie shook his head, as if he were trying to clear his mind. "Henry—who I met at Caroline's wedding? God, that was awfully quick, wasn't it?"

"Jamie, I've known him all my life. We had been together ten years ago and broke up. But I guess—"

"Why didn't you ever mention him?"

"I don't know. I should have. It was over ten years ago. It was completely over. We hadn't seen each other since then."

Jamie sat sideways on his desk. "You didn't know he was coming over here?" The sound of his low, calm voice reminded Eliza of the time he had told her about the day his mother had dropped him off at Ludgrove. He was eight, and after the tour of the school, he had turned to his mother and said, "But, Mummy, you aren't really going to leave me here?"

"No. Not at all," Eliza said. "I didn't even know he knew Caroline."

Jamie searched her eyes. "Are you in love with him?" His voice was even quieter.

"I think so."

"What do you mean, you think so? Eliza, either you are or—"

She leaned back against the office wall. "Yes."

Jamie had heard the answer he did not want to hear, and he was not certain where to go. "Well, Eliza, that changes everything." He stood up and moved back behind his desk. He searched for something under the papers scattered across the top. "I guess there isn't anything more to say," he said without looking up at her.

"Jamie, I'm sorry."

"You could have told me before now. You left me a message that you would be staying two more weeks, but that was it. For almost four weeks I've been waiting for you to come back. I only called you once. I didn't want you to feel any pressure. You never responded to my letter." He opened a drawer and retrieved a set of car keys.

"Jamie, I just didn't know."

"So you sort yourself out, but keep me on hold until you do."

"No, I left here because I wasn't sure we were right together, and you told me I was making a mistake, that it wouldn't be good for us, but I left anyway. That's how unsettled I was about us." She reached out to touch his arm.

"Don't." He held his hand out, as if he were pushing her words away from him. "I've got to get out of here." Before she could say anything, Jamie had disappeared. Eliza stood in the middle of his office.

She sat down. She had said none of the words she had planned or wanted to say. She had wanted to make Jamie understand. She clung to the arms of her chair because she felt if she didn't, she wouldn't exist. Everything in her body felt disconnected, and she didn't know how to put any of it back together.

ELIZA WALKED DOWN FLEET STREET AND FOLLOWED THE Strand until she found herself in Trafalgar Square. If she concentrated hard enough, she could keep all the turbulent feelings locked from her mind. The square was filled with tourists who had been discharged, then reabsorbed, by the large air-conditioned buses that carted them around to all the sights of London.

Eliza walked down the long sycamore-lined avenue of the Mall. The south side of the Mall along the park was quieter. She wanted to get away from the confused sounds of the afternoon traffic. Jamie would probably be arriving about now at Christopher's, and he would have a few drinks and play tennis or sit by the pool, and Christopher would have several unattached trainees from Christie's art program—Devinas or Isabellas or Leonoras—who would listen with doe-eyed attention to stories of Jamie's latest travels.

It was one of those rare English days when the sun was strong, and everything seemed brighter than normal—the green grass and red geraniums and yellow daffodils. Even the tourists who always seemed to blur in a murky grayish blue swath of color seemed clear and loud and clamoring for photographs. She no longer belonged here. She knew that after this summer she would never come back.

When she got home she checked her messages, but there were none.

DURING THE FOLLOWING WEEKS, ELIZA MET WITH HER adviser at his home in Ladbroke Grove at nine thirty every morning. Sometimes he would take her to lunch at his club, but more often they would have a sandwich and coffee bought from a shop around the corner and continue working with only a short break. Together they reviewed the final draft of the four-hundred-page Magritte manuscript page by page, double-checking one last time for typos and accuracy. Most evenings they finished at seven, and Eliza would return to her flat to continue compiling the permission list required by the legal department of the publisher. She was grateful to have something in front of her that required all of her time and attention. She organized and completed applications to various art institutes in America, but she decided to wait to send them out.

Henry called every few days, and they spoke about her work, and he always had things to tell her about Lawton. He was teaching Lawton how to surf and to water-ski, and, of course, they played tennis often. Lawton came to the paper a few times and was given "jobs," which thrilled him. Mrs. Heyward was taking Lawton soon for a week to visit her brother in Wyoming. Henry had hired the Baldwin Brothers, a local Folly Beach earth-moving company, to fix the washed-out area at the Folly Beach property. A lot of Charlestonians had already left the city for summer houses in Flat Rock, North Carolina, and he said the controversy over the Port Authorities' plans had died down with the heat. It was as if no one had any more energy left to fight.

On July 15, and for each of the fourteen days thereafter, Eliza received in the mail a photograph from Henry that he had taken on that early morning they had spent together on the Edisto. The photographs were elegant and serene and made Eliza think about the beauty of that morning. She had avoided going to the Tate to check the files on the Bonnard picture because she knew it would make her sad to think about Jamie. He was the one who had told her she was looking at the wrong picture. And she knew if she found the right picture, she would want to tell him. She first made an appointment to speak with the archivist at the National Portrait Gallery. She wanted to see what they had on Henrietta Johnston.

And then she did go to the Tate. A dour, assistant keeper of the collection dragged out the massive four-volume catalogue raisonné. Eliza started with the third volume, which covered the nineteen-year period between 1920 and 1939, and read the exhibition history of every painting page by page. When she reviewed the year 1923, she passed the painting she had identified earlier. But instead of stopping, as she had done the first time, she kept working her way backward. By late afternoon she had finished volume III and started on volume II, which covered the period 1906 to 1919. At quarter to five, the assistant keeper of the collection appeared and ushered her out. She had worked her way only through 1918 and 1919. She would have to come back the following day and begin with 1917.

That evening she worked for several hours packing up papers and books to ship back to Charleston. She found a book of essays by Joseph Brodsky with a slip of newspaper marking a spot. The book was not hers. It must have been one Jamie had left behind. She opened the book to the marked spot and read the passage underlined in pencil.

No one can tell you what lies ahead, least of all those who remain behind. One thing, however, they can assure you of is that it's not a round trip. Try, therefore, to derive some comfort from the notion that no matter how unpalatable this or that station may turn out to be, the train doesn't stop there for good. Therefore, you are never stuck—not even when you feel you are; for this place today becomes your past. From now on, it will only be receding for you, for that train is in constant motion. It will be receding for you even when you feel that you are stuck. . . . So take one last look at it, while it is still its normal size, while it is not yet a photograph. Look at it with all the tenderness you can muster, for you are looking at your past.

Jamie had once told Eliza that he never tried to find anything he had lost—he had learned there was no point—absolutely none—looking for it. Jamie made decisions based on that belief. He had learned to look forward, not sideways, and never backward. She felt with Henry that she could be lost forever and he would still try to find her. After ten years he had not given up hope of their being together. Despite what had happened, she felt safe with him. Maybe it was as simple as Jamie having taught himself, out of necessity, to see without memory. She wondered if going off to boarding school at age eight had taught him a way of navigating an emotional world that required always going forward. She thought about Jamie and how angry he had been. She understood his anger, but she knew he would be all right soon. Maybe that is what frightened her about him.

The following morning, when the second volume was delivered to her, she resumed where she had left off. By lunchtime she had found a second painting that had been exhibited at the 1939 Golden Gate Exhibition. This one, titled *Salle à manger à la campagne*, had been painted in 1913, ten years earlier than the one she had previously identified. Here was the woman standing outside a house, leaning with her elbows on the windowsill, looking in. There was even a cat with light green eyes. She put the volume down and rested her head in her hands and rubbed her eyes. How could she have ever thought the first painting was the correct one? She felt slightly sick to her stomach with how close she had come to making such a bad mistake. In the same way that she had tried to convince herself that the first painting she identified was the correct one, hadn't she tried, for a period of time, to convince herself that she and Jamie were right together? In both cases she had pretended that what wasn't there didn't matter. But why had she needed someone to act as a catalyst for her to take action? She had always allowed things to come to her, never the other way around. She wished she could call Jamie to tell him he had been right, but she knew she couldn't. Eliza returned the volume and waited for photocopies of the images to be made.

As she walked home, she thought about how Williams had interpreted this second painting of Bonnard's. Williams had imagined that the woman was waiting for a man to come, and that this man, who was watching her from the garden, wanted to be with her but was held back by something mysterious that even he didn't understand. Eliza thought about how Williams had included the theme of waiting and the sense of mystery between two people in many of his Delta plays. Laura waits for gentlemen callers who never come, Blanche waits five years at Belle Reve for her situation to improve, and Maggie waits for Brick to make love to her. Eliza tried to remember the exact lines from *Summer and Smoke* when John tells Alma that they had come face-to-face several times and each time they seemed to be trying to find something in each other without knowing what it was they were looking for, but she couldn't quite get the lines right. She would have to look them up when she got home.

Sometimes she wondered if Issie had not existed, would she and Henry have stayed together. They had been so in love, but they had been so young. And sometimes she found herself asking that question as a way of consoling herself about the loss of ten years.

But now she didn't have any more patience for questions. She felt desperate for Henry—for his touch, for his voice. The boundaries between them had blurred, and it hurt to wait. That afternoon Eliza sat at her kitchen table and adjusted the text and finished her essay. She knew it was the last thing she would ever write in London.

On July 29, Henry's thirty-second birthday, he sent her a black-and-white photograph that on first glance appeared to be an image of a dark, rough-textured surface. Eliza studied it carefully and then realized it was an image of the surface of what she guessed was the harbor at night. In the far left-hand corner was the curved fin of a dolphin. When could he have taken that? she wondered. She turned the photograph over. On the back was written in Henry's hand, "STILL—'NO FUN WITHOUT YOU.'" Those were the letters. That was what the list of the letters on the back of the photographs had spelled.

THE FOLLOWING EVENING, ELIZA'S ADVISER TOOK HER TO his club for a farewell dinner. She handed him her essay, which he read over a glass of champagne and pronounced it "Fine indeed." He said that Macmillan was planning to bring the collection of essays out in the spring of the following year. She would need to get a high-resolution image of the painting to them by October 1. He reminded her that she might be making a mistake to leave London, but that he knew his advice was no match for an affair of the heart.

A few days later, Eliza took a taxi to the airport. When she got to Heathrow, she called Henry. It was six in the morning in the States.

"Hello." He didn't sound like himself.

"Henry? Did I wake you up?"

"Eliza. Where are you?"

"I'm at Heathrow."

# CHAPTER THIRTEEN

Eliza arrived in Charleston three hours later than originally scheduled. She looked out the window into the darkness and wondered if Henry would still be there. As she approached the entrance to the waiting area, she saw him one beat before he saw her. He was leaning against one of the columns off to the side, just as he had on that early Sunday morning in June when he was waiting outside her house.

"Eliza." He held her away from him. "You're finally here."

"I am."

Henry moved his hands from her arms to her face and kissed her. "I began to think the longer you stayed, the worse the odds of your coming back."

"No," she said into the soft folds of his shirt. "I was always coming back."

They walked to the baggage carousel and waited for her bags.

"How's Lawton? How is he about my coming back?"

"Fine, he's seems okay, but it will take time."

"So he's still . . ."

"No, I didn't mean it that way. Lawton's just not great with change, he needs time to adjust. But he's good. He spent two weeks at tennis camp and now is in Wyoming with my mother. They're coming back in a few days so he can get ready for the State Tennis Championships. He's spent the rest of his summer researching dogs. He's checked out every book the library has multiple times. He's desperate to have one."

"But I thought you already said he could."

"I told him he could have one for his tenth birthday—in May, but not before, I just can't handle it with all the travel I'm going to have to do over the next couple of months. He's been trying to move the date forward to Christmas."

"I just have those two duffel bags." She pointed as they came around on the carousel.

"That's all?"

"I shipped everything else back."

He lifted her large bags off the carousel. "Good Lord, Eliza, books or bullion?"

"Clothes, books, and a present for you."

"Well then, that changes everything," Henry rolled his shoulder forward to balance the heavier bag.

They walked out into the soft warm air of a Charleston summer. The lights from the lampposts were diffused and blurred in halos around the posts. The dry fronds of the palmettos rustled in a slow breeze. "I'm parked way down there," he said, jutting his chin to signal direction.

Henry lifted her bags into the back of the Jeep. "Do I need to get you home right now?"

"No, no one is home," she said. "My mother and Ben stay in Middleburg all summer, and Sara's still in Europe."

"Everyone's gone—it's so hot." Henry looked at Eliza as he turned the key in the ignition. "So where to?"

"Depends."

"On?"

Eliza leaned against the door to face Henry. "Are we playing for keeps?"

"Completely." Henry's voice and laughter were intertwined. He put his hand on his chest. "I've been all in since the beginning."

"Okay," Eliza said, "then I'm all in, too."

HENRY PULLED UP TO THE FRONT OF 14 LEGARE. THE STREET was empty and dark. He led Eliza through the large brick piers down the pathway to the carriage house. The only sound Eliza could hear was the crunch of their feet on the oyster shells. Henry fished the key from the back pocket of his jeans. He opened the door and flicked the light switch, but no lights turned on. "I keep forgetting to fix that light," he said. "Here, hold my hand. Here's the first step." He paused for her to find it. She followed him up the narrow steep stairs to his bedroom in what had once been the hayloft.

He patted the wall at the top of the stairs. "Light," he said as he flicked the switch on. The loft was small—barely enough space for a double bed, chest of drawers, and an armchair. A black-and-white photograph of a little boy playing with Matchbox cars around a round wicker garden table was propped against the mirror over Henry's chest of drawers. Eliza walked over and looked at the photograph. She bent toward it to look carefully. "Is that you?"

"No, no, it's Lawton." Henry paused and looked at the photograph. "Lawton was mad about cars when he was little. It's all he ever played with. He would spend hours moving those two cars around that table. Here, I'll show you something." Henry took the frame and turned it over and opened the back. He handed her a photograph that had been hidden behind the back plate. "You have a good memory." A small boy played with a toy car on top of what looked like the same wicker table. "That one is me. Turn it over."

Eliza read, "Henry, age two, April 1961." She held the two photographs side by side. "God, Henry, he is the spitting image of you."

"I know."

"You even hold the car the same way. The only difference is that Lawton has two cars and you have only one."

Henry leaned over and looked at the second car on top of the table. "I never really noticed that." He sat on the edge of the bed and kicked off his loafers and reached toward Eliza and took her hand and pulled her toward him. "So when are you going to tell me how much you missed me?" He turned her wrist over and unbuckled the strap of her watch and set it on the bedside table. "Before you answer—bear in mind—we wouldn't want this perfect nose"—he ran his finger lightly down the bridge of her nose—"to, in any way, come to resemble Pinocchio's." She laughed and shook her head.

FOR A LONG TIME, ELIZA LISTENED FOR THE SPACES IN BETWEEN the sounds of the night. When she was in his arms, everything became easy to think about. "Was he meant to be the lighthouse keeper—the little man?" she asked.

Henry didn't answer, he had fallen asleep.

WHEN ELIZA WOKE UP THE NEXT MORNING, THE SUN WAS HIDden by a sky that looked like an ocean turned upside down. Henry was gone. Her duffel bags had been set side by side in the corner. On the mirror was a handwritten note. "Good morning, Sunshine. Call me at work."

Eliza unzipped her duffel bag and pulled out a tee shirt and summer skirt and wandered down the steep stairs to the kitchen and made coffee. She opened the kitchen door. The back garden—a simple lawn with pear and orange trees—was still. She could hear a faint drone of a lawn mower somewhere down the street. The heat had not yet stilled the birds that flitted back and forth in the fruit trees. Eliza drank coffee and returned upstairs. She looked again at the note on the mirror. Henry's style of starting letters from the bottom gave the words a lean and elegant form. She walked into Lawton's room. His drawings of airplanes were pinned to a cork-board. Their papier-mâché screech owl was stationed on the top shelf of his bookcase. It made her smile because she knew Lawton would have thought seriously about the best and most appropriate place in his room for his screech owl to rest.

In the corner on the floor were two opposing armies of plastic knights and horses. Lawton had left them in an orderly formation. For each cavalry, he had arranged six rows of ten warriors on their horses. Eliza bent down and examined the horses, which were draped in colorful coverings ornately decorated with images and symbols that indicated the identity and status of their rider. The horses reared and charged, and the riders, in armor that matched their horses, blocked with shields and attacked with lances and swords. Lawton protected his heart with the fierceness of his soldiers. But the passion of a nine-year-old boy, like that of his toy soldiers, had no power in an adult world. His stubbornness was his last defense against this understanding. Henry was right. It would take time, but it would be Lawton who decided how close she could come. A Viking longship, with a bow in the shape of a red dragon head and a square red-and-white-striped sail, was stationed a few feet away. She knew Henry had left Lawton's battlefield untouched because he missed Lawton so much.

When she called Henry, his secretary said he was in a meeting.

"He can call me back, nothing urgent, at his convenience." Eliza fiddled with the telephone cord as she put the receiver down. She picked up the photograph of Lawton playing with cars on Henry's dresser and looked at it carefully. She remembered a short story about a family sledding together and the author ending the story with the line that when you have children it opened up whole new rooms in your heart. She remembered telling Henry when he had driven her to the airport a month ago about imagining running into him surrounded by her beautiful children. It was odd that she could imagine children but that she had never thought about to whom she would be married. Was it because deep in her heart she could never imagine being with anyone but Henry? And yet in those reveries, Henry had always been alone, never with a son. Had her imagination tried to protect her from the painful parts of the past? But now as she thought about it, it had the reverse effect. Instead of denying Lawton's existence, it made her want to put her arms around him and hold him close. He had been trying to protect what was his in the only way that he knew how. When the phone rang, she put the picture frame back in its place, as if she had been caught looking at something forbidden.

"You were so asleep when I left, I couldn't bring myself to wake you up. Charlotte and Lucas Pinckney called and invited us over for a drink. Actually they invited us for dinner, but I was looking out for you—I said we had plans. We can walk over there around six thirty."

"But, Henry, I thought . . ."

"I know, apparently they're back together. No one quite knows the story. Louisa has her theories—she's not writing—no, of course not—well, I say that—she would if she could. She wouldn't dare. Charlotte is our second cousin."

Eliza wanted to tell Henry that she had discovered the small battlefield in Lawton's room, but he seemed preoccupied and in a rush.

"I'll try to leave work a little early, see you around six?"

When Henry returned home, Eliza was sitting at the small kitchen counter with the newspaper spread open in front of her. Henry kissed her and put his arms around her and looked over her shoulder. "Classifieds? Looking for a job so soon? You just got here."

"No"—she laughed—"at least not yet. Actually I was reading the *Antique and Collectible* ads—have you ever looked at these? Some are really pretty intriguing. Here's one—'seaman's chest with sundry articles of clothing and papers.' And another—'collection of photographs pertaining to the forestry operations of McLeod Lumber Company on Fripp Island and Caw Caw Swamp.' I love the word *sundry*—who uses that word anymore? And 'pertaining to'—it sounds so official. And the name Caw Caw. What a perfect name for a swamp."

Henry leaned closer and read, "'Alkaline-glazed storage pot in the manner of the Edgefield slave potter Dave.' Why did you circle that one?"

"Do you know anything about a slave potter named Dave? Didn't you say the bowl Cleve had given you was made by a slave?"

"He said it was. I don't know anything more than what he told me. He never mentioned the name Dave. But you know who would know is Matthew Cuthbert at the Charleston Museum." Henry checked his watch. "Let's take the long route to the Pinckneys. We have time."

"What's the long route?"

"Mmm, how about South Battery to East Battery to Queen to Logan to Montagu."

"Do you know who'll be at Charlotte and Lucas's?"

"Don't know—I think it might just be us." They walked past the Edwards house at the bottom of Legare.

"How is Cal getting along on his painting?" Eliza stopped to look at the side of the house. "He was just beginning when I left."

Henry turned and looked, too. "I don't know. I haven't seen him out here. It doesn't look as if anything has changed."

As they turned onto South Battery, Henry looked up at the sky. Dark clouds were gathering from the west. "Doesn't look great," he said. "How lucky are you feeling?"

"Incredibly lucky," Eliza said, looking up at the sky.

"Good, so am I."

"I've got my sunglasses just to prove it."

HENRY TOLD ELIZA THE THEORY ABOUT THE MORSE CODE still being up in the sky. "They are still bouncing around up there. Many of the messages—it's true, really." He looked up at the sky. "Think about it—it just has to do with starting sound waves in motion that never stop."

"But I thought they came over transatlantic cables—the dots and dashes."

Henry looked back up at the sky. "Maybe they did. Maybe you're right. It's still a lovely idea. I guess I'll have to put them up there with all of Cleve's souls."

Henry waved to a tall thin man with pale skin and wild strawberry hair who was walking toward them on the opposite side of the street. He was dressed in a shirt and tie and held his suit jacket folded neatly over his arm. He walked with perfect posture and showed no signs of feeling the heat.

"Who was that?"

"Chick Stobo. You probably never knew him. He's a good bit older than you. His parents were Charles and Sara Stobo. They lived year-round at Rice Hope Plantation up on the Cooper River. His father and my father were at Yale together, and once a year they'd have dinner at the Yacht Club. I think it was the only time he ever came to town. Chick was an only child. He is or was brilliant. He studied classics at Harvard and apparently had one of the most remarkable records of any student there. After Harvard, he tried to write, and I think had some success—I mean, he published a story or two, but it wasn't as if he were succeeding the way he had at everything before."

Eliza stumbled on the uneven flagstone sidewalk. Henry caught her arm. He lifted his chin toward the crushed oyster shell and sand perimeter of White Point Gardens that stretched the length of South Battery from King to East Battery. "Want to switch sides?"

"It's okay. So what happened?"

"After a few years, Chick went to Yale Law School to please his father, who had graduated first in his class. While he was there, Chick was found wandering the streets, not knowing who he was or where he was from—I heard it was pretty bad—he stayed in an institution until his father's death about four years ago. I ran into him several weeks ago and asked him what he was doing. He told me he was writing a book on Magnolia Cemetery. I asked him how he was doing it, and he said he was reading the cemetery's ledgers. He said he was trying to solve the puzzle of an entry he had just come across. In the 1880s, I think, a one-year-old child died and was buried in an unmarked grave. His name was 'King of the Clouds.' The brief entry noted that he was born in the Dakotas and had died of fever."

"I didn't know that anyone not from Charleston was buried at Magnolia." On the corner of King Street they passed a woman who had stopped to open her umbrella before walking on. Eliza looked up at the sky and wondered if they had made the right decision.

"Don't know." Henry shook his head. "I asked Chick if he

thought the infant could have been an Indian. He said it was unlikely, given that only white people could be buried at Magnolia. He thinks the child may have come to Charleston with parents who were part of one of the Wild West Shows that used to travel around the South. He said he was looking through all of the archives at the Historical Society. I am surprised you haven't come across him when you've been there."

They crossed the bottom of Meeting Street.

"That's sad."

"What?"

"The child, that he didn't have an ordinary name."

"Or maybe his parents gave him such a name to cope with their grief."

"I guess," Eliza said, "but the image of such a small child as the King of the Clouds, something so vast and far away—seems almost more painful."

"Yeah, I know."

"Is everything okay?"

"Sorry?" he asked.

"Are you okay?"

"Yes, yes, of course."

"You seem to be somewhere else."

Henry put his arm around Eliza's shoulders. "I'm right here."

They passed Villa Margherita. Eliza noticed the yellow DO NOT CROSS police tape in front of the decaying white Greek Revival mansion. "When I was little, I never had the courage to come trick-or-treating here. Does Mrs. Mackay still live here?"

"She does, but she's become even more of a recluse. I think her daughter lives with her now. They never come out in the day. It's pretty sad. They live on bourbon and Campbell's soup." They turned for a moment and looked at the crumbling facade. They crossed East Battery and climbed the stairs to High Battery.

"So do you recognize where you are?"

"Yes."

Henry dipped his head forward and held his palm out to her to indicate he wanted her to say more.

"We're on High Battery."

"Wrong answer. This is where I took that last photograph, the one I sent you on my birthday."

"Oh, Henry. Sorry, I loved it. The last one you sent me. I forgot to thank you."

Within minutes, heavy clouds darkened the sky, and the air cooled ten degrees.

"It's going to pour in a minute." Henry held his hand out and caught a few raindrops. "In less than a minute." He looked toward White Point Gardens. "We can take cover under the bandstand. Come on, let's go." He grabbed her hand, and they ran down the steps and across the street.

The rain was coming down hard now, and the sound of it crashing down took over everything. Eliza and Henry ran under the canopy of the live oaks and made it to the bandstand. Eliza, out of breath, leaned against one of the columns and pulled her wet shirt away from her body. "I don't think I've sprinted that fast since my last track meet at East Bay Playground when I was thirteen." Eliza turned and looked out at the thick rain that pelted hard against the earth. "Think there'll be lightning?"

"Don't know," Henry said and walked to the edge of the bandstand and looked out. "Hard to say." The fury of the rain had softened into a steady beat.

Eliza pushed her hair back and then felt the top of her head. "My sunglasses. They must have fallen off when we ran down the steps."

"I'll go look for them."

"You'll get soaked."

"It's okay. Death by rainstorm could be considered a noble end.

I'll be right back." He smiled and sprinted in the direction they had come.

HENRY, WHO LOOKED AS IF HE HAD JUST PULLED HIMSELF out of a swimming pool, took the stairs four at a time. He leaned over and kissed her and produced the glasses from his pocket. "The equivalent of Prince Charming returning Cinderella's glass slipper. Now let's see if they fit."

"Hooray." Eliza slipped the sunglasses back on top of her head. "My favorite sunglasses. I've had them forever. Where were they?"

"Come with me, I'll show you."

Henry ran down the steps. He turned. Eliza stayed where she was and looked out at the rain. "But, Henry, it's raining."

"Believe me, I know."

"You can just tell me. Promise, I'll believe you."

"No, really, I want to show you something. You won't regret it. Come on." He motioned with his head. "Quick. You might miss it. And I'll show you where your glasses were."

They ran under the live oak trees to the edge of the park. Henry checked for cars. Now unsheltered, they braced themselves for the rain and ran across the street and up the steps to High Battery. The rain, like a sharp curtain, ended. The slate promenade was dry, but a few inches from its border, the rain came down hard.

"We're at the edge." Eliza held her hand out to feel the rain.

"Exactly," Henry laughed. "We are on the edge, on the edge of a rain cloud—where the rain begins and where it ends. I've never seen this before. So sharp, so definite. It just stops, no tapering off. It's as if there is a whole other world over there—over that wall of rain."

Henry pushed his hair back from his forehead. "I found your sunglasses up here just as dry as they could be."

Eliza turned to look where he pointed.

"And what is even more extraordinary is that the curve of the rain follows the curve of the Battery. Come. I'll show you."

They followed the promenade as it curved and headed west, and just as Henry had described, the promenade remained dry.

Henry stood at the corner and said to Eliza, "I just hope the significance of this event is not lost on you. I just hope you realize that you are with a man who can find—not only the edge of a raincloud—but its corner."

When the rain finally stopped, they walked back to Henry's to change. The rain had relieved the air of its heaviness. The streets had been emptied of tourists and smelled faintly of salt and over-ripe vegetation. A few crickets joined the soft sounds of the humming and pulsing air-conditioning units. It was as if they had been transported back to the Charleston Eliza had known as a child. The sound of a car tearing softly through a puddle of water on the street made her take notice. She wondered if the tide were high or if it had rained so much that the water had no place to go.

"WE THOUGHT THE DELUGE HAD CARRIED YOU AWAY," LUCAS said as he opened the door.

"Sorry," Henry said. "Actually, we did get caught and had to go back home to change."

"Do come in. Eliza, dear, how are you?"

The Pinckney house was built in the third quarter of the eighteenth century with a wide hall and two large rooms on each side. Lucas turned and fluttered his hand toward the unmatched chairs lining the hall. "I've just inherited some chairs from my great-aunt Lavinia, and I'm afraid it rather looks like a funeral parlor. Oh, and what Charlotte and I think is a wonderful picture. Remind me to show it to you, Eliza."

Lucas led them into the double parlor painted a light blue gray and directed Eliza to sit on a Chippendale sofa covered in a persimmon silk damask with matching cushions. He apologized for serving them cheap grocery store wine and added, "Charlotte will be down in a minute. She's gone up to the attic to check the roof—we've had a leak, we think it's been fixed, but she just wanted to check."

Charlotte appeared as if on cue, hair twisted into a loose bun and wearing a long, unfitted floral print dress that could have belonged to her mother. She greeted everyone and then disappeared to retrieve a tray of shrimp paste sandwiches. The phone rang, and Lucas fluttered the air with his hand again. "Charlotte will get that."

Charlotte returned, and Lucas asked her who called.

"Mary Elizabeth."

"Oh my," Lucas said, "don't tell me. She was calling about either your artichoke pickle relish or your fig preserves. What Bible verse was she quoting now? My sister, Penelope, told me Mary Elizabeth cornered her last week before the afternoon service at St. Michael's and began a monologue about how 'God loves a cheerful giver.' The week before she was quoting the passage in II Corinthians about 'whoever sows generously will also reap generously.' Mary Elizabeth wants Penelope's recipe for a seven-layer Viennese torte. Lord, this city is wrecking her mental health."

Charlotte interrupted Lucas to ask Eliza about people in England whom she had met on various trips of the Georgian Furniture Society.

Lucas crossed his legs and leaned toward Henry. "Now, have you heard the latest about Charles Lowndes's ashes? Charles Junior swears his father wanted to be cremated and have his ashes put in one of the cypress trees at Ashley Gardens for all the tourists to honor as they paddle by in those silly canoes his father designed. I told him at least he could put up a plaque. There's a rumor going round that Charles Senior had no such wish, but that it's Charles Junior's attempt to punish his father for leaving him no cash and a second-rate plantation that has to be opened to the public and cannot be sold. Apparently to add insult to injury"—Lucas lowered his voice an octave—"so to speak, Charles Senior had a very valuable piece of South Carolina pottery that Charles Junior had lined up to sell to a collector for a big price until he learned that his father had donated it to the Gibbes weeks before his death."

Lucas stood up and promised to "return with more libation." He raised his hand in the air as he disappeared. "But we all know about nutty fathers in this town. I dare say it's a prerequisite for living here."

Lucas returned with another bottle of wine. "Poor Charlotte and I had just recovered from her father's escapades of encouraging children to soak bread crumbs in bourbon to give to the seagulls. Henry was gracious enough to let us know gently about Charlotte's father, but those dreadful people from Chicago, the Downings, the ones who moved into the Simmons house, and who correct people when they refer to their house as the Simmons house, are taking it upon themselves to report everybody who gets in their way. That Betsy Downing was downright hostile about Charlotte's father. If Mother were still alive, she would have made it her business to inform them that Charleston houses retain the name of the Charleston family who owned the house. And no doubt—she would have suggested that they move back to Chicago."

Lucas waltzed around the room "replenishing" everyone's glass. "Meanwhile, just yesterday, Penelope called to say that Father had sent off a letter to the new president of Duke with what could be construed as a racist comment. She is treating it as if it were a Family Tragedy. She is especially worried, as her eldest son, who shares Father's first name, is waitlisted at Duke. I told Penelope,

'Father's ninety-two, for goodness sake, everyone will just chalk it up to dementia.' More wine?" Lucas stepped around the room and insisted that everyone have their glass refilled. "Eliza, you went to Princeton, or was it Columbia?"

"Princeton undergraduate, Columbia graduate school in English and then art history."

"Oh my, well then, Henry, do let me borrow Eliza to get her opinion of this picture of Aunt Lavinia's. You can stay and keep Charlotte company. But when I return I want to talk to you about what we all can do to stop this idea of deepening the harbor."

Lucas held out his elbow to Eliza. He escorted her to a small library and pointed above the fireplace to an oil painting of a man and woman in eighteenth-century dress standing under a tree in a tropical setting. A spaniel, with its back to the viewer, sat next to them.

Eliza thought the picture was amusing but almost certainly painted by an amateur rather than a serious artist. "Intriguing," was the best she could do. "Do you know who the artist is?"

"It's not signed. But I think it is very important. Can you think of any painting you have ever seen, any portrait where an animal has its back to the viewer?"


"WAS THAT ENOUGH TO FRIGHTEN YOU FROM LIVING IN Charleston forever?" Henry asked after Lucas had shut the front door. Henry jumped ahead and walked backward, facing Eliza. "I knew I should have said we were busy."

The night air was cool and fresh from the rain.

"I don't know why Charlotte puts up with Lucas," Henry said. "I was running past their house a couple of weeks ago, after a bad storm, and she was pulling fallen branches and palm fronds from their back garden out onto the street. I stopped to help her. Lucas was nowhere to be seen. And while I was helping her, three toy arrows were shot over the wall. Charlotte picked them up and threw them back over and said loudly, 'Oh, my word, Indians are attacking,' and she smiled when the small band of boys on the other side of the wall squealed in excitement. And then she said very quietly to me, 'You know, I don't think I will ever get over not having children.' I didn't know what to say to that. Charlotte has always been such a private person and, as we all know, Lucas has been horrible to her. She told me she thought the boys next door were scaling the wall and picking all the fruit. She has lovely fig and pear and peach trees. She said she didn't mind, but that Lucas was getting angry. I told her it was probably rats, though her mother and my mother would say mice, even though mice are in the country and rats are in towns, especially ports like Charleston. She was surprised by that, but she said she would tell Lucas and it might make him less irritated by the little boys. I don't know why she stays with him, she would have been such a sweet mother."

"I guess she really must love him," Eliza said.

"Yeah, I guess you're right. Maybe it's not any more complicated than that."

As they passed the Walker house, the twins were running around with blue LED lights strapped to their foreheads. "William, Chisolm," Henry called to them.

"Hi, Mr. Heyward." They stood at attention.

"What are you doing?"

"Trying to catch fireflies." They held their Bell and Mason glass jars up as proof.

"Are your parents here?"

"No, they went out to dinner."

"Who's looking after you?"

"Hannah."

"Shouldn't the two of you be in bed?"

"Hannah said we could play a bit longer."

"Ask Hannah if you can turn the piazza lights off. Then wait ten minutes, and I bet you'll see them."

They nodded and turned to run inside.

"Wait," Henry called to them. "Do your jars have holes in the top?" They turned the jars sideways to show Henry the holes. "Okay, well, good luck. But be sure to let them go." They scrambled up the steps of the piazza and raced to the front door.

"They look just like Charlie."

"Yeah, they do, don't they?"


As THEY WALKED HOME, ELIZA THOUGHT ABOUT JOURNEYS. She had traveled wide to come back to Henry. And even though this world around her now was so familiar that she could navigate it blind, being back with Henry gave her access to a whole new continent of feelings. It was a world that could never be seen, but it was there—underneath the surface of everything—joyful and pure. When they made love that night, Eliza felt the contours of Henry's body as if she were mapping a secret area of the earth that would forever hold her and enthrall her. The way he kissed her made her feel as if she would always belong to him. She liked the thought of being the cartographer of Henry's body, but he would forever be the cartographer of her heart. She wondered if he knew that.


WHEN SHE WOKE UP IN THE EARLY MORNING, SHE REMEM-bered the line of a Wallace Stevens poem about the house being quiet and the world being calm, but she couldn't remember anything else. She turned onto her stomach and shifted her hands underneath her pillow. She heard Henry walking up the stairs. "Where have you been?" she asked him when he was at the top. His hair was wet.

"I went for a run."

"What time is it?"

"Early, ten past six."

"What time did you get up?"

"I don't know, early. I couldn't sleep."

Eliza pushed up on her forearms. "Henry, what's going on? What's the matter? Since I've been back, you've seemed preoccupied."

He sat on the bed and pushed her hair away from her forehead. "There's nothing to worry about. I just couldn't sleep, that's all."

Eliza stretched her arms forward and lay back down. "You know, I was thinking about my flight back here. There were these two young men—about your age—and they kept standing up and talking to each other, and they both had on wedding bands. And they were very straight-looking—investment banker types. You know, serious and mature and responsible and perfectly turned out. They talked with energy, but they weren't joking around, and I watched them. Their wedding bands somehow made them seem vulnerable, that somewhere in the world there was someone they loved. And I began to wonder what their wives were like. How differently did these men treat their wives? Were they soft and tender with them? Could they exist without them? And it made me think of you. Was I that person to you? If you were on a plane would you seem serious and would someone wonder about who you loved?" Eliza lifted her head up slightly to see Henry's reaction and then collapsed back down on the pillow. "What is it about the rain? I say things I shouldn't."

Henry moved his hand slowly down her back. "What are your plans today?"

"Sleep and more sleep."

"I don't believe you." Henry leaned down and kissed her.

"You shouldn't." Eliza turned over and pushed herself up on

her elbows. "Actually, I thought I would go by the museum, just to double-check that they don't have anything on Henrietta Johnston. I was also going to see if they have anything on the slave potter Dave."

"Want me to drop you off?"

"No, thanks, they aren't open until nine."

"Okay, I'll meet you back here after work. Do you want to go down to Folly or have dinner in town?"

"Can we decide later?"

"Sure," Henry said and kissed her a second time. "You should go back to sleep."

"I ALMOST CALLED YOU AT WORK TO COME DOWN TO THE museum," Eliza said when Henry returned at the end of the day. "You've got to see this," she said, waving images of clay pots. "The museum has a small but amazing collection of pots by Dave."

"Dave?"

"The slave who was a potter."

"Oh yes, of course." Henry ran his hand through his hair and looked around the room as if he were not sure where he was.

"He was an amazing potter, I mean, really gifted—his glazes are beautiful and clear. Some of his pots are almost twenty-four inches high. Do you know how hard it is to throw a pot that large? Here, look." Eliza sat down on the sofa and spread the images across the top of a trunk that served as a coffee table. "Matthew Cuthbert was away, but his assistant, Alida Reeves, helped me. I asked her if she knew of any bowls attributed to Dave, but she said she didn't think there were any. So the mystery of Cleve's bowl remains."

Henry sat down next to her and took off his tie and unbuttoned the top button of his shirt.

"Alida gave me a copy of their files. The museum has several pots, but only one is on permanent display. I have a picture of it somewhere." Eliza flipped through the photocopies. "Here it is. It's massive, and just here"—she pointed to the areas just below the rim—"Dave wrote these charming couplets. In 1919, this is the one that Colonel Stoney donated. It is what started the museum's collection. Can you see the writing?" She handed the image to Henry.

Henry squinted. "Not really."

"It's hard to make out from that copy. I wrote it on the back." Henry turned the image over and read, "Made at Stoney Bluff, for making lard enuff—13 May 1859."

"Alida said that Dave wrote these couplets on about twenty pots." Eliza shuffled through the papers. "Alida gave me a copy of the known ones. This is my favorite." She read from a sheet of paper, "'I wonder where is all my relations, friendship to all—and every nation.' He wrote that in 1857. Alida said there wasn't much published on him."

"That's great," Henry said.

"Why is that great?" Eliza felt as if she had just run over a hard bump.

"If not much is written, then you can write something, an article, maybe even a book." Henry picked up the images and looked through them. "So how many did you say had lines of poetry written on them?"

"Alida said twenty are known to have couplets, but there is always the hope that more will be discovered. These pots were used to store things—oil, grains, lard—so it could be that some have been passed down in families who don't realize how valuable they are."

"You'll have to take me to see them." Henry picked up the newspaper. "So how do you feel about going to see a movie tonight?"

# CHAPTER FOURTEEN

THE FOLLOWING MORNING HENRY GENTLY SHOOK ELIZA'S arm to awaken her. "Eliza, listen, I need to talk to you. I need to tell you something." He was already dressed for work.

"What time is it?"

"Quarter to seven."

Eliza sat up in bed and pushed her hair out of her eyes. Henry was standing with his hands on hips and looking down at the floor.

"Henry, what, what is it?" She felt as if her skin were made of thin sheets of metal that were about to pull apart.

Henry sat sidesaddle on the bed facing Eliza. "I received a letter from Issie's lawyer saying she wanted to meet with me and see Lawton. She came back into town for a few days at the beginning of June and then left. I didn't see her, but . . ."

"Louisa did," Eliza said. The image of Henry and Louisa talking by the fireplace at Anne's returned to her. "That's what she told you at Anne's party that night."

Henry said, "Louisa said she had heard Issie was in town, but she hadn't seen her. I should have told you, but Louisa doesn't always get it right. And I wanted to find out the facts before I let a rumor—I don't know—well, I was afraid it would unsettle you. Things were going so well for us that I didn't want anything to jar us, and I thought if I brought up Issie's name, it might send you running."

Eliza pushed her back farther against the headboard. "God, Henry—I've just broken up with Jamie, turned down a research fellowship at the Courtauld, come back to Charleston without any-thing to do—all just to be with you. What more proof could you want from me?"

"Nothing, nothing more. I should have had more faith in you. I should have. Listen, you've been wonderful."

"Is that everything?"

Henry's voice was subdued. "Yes. There's nothing more."

"Does Lawton know any of this?"

"No, not yet. I'll have to tell him when he gets back."

"Does Issie have the right to do this?" Eliza pushed her hair from her face.

"Technically, no. I mean, she gave up all rights to him, but in a way, I guess, it doesn't matter. Lawton is going to find this really difficult." Henry looked down at the floor before looking back at Eliza.

"Is she moving back here?"

"I don't know. Her lawyer said she was here visiting. I haven't seen Issie since Lawton was born. She hasn't tried to contact me. She's never written me or tried to call me. I just got a letter from her lawyer saying that she wants to meet next week."

"She can't take Lawton away, can she?"

"No, but she can make trouble and add confusion."

"Who is her lawyer?"

"Someone from one of the big firms in Boston. I don't know him."

"When is she coming back?"

"I don't know, I guess she could be here now. All I know is that she wants to meet with me next week and see Lawton."

Eliza looked down and traced the lines in the palm of her hand with her index finger. "Henry, I don't know what to say. What are you going to tell Lawton?"

"I don't know, but I've got to talk to him as soon as he gets back."

"Have you spoken to Elliott?"

"Eliza, the law doesn't really matter. The only issue is—how will this affect Lawton."

"Does she want to start being his mother?"

"I don't know. I don't know if Issie is married or has other children. I really don't know anything except that she's asked for a meeting with me next week."

They sat together without saying anything.

Eliza searched for the sounds of birds, but she could not hear anything. She felt as if all the relationships were being readjusted, and she feared her rapport with Lawton was in danger of slipping away. She didn't know what to say. Henry moved close to her and cupped his hand around the arch of her foot. "Eliza, I can't imagine my life without you." He leaned over her and took his watch from the bedside table. He checked the time. "I've got to get to the office. The owners of the paper in New Orleans are coming in this morning to sign all the documents. I offered Mr. Porcher a tour of our offices."

Henry picked up a tie that had fallen on the floor. Eliza watched him measure one side against the other. He pulled the ends down until the wide end was six inches longer than the narrow end. "Mr. Porcher told me that he and Edward McGee's father were roommates at Sewanee." Henry wrapped the wide end around the narrow end twice. "When Edward learned that we were buying *The New Orleans Gazette*, he wrote to Mr. Porcher and sent him his articles. Fortunately Mr. Porcher thinks Edward's ideas are not worth the paper they are written on—direct quote." Henry pulled the knot tight and centered it and looked up at Eliza. "We'll get through this."

"I know, it's just—why now, you know?"

He bent down and kissed her, squeezed her arm, and said, "I know."

THE RAIN HAD DISSIPATED INTO A SOFT MIST. AS ELIZA LEFT the garden, she heard the sweet hollow call of a mourning dove. She walked down Legare Street and watched an old blue station wagon pause in front of each house as an arm tossed a newspaper over the car with the precision of a juggler in a circus. Three runners passed, their feet slapping at the wet pavement, sounding like conversations, and disappeared down the street. At the bottom of Legare Street she turned east. Eliza concentrated on the sounds of the birds—she counted seven different ones—that ranged from plaintive calls to husky chirps, from high twills to low-pitched twitters. As she walked down South Battery toward her house, clouds, opaque and blue and tinted with the palest lavender around the edges, covered half of the sky.

BY MIDMORNING, ELIZA WAS AT HER DESK AT THE HISTORI-cal Society with the last six boxes of the Vanderhorst's family papers stacked beside her on a gray trolley. When Claire tapped her on the shoulder and asked if she were all right, Eliza looked down at the table and saw that the same folder had been opened for a long time. "Yes," Eliza said, "I think it's just the heat. I think I'll leave and come back tomorrow."

On the corner of Tradd and Legare, Eliza swung wide around a large, slow-moving herd of tourists who looked over each other's heads in different directions, as if searching for a sign to appear.

Their tour guide, practiced at such maneuvers, had stopped in front of the Sword Gate House and had begun to tell them the story of how the crossed swords were originally made in 1838 for the city's new guardhouse. Eliza slowed down to listen. "From 1819 through 1848, Madame Talvande kept a select academy for young ladies in the large house beyond the imposing gates," the guide revealed. "Her ghost is sometimes seen on the third-floor piazza looking down at the garden." The tourists all looked up to the third floor. As she passed, Eliza looked through the gates to see if Joe were sitting, as he always did, in the wicker rocker on the first-floor piazza. She did not see him and wondered where he had gone.

ELIZA WAS PACKING SOME OF HER THINGS WHEN SHE HEARD a knock on the glass-paneled carriage doors. The door opened, and Anne de Liesseline's voice called her name.

"Oh, Eliza dear," she said and clasped her hands together, "I was hoping I would find you here. You aren't going off again?"

"No, I just need to bring some things over to my house."

"Here, let me help you. I'll give you a lift, but only if you promise to come with me. I want to show you Sallie's portrait. I finished it last evening, and I want you to see it. I want your honest reaction."

Looking at a portrait of Sallie Izard was the last thing Eliza wanted to do, but she found herself waiting for Anne to move a collection of maps from the front seat to the back of her car. Anne's car was an old unidentifiable model. She didn't believe in airconditioning, so they headed for the Cooper River Bridge with their windows down and the air rushing past them. It suited Eliza. It was so noisy that it was impossible to talk without shouting. They ascended over the high arches of the twin spans of the Cooper River Bridge that connected the peninsula of Charleston to Mount Pleasant.

Anne's family had owned Landgrave Point, the land on the southeastern tip of the Isle of Palms, for as long as anyone could remember. In the early 1900s her grandfather had paid fishermen to bring huge piles of rocks to dump along the shoreline to fortify the land from erosion. The result was this glorious crescent of land surrounded by the Atlantic Ocean. Anne's father had somehow managed to get an old train car from one of the luxury trains and had it transported to their land. It was where he and his friends would retire and smoke cigars and play poker on Saturday evenings during the summers when most of Charleston had moved into beach houses on the adjacent Sullivan's Island.

As they pulled into the driveway, Anne asked Eliza if she remembered coming out to Landgrave Point.

"Vaguely," she said, "with my father. I remember the train car."

"Yes, that's still here, right over there," she said, pointing to the vintage train car shaded by several large oak trees.

"So it survived Hurricane Hugo?"

"Just. Hugo flipped it on its side, but other than that, it was okay. It's monstrously heavy. We had a dickens of a time getting it upright. My aunt Louisa used it as a study. It's where she wrote all those horrendous novels that had pictures of southern belles with their torn-off-the-shoulder gowns on the cover and some columned white plantation house smoldering in the background. I'd always see them in the racks next to the checkout counters at the Piggly Wiggly. It would have pleased us all so much if she'd used a pen name or at least her maiden name of Carter. But she was beyond thrilled with her success. Louisa de Liesseline. Big yellow letters splashed across the front covers. You know, your father used to stop by sometimes in the summer. I remember the day he designed that studio for me on a paper napkin," she said, pointing to the tall squarish building positioned on the north part of the land. "If I remember correctly, you were with him. You were very little. Come, let me show you."

Anne searched her purse for her keys. "*Design* may be too strong a word for a one-room studio, but he drew the most wonderful large window facing north. His sense of proportion was perfect. Every time I open this door, it makes me a little sad that he never saw what I built from his sketch."

Anne pushed the door open, and Eliza stepped into a double-heighted room with a large north-facing window that reached from the top of the cornice to two feet above the floor. The ceiling and floor were painted black and the walls white. Anne's work was scattered around. There was a long table with brushes and paints laid out in order, and in the corner was a tall white sculpture of a shrouded woman holding a baby upright in her arms. The portrait was positioned on an easel at the other end of the room. It was large—three-fourths life size. Anne had painted Sallie as she had requested—as a mermaid. Sallie Izard sat on a rock with her tail curled to the side and around her were mysterious wild vines and tangles. Behind her was a pond that Eliza assumed was the swimming pool she had converted for her turtles. Anne had chosen the medium of watercolor, and the green and blue and violet colors blurred and ran into one another as if the canvas had not finished drying. Sallie's eyes were painted with bold black smudge strokes and underlined in a liquid pale green. Her lips were a watery pinkish red that faded into the pale color of skin, and on one cheek was a rectangle of red that faded to pink and then to nothing.

It made Eliza smile. "Anne, it's really good. The technique reminds me a bit of Francesco Clemente's watercolors. I have to say that, when you first told me about it, I thought it would be, well, rather . . ."

"Horrible." Anne finished Eliza's sentence. "I know. I don't blame you." Anne walked around it and looked at it from several angles. "But I am rather pleased with the way it turned out. Sallie was adamant that she be painted as a mermaid, and I finally gave in and thought, well, here goes. Oh, here, let me make us some tea." Anne disappeared out the back and returned with a handful of leaves. "My own tea," she said. "I smuggled some back from Italy. Verveine." Eliza watched as Anne brewed a pot of tea and then cooled it with ice.

"You may have met the McMasters at my party—the couple who bought my great-aunt's house on Meeting Street. Or maybe you had already left by the time they arrived. Anyway, Angela has already spoken to me about painting a portrait of her girls. A painting of her three girls would be lovely over the fireplace in Aunt Zenobia's house, but I haven't had the nerve to show her this portrait. I'm afraid it will scare her off. Angela thinks she knows exactly what she wants—her three little girls in front of an arrangement of fruit. The trick for me is to find some twist she doesn't even recognize—it's the only way I'll be able to stay engaged." Anne handed Eliza a glass of iced tea and walked to the window and pointed to the tip of the property, which jutted out into the water. "We can sit down under those palmetto trees on the point. There's always a breeze there." As she led the way, they stopped to watch two shrimp boats slowly making their way back to their berths at the Shem Creek marina.

ELIZA ASKED ANNE TO DROP HER OFF AT THE FOOT OF Church Street. As she pulled over and stopped, she patted Eliza on the shoulder and said, "I ran into Henry. He needs you right now. He's not the least bit interested in Isabel. She is absolutely mad. She's a distant cousin, and my father always said, you know those Lartigues are as crazy as June bugs. No matter what she thinks now, she won't stay in Charleston long. She won't be able to take it here. Eliza dear— it's the wrong turns in life that get you—if you let them. Pain is bad, but regret is worse."

# CHAPTER FIFTEEN

When Eliza had finished unpacking her bag, she surveyed the landscape of her bedroom—no stacks of papers that needed to be organized. No more Magritte, no pages to be proofed, no letters to write. Nothing more to be considered on Bonnard and Williams. No applications to fill out and send off. Just a bound copy of her notes to give to Henry as a late birthday present. She had to see Mrs. Vanderhorst, but after that? She could hear the English voice of her adviser cautioning her that she was making a mistake to leave. His admonition didn't unsettle her, but just because she had made the decision not to stay in London didn't mean she had made the right decision to return to Charleston. She took the little lighthouse keeper out of her pocket and placed him on top of her mirrored box. She liked the way he looked, as if he were walking on water.

And then she heard Henry's voice calling her from the garden.

She raised her window to answer, but he was gone, and then she heard him sprinting up the back staircase.

"Eliza, God, there you are. I've been calling you. Did you hear me? I was worried when you weren't at the carriage house." He walked to where she was standing by the window. He rolled up his sleeves and wiped his forehead with his forearm. "Why did you leave?"

Eliza leaned her shoulders against her bedroom wall and looked down on the canopy of the magnolia tree. "I needed to come back here and start unpacking and getting settled. I had to do it at some point, and I don't know, well, it just feels safe here. I was going to call you a little later. You left work early?"

Henry turned Eliza toward him. "Eliza, listen, we've gone through the tough part. We can't change what has already happened. You're safe with me. You know that, right?"

Eliza sat down on the bed and smoothed the bedspread with the palm of her hand. "I do. I know. It's just harder for me than I guess it should be. I feel as if I am jumping off the Ben Sawyer Bridge—only it's a million times higher, and I have no idea what I am going to do next. It was difficult enough for me to get to the point to believe, I mean, to trust that we should be together. And now that Issie is back—she's no longer a vague abstraction from the past. I don't know"—Eliza looked around her room—"organizing everything around me makes me feel as if I, at least, have some control over part of my life. I know it makes no sense, but it helps me. Henry, I'm not going anywhere. You don't need to worry about me, you have enough to deal with. I just need some time to adjust, that's all. Maybe you should leave me alone for a while."

"Eliza, I'm not going to do that." Henry sat down next to her and put his arm around her. He reached across her and moved the small figure from the top of her mirrored box to the top of the table. He picked up the box. "Is this your treasure box?"

Eliza nodded. "It's where I keep the things my father found and gave to me or things we found together." She pushed her back against the pillows and took the box from Henry. The pieces of mirror that covered the sides were beveled on the edges. She opened the drawer carefully and laid the pieces on her bed. "A Victorian marble, an eighteenth-century shoe buckle, bits of china, some shards of Indian pottery, pieces of blue and white delftware, a quartz arrowhead, a—"

"Let me see that." He reached for the arrowhead. "Quartz. Not from around here. Where did you find this?"

"On the banks of the Stono. My father and I were crabbing one afternoon, and we found it lying on one of the sandbars. My father said he thought it must have been from Indian traders. He said just what you said—there is no quartz in South Carolina. He guessed that Indians from North Carolina must have come down here to trade. This is my favorite." Eliza pulled a small wrapped bundle from the back of the drawer. She unfolded the delicate cloth, a child's handkerchief with the monogram of *E*, and held up a delicately carved figure of a cat, about the size of a dime. "A little girl's necklace or a charm from a bracelet." The cat was carved out of bone, and its eyes and nose were painted with tiny black dots. She handed it to Henry, who turned it over in the palm of his hand and then handed it back.

"Where did you find it?"

"In our garden. My father was overseeing a trench dug for my mother's roses, and he gave me the task of sifting through all of the dirt. It was in a layer about eighteen inches below the surface."

Henry watched Eliza carefully place all of the pieces back in the box. She knew where each piece went. She closed the drawer and placed the box on top of her dresser. After her father died, the weekend trips to the country stopped. Eliza remembered being upset that her mother had sold their share of the Poinsett plantation to her father's brother, but she later understood it wasn't a choice but a necessity.

Eliza looked up at the map her father had painted of Charleston and the surrounding areas. "My father had his own plane, and he and his brother would fly to different properties to go hunting. I always wanted to go with him, but my mother never would let me, she thought it was too dangerous. And I would always ask my father what it looked like so high up in the sky. So for my seventh birthday, he drew what he saw looking down from the plane. He told me when I went to sleep at night, I could look up, and I would see what he saw when he went flying. I figured if I memorized the images, then I would be the best copilot he ever could have. I've forgotten how much it meant to me. I used to get scared at night. And he would come up here and sit in that chair over there and speak to me as if we were in the cockpit together. He would tell me to look down and follow the Edisto—'See where it widens— that's Willtown Bluff.'" Eliza pointed to the ceiling to the place she mentioned. "He would tell me about the group of settlers who left England and landed on that spot and first called it New London. He would tell me how they set up plats of land and squares and how children would spend their time looking for arrowheads and shards of Indian pottery, and I would fall asleep dreaming that I was on that treasure hunt with them. After my father died, my eyes would always go to the spot where he died—right there along the Ashley River. We have always assumed that a deer must have jumped out of the woods, and he swerved, and that is why his car crashed into one of those large live oak trees that line the road, but, you know, we will never know. It's hard—the not knowing." Eliza was telling Henry things she had told him many times before.

"Slip over," he said. He lay down next to her and studied the ceiling with her. He turned to look at her.

"You know, sometimes an inconsequential thing—even a small

mistake—can wreck the rest of your life. It could be driving too fast on a slippery road or falling asleep at the wheel or not turning back in a sailboat when storm clouds appear or trying to swim too far when you are tired. It only takes one small error." He pushed her hair back from her face. She looked back up at the map. The destruction of a life by one small gesture of motion or mind—Eliza understood that. Even what had happened between Henry and Issie had held—and possibly still did—the potential for destruction and ruin. Second chances were rarely offered, but she and Henry, either through the bizarre randomness of coincidence or the tight control of Fate, had been given one.

# CHAPTER SIXTEEN

W HEN ELIZA CALLED, RANDOLPH TOLD HER THAT HE would be delighted to see her and invited her over for afternoon tea.

Eliza rang the bell at 103 Beaufain Street, and a large dog began barking and jumping at the front door. Eliza heard Randolph's voice, "Scarlett, shush; shush, Scarlett." A short, pale man in a white starched shirt and gray linen trousers opened the door. He braced backward on a thick, short leash to prevent the shaggy gray wolfhound from lunging at Eliza.

"Do come in." Randolph tried to smile, but all of his energy was concentrated on restraining Scarlett. "I'm just going to put Scarlett in the garden." He wrestled the large dog to the back of the house. Eliza heard Scarlett's toenails scramble against the hardwood floors. Not certain where she should go, Eliza stood in the hall and waited for Randolph. She heard a back door open, more scrambling, and then the door slam shut.

Randolph returned. "I must apologize for Scarlett. She's still a puppy, and she gets so excited whenever I have visitors. I've just registered her for obedience class, but class doesn't start until September." He held out his arm toward the parlor. "After you." He beamed and waited for Eliza to pass in front of him. "I've always had wolfhounds, but Scarlett is the most rambunctious one I have ever had."

Eliza walked into a small room painted a dark crimson and furnished with a large Victorian settee, four matching chairs, and a piano. It was a room Jamie would have described as "overfurnitured." With a hopeful expression, Randolph asked Eliza if she would prefer sherry or tea. When Eliza turned and said, "Tea," the hopefulness left his face, and he returned with a tray set for tea and a tiered plate of petits fours.

"So Henry tells me you're researching Henrietta Johnston."

"Yes," she said. "Mrs. Vanderhorst has a pastel drawing that she thinks might be by her but isn't sure."

"It's not signed, then?"

"No, it's not. I brought a photograph of it." Eliza opened her notebook and handed Randolph the image tucked inside the front cover.

Randolph pulled a pair of reading glasses from his shirt pocket and adjusted them on his face. He studied the image. "It's lovely," Randolph said. "There's no family history about the picture?"

"No, none that is known. It was passed down in Mr. Vanderhorst's family and has always been attributed to Johnston, but Mr. Vanderhorst didn't know who the sitter was."

"Curious," Randolph said and gave her back the photograph. "Sugar, lemon?"

"Just lemon."

Randolph handed Eliza a cup of tea. "Most of the ones I've come across, the sitter is known. Of course, I'm sure you have read Margaret Simons Middleton's book."

Eliza nodded. "I even looked through her files at the Library Society."

"May I tempt you?" Randolph offered Eliza the plate of petit fours. "The ones with the sugared violets on top are my favorite." After Eliza had chosen, Randolph helped himself to two. "I suppose there are no record books where Johnston made notes?"

"No, none that are known. And I haven't come across anything to suggest she might have kept a record. All I've found of Henrietta Johnston are a couple of letters she wrote, but she doesn't mention anything about her art. Her letters mainly deal with needing money. I've checked the newspapers and some family papers of people who sat for her. I've looked through all of the Vanderhorst family archives at the Historical Society. I was hoping to find a will or letter that might mention the portrait, but I haven't found anything yet."

Randolph pinched his forehead with his thumb and index finger. "Vanderhorst is a Dutch name, but William had a number of ancestors who were French Huguenots. Johnston was descended from French Huguenots, her maiden name was . . ." Randolph tapped his forehead with his fingers.

"De Beaulieu."

"Exactly. And a number of her sitters were also French Huguenots."

"Mrs. Vanderhorst said that Mr. Vanderhorst thought she might be one of the Guignard daughters who married into the Bruneau family."

"Now that is very interesting. If I remember correctly, William's maternal grandmother was a Bruneau, and before the Revolutionary War that family owned a vast plantation on the Santee."

"Yes, they did, but then something happened, and they all disappeared. Mrs. Vanderhorst thinks that part of the family either died off with yellow fever or lost their fortune after the Revolutionary War. I looked through what the Historical Society had on both the Guignard and Bruneau families."

"Nothing?"

"No, nothing in their archives."

"Hmm," he said. "And are there no experts on Henrietta Johnston?"

"Helen Halsey at the Gibbes was helpful. She is knowledgeable, but it's not really her field. She thinks it, very likely, could be a Johnston, but is quick to say her opinion should not be relied on."

"I suppose there really is no one else."

"Someone mentioned Peter Marshall but . . ."

Randolph shook his head and scrunched his face into a knot. "Don't do that. He will tell you it is not a Johnston, and then will go around your back to Mrs. Vanderhorst and try to buy it from her for a song, and then he will come up with some trumped-up research story declaring that it is indeed a Johnston and sell it to some newcomer who wants to own important Charleston pictures."

"I was afraid you were going to say that," Eliza said. "Who is he?"

"Peter Marshall?" Randolph asked. "I don't really know anything about him except that he came down from New York and has developed a reputation for exaggerated attributions and high prices. He got reined in last year when he tried to pass off a portrait of an eighteenth-century gentleman as Arthur Middleton, who, as you know, was one of the signers of the Declaration of Independence. One of Middleton's direct descendants produced a portrait of his ancestor that looked completely different. One had a rather large hook nose, and the other a small straight nose. One had blue eyes, the other black. It wasn't even close. I had heard that Mrs. Morton had all but signed the check. Peter Marshall has been lying low since that incident. But never mind about him, let me show you mine."

Randolph left the room and returned with a framed pastel of a young woman with auburn hair, brown eyes, and a fair complexion. "It came from Mother's side of the family. Her mother was a Prioleau."

They looked at the drawing together without speaking. The sitter wore a loosely draped blue gown with a narrow inset ruffle and shared with all the other Johnston women unusually large and expressive almond-shaped eyes. As with all the other Charleston portraits Eliza had seen, only the shoulders and head of the sitter were drawn.

"It measures just under eleven by fourteen inches and, I'm told, is the largest size known." Randolph turned the portrait over and showed Eliza the pastel signature on the rough backing board. 'Henrietta Johnston Fecit Carolina Anno 1714.' The fact that yours is not signed is not dispositive. Many don't have signatures. If the frame got damaged or were changed, the signature and date disappeared." Randolph handed the portrait to Eliza.

"Mrs. Vanderhorst's picture is a little smaller than yours," she said, "but the paper seems to be the same quality and texture, and the colors are very similar." Eliza leaned closer. "The technique of shading in the background is almost identical. According to Mrs. Vanderhorst, this portrait has never left the Vanderhorst family."

"Odd that it wasn't mentioned somewhere in a will."

Eliza handed the portrait back to Randolph, who propped it up in a chair so they could view it together. "Yes, unless it was given before death."

"True, true." Randolph offered Eliza more tea.

"From what I can gather, Johnston's work in Charleston can be divided into two distinct periods." Eliza paused to take a slice of lemon. "The first eight years when she was living with her husband in Charleston, and the eleven-year period after her husband's death. I was hoping to be able to place Mrs. Vanderhorst's drawing in one of those two Charleston periods as a way of narrowing my search."

"And?" Randolph offered Eliza the tray of petits fours.

She declined and said, "It doesn't fit neatly into either one."

"How so?" Randolph asked, as he waved his hand over the plate of small cakes before deciding on two more.

"In her earlier Charleston drawings, such as yours, the women wore their hair swept up. In her later ones, the women wore their hair down, loosely tied back. The expression of the sitters, the quality of the detail, and even the shading of the backgrounds are much more carefully rendered in the earlier period."

Ralph considered what Eliza was telling him. "Perhaps after the death of her husband she was very sad and did not have as much time or desire to devote to her drawings."

"Yes, maybe," Eliza said. "The quality of the rendering of Mrs. Vanderhorst's portrait is comparable to yours, yet the hairstyle dates it to the later period."

"I see. But perhaps it was someone who had been very kind to her, and she was able to give it her best effort."

"Could be. But then there are the eyes."

"The eyes?"

"The eyes of the sitter in Mrs. Vanderhorst's portrait are rounder and larger than the eyes of Johnston's other women. Even Johnston's men have the same eyes. When I was in London, I looked at the collection of portraits the National Portrait Gallery has. Before she came to Charleston, Johnston was living in Ireland and drew a group of titled Irishmen, and they all have the same oval eyes. Also in all of the documented Johnstons, the eyes are the same width as the mouth. In Mrs. Vanderhorst's pastel, the eyes are larger than the mouth."

Randolph leaned over and picked up his portrait and compared it side by side to the photograph. "Perplexing. But I would think if everything else is similar—the paper, the dress, the colors, the technique—especially the technique—it would be hard to say it wasn't a Johnston. It would help Kit so much. I just can't imagine her not living on Tradd Street."

The reference to Mrs. Vanderhorst as Kit jarred Eliza. Even though Randolph was closer to Mrs. Vanderhorst's age than to hers, Eliza could refer to him by his first name whereas parents of childhood friends would forever be addressed formally. She asked Randolph what he meant by his last comment.

"Well, I hope I am not talking out of school"—Randolph leaned forward and lowered his voice—"but I think everyone knows. Kit is going to have to sell her house. Whatever William left her is all but gone, and well, you know how expensive these old houses can be."

"What will she do? Where will she go?"

"Do you know Marianne Bowman who is in charge of the Confederate Home on Broad Street? She does the flowers at St. Michael's, and she told me she could find a little apartment there for Kit. The apartments are primarily for artist studios, but its founder, Amarinthia Snowden, was Kit's great-great-great-aunt on her mother's side, so Marianne can slip her in." Randolph handed the photograph back to Eliza. "You know, Eliza, Charleston needs someone like you. You know better than I how Charleston is filled with stories. No one here can bring this sort of scholarly analysis to all of, well, our lore."

Eliza thanked him. "For the moment, I think I have my hands full." She kept her mind steadied and stopped on "for the moment" and did not let herself think past the phrase.

Eliza left Randolph's house and rode her bicycle up Meeting Street to the Gibbes. With Randolph's picture so fresh in her mind, she wanted to look at the three Johnstons the Gibbes had on reserve for her.

An hour later Eliza left the Gibbes. She walked around the side of the museum where she had locked her bike. A car line had formed outside the museum's annex. Mothers waited for children to be dismissed from afternoon art classes. Eliza overheard fragments of sentences about the Junior League auction planned for late Octo-

ber and the upcoming election at the Garden Club. Just as the bells
of St. Michael's marked the late afternoon hour, a line of tradition-
ally dressed young children emerged holding plaster medallions
in the shape of hearts painted in blues and greens and pinks and
strung with a ribbon. They marched forth as if transporting newly
hatched birds in the palms of their hands. Eliza waited for them
to pass before she moved her bike out into the street. The air was
heavy and reminded her of the summer refrain she had grown up
hearing, that "the air was so thick, you could cut it with a knife."
As the summer moved toward the middle of August, the afternoons would be broken by thundershowers that washed the air of
its heaviness.

Eliza was still thinking about the three Johnstons she had just
examined, when she saw Issie. She was walking across Broad Street.
Issie looked as Eliza had remembered her—slender, curvy, with
long, wavy, dark blond hair tied back with a scarf. A feeling of dis-
location and alienation stunned Eliza. Lawton was Issie's son. He
looked like Henry, but he had his mother's thick wavy blond hair.
The three of them would always share something she could never
be a part of. Issie was dressed in jeans and a white tee shirt. She
had always been beautiful, but as beautiful as she was, she never
seemed to notice. Even now as she walked across the street, Eliza
saw how people turned to look at her. Fifteen years ago, *Town &
Country* had done a feature on Charleston, and they had chosen
Issie for the cover. The magazine had used an image of her in a pale
blue, silk taffeta ball gown being escorted by several Citadel cadets
across Summerall Field. Whether the photographer had asked her
to or not, Issie had mischievously kissed her escort on her right, and
that was the image the magazine had chosen.

Issie stopped in front of an old dark blue Mercedes coupe and
searched her satchel for her keys. There had always been something
slightly wild and lost about her that made men want to claim her.

Eliza paused her bicycle and pretended to look at the sweetgrass baskets that the flower ladies were selling outside of St. Michael's Church. Eliza reversed her direction and walked her bicycle west on Broad Street past the building where the Piggly Wiggly used to be—now replaced by a large art gallery selling bright pictures of palmetto trees and marshes and dreamy skies—and past the formerly run-down facade of the plumbing firm Mr. Julius E. Smith and Sons that had been restuccoed and painted a strong stone color and turned into a private office. The sight of Issie had made everything Eliza had been thinking about disintegrate.

At home, Eliza unpacked her notes from the afternoon and organized them into a neat stack on the kitchen table. She walked outside and sat in the garden and listened to a lawn mower's drone, a car door slamming, a mother calling her children to come inside for supper. She needed to hear Henry's voice.

"I am sorry, but Mr. Heyward is in a meeting." Eliza did not recognize the woman who answered the phone.

"It's Eliza Poinsett. He asked me to call him. Do you think he will be long?"

"I really couldn't say. I can have Mr. Heyward return your call when he is finished."

"May I speak to his secretary?"

"Dorothy's just stepped away. Oh, no, wait, here she is."

Dorothy answered the phone, and Eliza asked her if she thought Henry would be long. He had asked her to call him. Dorothy paused for a moment, as if considering what to do, and then whispered into the phone. "He is with Miss Lartigue, and she seems very upset."

Eliza returned to her spot in the garden. She thought about that Sunday in June when she had entered the house at Oakhurst and how unnerved she had felt and how Henry had talked about things that had nothing to do with her as a way of trying to make her feel safe. Was that what he was doing now—not telling her things that might unnerve her? Weren't they past all of that? She knew there were no more smooth surfaces. Nothing could be perfect anymore. She had to stop hoping it could be. She couldn't even pretend. But she didn't doubt Henry—that was the most important thing. He had done his penance, he had stayed in Charleston and taken responsibility for the consequences of a wrong decision. And his love for Lawton had made her believe in him beyond where she had before. The most they could hope for was a chance to continue. She had to stop looking for order and perfection where it could not exist. The point was to keep going forward. She was still sitting outside when she heard Henry call her name.

"Eliza. Didn't you hear the phone? I thought you were going to call me."

"I did, but you were tied up."

"Next time ask Dorothy to interrupt me." Henry turned and looked at the garden and then turned back to Eliza. "Did you see Randolph? Did his picture give you any clues?"

"Yes, I think so."

"Eliza, what's wrong?"

"When were you going to tell me that Issie came by your office?"

Henry sat down next to Eliza. "Oh, Eliza, is that what's bothering you?"

"You didn't tell me she was coming by your office. Henry, I can't do this if you keep anything from me."

"I didn't know she was coming. She just showed up."

"She just showed up?"

"Yes. I was waiting to hear back from her lawyer about a day next week. Issie came by without my knowing and asked to see me."

"What did she say to you?"

"She said she's considering moving back to Charleston and wants to meet Lawton."

"And you told her?"

"I told her we should be very careful about him."

"What did she say?"

"She was surprisingly controlled. She said she understood, but that she was his mother and that she had the right to see him. I told her I was sure we could work something out, but that we should be careful. I also told her she should be sure of what she was deciding because it would be devastating to Lawton if she came back and then decided to leave a few months later."

"That was all?"

"That was about it. She said her lawyer would be in touch to set up a meeting, and then she left."

"Did she mention me?"

"No, and I didn't volunteer anything."

Eliza picked a leaf from a gardenia bush and folded it in half along its stem.

"Eliza, sweetheart, listen, Issie is Lawton's mother." Henry put his hands on her shoulders. "You have to listen to me. Issie is Lawton's mother, and I have to deal with that for him. She is a very fragile person. Her mother committed suicide when she was fourteen. Life hasn't broken her way. And I'm not going to do anything to make things worse for her. I just can't."

"I know. I know. I do. I don't know why I'm having such a hard time. When I saw you, I had planned to tell you how dear Lawton's battlefields were, that I understood why you had left all those plastic soldiers and horses on the floor, why you weren't able to put them away."

"I miss him."

"I know." Eliza brushed the back of her hand across her eyes.

"And I missed you, and I am not going to let anything get in the way. Just please don't be upset with me."

"I'm not, Henry. I'm just, I don't know. If I weren't so in love with you, all of this wouldn't matter so much. We both know"—she laughed across a sniffle and wiped her face—"I'm not very good with risk."

Henry stood up. "Listen, Eliza." He took her wrist and pulled her close to him. "There is no risk." He smoothed her hair from her forehead. "I'm so sorry for all of this. But the answers aren't in the reasons. They are all around them—blurred, smudged. Everything will be okay."

HENRY CAME BY ELIZA'S HOUSE THE FOLLOWING AFTERNOON and said, "I've had an awful time today." He looked as if he'd been outside in the heat all day. "Things with Issie are blowing up." He ran his hand through his hair and looked at Eliza and then out the window to some unknown place.

"What do you mean?"

"She's just becoming unreasonable and emotional about everything."

He was distracted and paced back and forth with his hands on his hips. "It's just impossible to have an unemotional conversation with her." He spoke more to himself than to Eliza. "It was a mistake." He sat down but stood up almost immediately and began walking back and forth again. "It was a mistake thinking I could or should talk to her. I thought we could sort all of this out between us, but it was a real mistake. When she came by yesterday, she was very pulled together, unusually so. She called this afternoon and asked to see me for fifteen minutes."

"What did she want?"

"She said that she wanted to see Lawton now and that she didn't want to wait for our lawyers to speak."

"What did you say to that?"

"I told her I understood, but that we should think about Lawton, and she got visibly rattled and angry and said that no one ever thought about her feelings. She said she had given birth to Lawton, he was her flesh and blood, she had every right in the world to see her son, that no one else, including you, needed permission to see him. No lawyer was going to tell her how and when she could see him. I told her that of course she could see Lawton, but that we needed to think through what was in his best interest as well as hers. That we should handle things in such a way as to get the outcome we all wanted. I reminded her that Lawton was away with my mother and that I needed time to speak to him when he came back. After that we could figure something out together."

"How did she react to that?"

"She calmed down, and then I asked her what had happened to make her change her mind, and she started answering in an unemotional tone, but then within ten seconds she became hysterical. She said after Lawton was born, her father had threatened disinheritance if she returned to Charleston. Now that he has died, she could return, and how I didn't understand what that was like. It was strange, as if a switch had been flicked."

"How did you calm her down?"

"I told her I didn't want her to be in such pain, that I would think about what she had said. My editorial board was waiting for me. I told her I had to meet with them, but that I'd be out in an hour. She could stay and wait for me, and we could continue talking, or I would call her tomorrow. She said she would wait, but when I returned she had left." He sat down in a chair and pressed his thumb against the bottom of his front teeth. "I've got to figure out what to do."

They drove down to Folly Beach. Henry stopped in front of the washed-out area filled with water from the incoming tide.

"It looks worse than last time," Eliza said.

"Ricky Baldwin should've finished this last week." Henry

shifted the Jeep into neutral and set the brake. "Let's have a look." They got out of the Jeep and walked to the edge of the submerged road. "Doesn't look good," he said.

"How about the back road?"

"It's torn up with a four-foot ditch across it. Ricky dug up the old culvert to replace it, but the wrong size pipe was delivered, so he's waiting for a new one. When I met with him last week he said he was going to start straightaway on this road." Henry stood with his hands on his hips and then walked as far as he could around the washed-out section.

"I have some two-by-fours in the back that I picked up to fix the dock at Oakhurst. I can lay them down to make a track." Henry walked to the back of the Jeep and pulled out two of the eight-foot boards. "I can lay these down, and they should give me enough traction to get across." He leaned the boards against the hood of his Jeep. He unbuttoned his cuffs and rolled up his sleeves, slipped off his shoes and rolled up his trousers. He picked up the two boards and held them upright like ski poles and surveyed the area.

"Can I help?" Eliza asked about the makeshift tracks, but she was asking about much more. She wanted to make things easier for Henry, but she didn't know how. He was worried about what could happen between Issie and Lawton. She could tell Henry assumed he would be the one who would have to sort everything out and get everyone through this difficult period.

"I'm just trying to decide whether to lay them single file or side by side. Side by side would be better, but I don't think I have enough." Henry laid the first board down and then felt with his foot to its end. He lowered the second board gently down into the water and stood on it to secure its place. "There," he said, pointing to the side of the road in line with the end of the second board. "Just stand there, so I know where it ends."

Henry walked back, balancing on the two boards. He laid two

more planks one after another in the water. Eliza moved to mark the submerged end of the fourth plank. She followed his instructions until he positioned the last one. "That should do it." He balanced on the submerged boards and walked back in line with the yellow beam of headlights.

They got back in the Jeep. "Okay, remember the drill?"

"Yes." She buckled her seat belt.

"How lucky are you feeling?"

"Not sure."

"Yeah, me neither." Henry slipped the Jeep into four-wheel drive. "Here goes." He drove fast and kept the wheels on the planks. He stopped when they reached dry land and looked in his rearview mirror. "And I thought we only had about a fifteen percent chance of making it through."

"Do we have to worry about them floating away?"

"We could, or we could live dangerously and not worry about it."

"Henry, I'm being serious."

"I know you are, and I find it endearing that of all the things we could worry about . . . Okay, seriously, the bottom is muddy, and the Jeep pushed all those planks into the mud, so they aren't going anywhere, they'll be there when we return."


THEY SAT ON THE PORCH OF THE COTTAGE. THE BREEZE coming from the ocean was warm and salty. Henry spoke that night as if he were in a trance. "You know, if Issie is planning, as she says, to move back here, she may ask for joint custody of Lawton. From what I can tell, she's led a pretty unstable life for the past ten years. If Lawton didn't exist, it would be as if I'd never known her. I can't imagine a judge thinking she's a stable mother and granting her request. My guess is the reason Issie is back here is because she and this painter have split, and she came back because she's tired. That's why a lot of people come back to Charleston. When they're tired. Elliott says she has a twenty percent chance of winning, but it's the trauma of a court case and dragging Lawton through it all—that's my worry. Issie contends that the arrangements about Lawton were her father's design, and it was not what she wanted, and that it has haunted her ever since, and she is his mother, and it's not too late, and she is from here, and now that her father is dead, she can do what she wishes."

"Do you think her father was the reason she never came back?"

"I don't know, but I doubt it. My guess is that Issie would have come back if she had wanted to. I don't know if you ever knew her father—he was formidable—but Issie has always done what she's wanted to do. Issie is remembering things as she wishes. At twenty-two, she had no interest in becoming a mother, and there was nothing between us, and she wanted to be free and run around the world, and now she is tired and at a dead end, and she wants to come back home. She has nothing else. And I think she honestly believes she has Lawton's best interest at heart. I told her, 'Look, you just can't come back here and expect Lawton to accept you. It will take some time and some work.' And she said to me, 'But why not?' And I do believe that's how she feels, at least at this moment. Issie says she's going to stay, but she won't. She'll stay long enough to shake things up, create some confusion, and then she'll leave. She'll be off again."

Henry talked for hours that night. Eliza understood that he was speaking more to himself than to her, trying to understand all that had been said that day. He went backward and forward and sideways and did not get very far except to say, "I made the wrong assumption thinking that Issie would never want to come back." Henry checked his watch. "It's late. We should get some sleep. Lawton comes home tomorrow, and I need to deal with some things at work so I can spend the afternoon with him."

# CHAPTER SEVENTEEN

The following morning Eliza sat with Mrs. Vander-horst in the small cypress-paneled living room of her house on Tradd Street. Eliza pulled several manila folders from her satchel and spread them in front of her on the floor. The portrait now hung over a small eighteenth-century walnut desk. "Oh, there she is," Eliza said a little surprised.

"Oh yes, that was William's desk," Mrs. Vanderhorst said, but her eyes were on all the folders spread out on the floor.

"I have your photocopy here." Eliza referred to the image of Mrs. Vanderhorst's portrait. "But I'm glad we can look at the actual portrait. I'll start with what I've learned and then explain how I got there, does that sound okay?"

Mrs. Vanderhorst nodded.

"I'm not sure if the pastel is a Johnston," Eliza said. "The best I can say is that it is 'in the manner of.' What throws me off are her eyes—they are a little too large and round compared to eyes in other portraits. Here, let me show you." Eliza leaned down and picked up a folder and moved closer to Mrs. Vanderhorst and opened it. "Helen Halsey at the Gibbes shared her files with me. She thinks this is a complete set of all of the documented portraits Johnston did when she was in America." Eliza slowly turned the images of young women and a few young men. "See how almond-shaped all of the eyes are?" Eliza traced the eyes with her index finger. "The eyes in your portrait are more rounded." Eliza held the photocopy next to the ones in her folder. Then she stood up and held several of the Gibbes images next to Mrs. Vanderhorst's portrait, which hung on the wall.

Eliza sat back down. "Do you see the difference?"

"Yes, dear. I do."

"And there is another difference that concerns me." Eliza took a small ruler from her bag. "The eyes in all of the documented Johnstons are almost exactly the same width as the sitters' mouths. See?" Eliza slid the ruler across the photocopies to demonstrate her point. Eliza stood up again and held the ruler in front of Mrs. Vanderhorst's picture. "In yours, the width of the eyes is about fifteen percent larger than the mouth. When I was in London, I went to the National Gallery and looked at the portraits Johnston did in Ireland before she moved to Charleston. They're not any different. Here let me show you." She leaned down to pick up a folder from the floor.

Mrs. Vanderhorst untucked her handkerchief from her belt and began smoothing it out across her lap. Four tiny bouquets of violets were embroidered in each corner. "Oh, Eliza dear, I think I may have sent you on a wild-goose chase. It's not necessary to explain any further. I think I understand. It's just that William was so sure she was by Johnston."

"Well, she still may be, but I failed to find any conclusive evidence. I should tell you that someone has recently been going through the Johnston files at the Library Society and the Historical Society. I don't know if it has any connection to you."

"Yes, I believe it was that nice dealer from New York. He said he would see what he could find, but I don't think he found anything."

Eliza was not surprised. She had remembered Mrs. Vanderhorst mentioning Peter Marshall when she had first shown her the portrait.

"Well, Eliza, what do you think we should do?"

"The only other thing to do would be to have the paper of your portrait analyzed. If it matches the paper of her other pastels, I think it would be hard to say that someone in Charleston at the same time was copying her, so then it would be more than reasonable to attribute it as a Johnston, and your portrait is worth a lot. If the paper is not the same, then it is much more likely that your portrait is not by Johnston and is not that valuable. But it is also possible that Johnston bought paper from different sources and so not all the paper is the same. But the chances of that are small."

"And what do you think it would be worth then?"

"I don't know the market, but it would be worth considerably less, possibly by a factor of ten, and its greatest value would be sentimental—you know—a portrait that has been passed down for generations in a family."

"Well, you see, dear"—Mrs. Vanderhorst folded her handkerchief into squares as she spoke—"after me, there is no one to whom sentimental value would mean anything. Both William and I were only children—there aren't any nieces or nephews."

"It may be better to leave its attribution unsubstantiated and ask Peter Marshall to sell it for you. But have him sell it on commission. You might want to ask your lawyer to draw up a contract for you so you are treated fairly. But let Peter Marshall take on the responsibility and risk of the attribution."

"What do you think he will offer?"

"Remember he is not buying it from you, he is selling it on commission. I asked Helen what she thought the value of your portrait would be if it were a Johnston, and she said about four years ago, a portrait of a man came up at Sotheby's and sold for $85,000. She said a portrait of a southern woman is much more desirable. She couldn't think of when one last sold, but she thought it would be worth at least double."

"And what would I have to pay Peter for selling it?"

"Helen said standard commissions down here are high—about thirty percent, but I think you could offer him twenty percent. This may be his only chance to have a Johnston or one attributed to her, so my guess is that he'll take the twenty percent."

Mrs. Vanderhorst considered Eliza's advice. "This is so difficult without William."

"I know," said Eliza. She handed Mrs. Vanderhorst a folded piece of paper. "I've written all this down for you. I'd be happy to make an appointment to see Peter Marshall if that would be helpful."

"HOW IS LAWTON?" ELIZA ASKED HENRY WHEN HE CAME BY later that afternoon. They sat on the steps of the piazza that led to the garden.

"Not good. I've just been with him. I told him about Issie. He didn't say a word. He just sat there. I tried to get him to talk to me, but he keeps saying he doesn't want to. I didn't force him."

Eliza understood the stillness, the quietness. She remembered the moment her mother had learned of her father's death. Someone had come to tell her—she couldn't remember who—all that she saw now was a dark shape and her mother crying out and almost collapsing and the dark shape catching her mother and trying to comfort her. Eliza remembered standing as still as she could on the stair landing, trying not to breathe. But as much as she understood the stillness, she knew she could only guess at the turmoil in Lawton's heart. It was one thing to understand that your mother had given you up when she was an abstract concept, but it was quite another to comprehend when she was standing in front of you. He had always believed it was just he and Henry. Eliza had watched him, knowing that he had no choice, struggle to accept her. And now Issie. Eliza suspected that Lawton now no longer worried that he would have to share his father, but that he could be taken away from him.

"I don't know how to make this any easier for him." Henry stood up and sat back down on the bottom step and pulled at blades of grass. "I know he's suffering and is confused. He isn't old enough to know how to think about this. Maybe I'm wrong about Issie, maybe she's changed, but I don't think so. I wish I could say 'Let's get the hell out of here,' but I can't leave Lawton."

# CHAPTER EIGHTEEN

WHEN ELIZA ARRIVED AT PETER MARSHALL'S GALLERY, a young woman, who introduced herself only as "Mr. Marshall's assistant," told her that he was still in his 4:00 P.M. meeting but would be finished shortly. She welcomed Eliza to have a look around. Eliza surveyed the paintings hung on the walls of the gallery—landscapes of the Lowcountry, Charleston houses and street scenes, and several eighteenth-century-style portraits. The assistant, eager to tell Eliza about any picture that caught her attention, shadowed her as she moved from one to the next. Eliza stopped in front of an oil of a three-storied Charleston single house. In a field next to the house, five figures played baseball.

"We just got that in," the assistant said. "Andrée Ruellan."

"I knew Ruellan made a few trips to the South, but I didn't know she came to Charleston," Eliza said.

"Yes, in 1936."

"Did she paint other images?"

"Mr. Marshall knows of a few, but he is always on the search for more." The assistant ended her sentence with the enthusiasm of a weather forecaster predicting sunny skies for a holiday weekend.

Eliza took a few steps back then turned and asked, "Isn't this the same house Edward Hopper painted? The one in, oh, you know, the neighborhood north of Calhoun that runs down to the Cooper River—Mazyckborough?"

"Yes, yes, it is. Hopper's watercolor was painted in 1929, seven years before this one."

Eliza turned back to the painting and leaned forward to look more closely. "Do you know why Ruellan painted the same house?"

"We don't. Mr. Marshall is trying to find out."

"The Hopper doesn't have this metal structure behind it. Do you know what this is?"

"You'd have to ask Mr. Marshall."

As if on cue, the door to Peter Marshall's office opened. Issie walked out followed by Peter Marshall. Issie was dressed in a pale pink tank top and a long flowing skirt of Indian fabric arranged in panels. She wore large gold hoop earrings, and her hair was pulled back in a loose ponytail. Eliza couldn't decide if Issie dressed in such a Bohemian style to define herself as an artist or to signal to Charleston that she rejected its conservative sense of decorum. She carried a large portfolio case in her right hand. Peter Marshall was dressed in a seersucker suit and colorful bow tie. A shiny alligator belt with a large antique silver buckle was cinched around his sizable girth.

"Give me a week or so with these watercolors, and I'll let you know if we can do something. Now don't forget"—he patted Issie on the shoulder—"if you happen to come across anything in your grandmother's collection that you have questions about or need help in making an attribution, we are here to help."

Issie wore no makeup, which only added to her allure. Her left wrist was covered in three inches of beaded bracelets that made a light jingle-jangle sound as she moved. "Thank you, Peter." Issie smiled, and Eliza understood that the tone of her voice would result in Peter doing more for her than he might otherwise have done.

"Mr. Marshall," his assistant stepped forward, "Eliza Poinsett is here to speak with you." The assistant faded back away from the middle of the room.

Peter Marshall pulled up sharply and held out his hand. "A pleasure to meet you, Eliza, presumably you know each other," he said and turned to Issie.

Eliza looked at Issie and wasn't sure what to do except to nod an acknowledgment. Issie took a few steps back and pivoted toward the door, as if turned by a strong breeze. "I should go," she said.

Eliza felt as if she had just walked through a glass door that was shattering all around her. She couldn't hear anything. She had never meet Issie. Many years ago, when Issie had come down from Boston to visit her grandmother, Eliza had seen her once or twice at a beach party or regatta, but Issie was a few years older and always had a crowd of the older boys around her.

Peter Marshall was now standing by the Ruellan painting, pointing out aspects of it. Was he speaking to her? Eliza turned to face him—something about the large metal octagonal structure behind the house being an oil tank owned by South Carolina Electric and Gas. She nodded, as if taking in his words and considering them, but she could not comprehend one thing he was saying. Could Issie not know who she was? Could that be possible? The assistant had said her name, and Peter had said only "presumably the two of you know each other." How innocent or how calculated was his use of the word *presumably*? Eliza dug her fingernails into the palm of her hand to try to brake her thoughts, to shock herself into focusing on what Peter was saying—something about the house being owned by an African-American dressmaker.

"I was hoping to speak to you about Mrs. Vanderhorst's painting." Eliza cut across his perfectly rehearsed paragraph.

Abruptly Peter stopped speaking and made a small lurch backward. "Yes, yes, by all means," he said. "Let's go into my office. Can I get you some coffee or iced tea? Water? You know, someone mentioned you to me the other day. I, for the life of me, can't remember who." He pressed his fingers into his forehead. "Maybe it was Kit come to think of who. No, maybe not," he said as he shuffled through his memory. "Well anyway, tell me what I can do for you."

As Eliza took him through her research, she felt herself steady. Peter never let on that he had sent an assistant to do research. When Eliza had finished, he asked her what she thought Mrs. Vanderhorst wanted to do.

"Depending on your offer, either sell it directly to you or sell it through you on commission."

"Let me give this some thought. I have a couple of clients who would love a Henrietta Johnston, but I'm not so certain they would buy one that doesn't have a rock solid attribution. It's such a pity, Kit's portrait would be worth so much more if we knew for certain it was a Johnston or even if we knew the identity of the sitter. That would help, too."

Eliza stood up to leave.

"Before you go, I would love to get your opinion on some pieces I just got in." Peter picked up a stack of watercolors separated by pieces of tissue paper. He showed Eliza the first watercolor and then moved the painting over and removed the tissue paper to reveal the second one. Eliza looked without saying anything as Peter neatly restacked the images of primitive tropical scenes rendered in shades of brown. He was careful to place the tissue paper uniformly back on each painting. "They aren't very good, are they?"

Eliza pressed her lips together and shrugged her shoulders. All she wanted to do was to get out of the gallery and back to her house.

"I didn't think so," Peter said. "I fear my cat could do better. And the colors are so dreary. If these scenes were brighter, I could sell them to all those people at Kiawah who don't care what they put on the walls as long as it is upbeat."

WALKING DOWN CHURCH STREET, ELIZA FELT AS IF SHE were being carried away by a rip current, and no matter how hard she tried to push her way back, the current took her out farther and farther. The trick was to give up her instinct to fight and let the current take her where it wanted. She had to concentrate to keep her mind in one place and to be patient and not overreact. Unlike Issie, she had always followed the rules. She had never crashed into other people's lives. She would never take what wasn't hers. Was Issie panicked that Eliza could replace her as Lawton's mother? If she did fear that, then Issie didn't understand her son. Lawton had made it clear he could not be won over easily. Eliza wasn't even sure he could be won over at all. Issie was still mesmerizingly beautiful, and she used her looks to get what she wanted. She had done it ten years ago, and Eliza could only assume she was doing it now. And even though Henry had done his best to reassure her that nothing could change between them—that what had happened between Issie and him was an impulsive mistake—if it had happened once, it could happen again. And even if it couldn't, couldn't Issie's presence recalibrate equations among them all and make it all but impossible for Eliza to stay? She didn't know what Issie wanted, but she felt sure she wanted something. Maybe Issie dreamed that she could come back to Charleston and start a life with Henry and Lawton. Maybe Charleston was where she thought she had a rightful place, and Eliza knew, despite the agreement signed when Lawton was born, she did. Didn't Issie really belong here more than she did? She was Lawton's mother. And ten years ago—Henry not wanting her had made her run far away—and Eliza understood that, too. Hadn't she done the same thing? Eliza remembered the feeling that had jolted her when she had seen Issie two days ago on Broad Street—the realization that the three of them—Henry, Issie, and Lawton—shared something she would never have access to.


HENRY WAS WAITING FOR ELIZA WHEN SHE RETURNED. TRYing to keep her voice even and unemotional, she told him she had run into Issie.

"Where?"

"At Peter Marshall's gallery. I went to see him about Mrs. Vanderhorst's portrait, and when I arrived he was in a meeting with Issie. When they came out of his office, he didn't formally introduce us, he just said, 'Presumably the two of you know each other.'"

"How was she?"

"Sort of skittish, like she didn't want to meet me."

Henry nodded. "Why was she there?"

Eliza knew Henry was collecting information before he formed an opinion. She had seen him do this before. But it still felt cold. And yet, she did not know how else she wanted Henry to act, what more reassurance she needed. Talking about Issie was hard for both of them. "I don't know, but she did have a large portfolio case with her. And at the end of my meeting with Peter, he showed me some very primitive, not very interesting watercolors of beach scenes with palm trees. He asked me what I thought of them. They weren't very good, but I didn't say anything because I suspected they came from Issie. I wonder if they were done by her boyfriend, didn't you say she was living with a painter or art dealer in Tangiers?"

Henry shrugged his shoulders. "Could be, but who knows with Issie. I doubt Peter is too interested in them—whatever they are. He's probably feigning interest as a way of getting his hands on some of her grandmother's pieces. Mrs. Estabrook had a wonderful collection of Alice Smith watercolors of rice fields and cypress swamps and a complete set of Mark Catesby engravings." Henry fiddled with his watch. "After all this time—we are finally together and she appears. I don't want to leave, but I should get back. I asked Cora to stay an hour longer, so I could come see you. She is cooking chicken pilaf and fried okra for Lawton. Come for supper."

"Thanks, but maybe it's better if it's just the two of you. Maybe he will open up a little more."

"I don't know." Henry took a slow deep breath and shook his head. "Whenever I mention Issie, he shows very little emotion. He doesn't say anything or ask any questions, and when I told him I thought we should have dinner with her, he just shrugged his shoulders. I would have thought he would have wanted to meet her, but so far he hasn't expressed any desire to do so. Issie's lawyer called today about coming by with her tomorrow afternoon to try to agree to a schedule of visits. I think the best thing is to go slowly, let Issie meet him, let them spend some time together, and then if she wants to collect him from school or take him to a tennis practice, that's fine. But what I don't want to happen is for her to try to be his mother and then lose interest and decide to leave. That could be devastating for him."

"Can you prevent that?"

"No, but I can control things up to a point. Issie did legally give him up. So I could prevent her from seeing him."

"But you aren't going to do that, are you?"

"No, I'm not, but I want to go slowly, let Lawton get comfortable with the idea or as comfortable as he can with the fact that his mother has come back and not try to force things too much. But Issie, if she is anything, is very headstrong and, in some ways, spoiled, so even if we agree on a schedule, I'm not sure she will follow it. I guess I can only try." Henry looked away for a moment and then back at Eliza. "You sure I can't persuade you to come?"

"I think it's better if Lawton has you all to himself. All of this has to be incredibly confusing for him."

"You've been great with him."

"He's dear, but he's fierce." They both laughed.

"He is, isn't he? All seventy-two pounds."

"He's good company. I enjoyed working with him on his owl project."

"I should warn you. I sense he is plotting to include you in his campaign to get a dog sooner than his birthday."

"Too late."

# CHAPTER NINETEEN

THE FOLLOWING DAY, WHEN HE STOPPED BY AFTER WORK, Henry found Eliza with her papers and books spread out on the kitchen table. "This looks serious. Like you're planning an assault."

"I'm giving it my best shot," Eliza said and pushed her chair back. "So how did your meeting go?"

"With Issie?" Henry took his jacket off and hung it on the back of a chair. "Who knows. I told her we could start with a few visits, and then if that went okay, she could collect Lawton from school some days."

"How did she react to all that?"

"She seemed fine with it. Her lawyer did most of the talking. My goal is to keep everything as calm as possible. Fortunately, I suppose, right now much of Issie's time is taken up with getting her family's plantation on the Combahee River ready for sale. Apparently, according to her grandmother's will, the plantation was left to seven grandchildren, but Issie's father had been given sole use of it during his lifetime. Issie said, of her six cousins, five had no interest in owning property down here, and so the only option is to sell it. Who knows what she will do when everything is sorted out. I assume when her grandmother's estate is settled, she will inherit quite a bit. Though whether she will get it outright or in trust, I don't know."

"Do you think that's the reason she came back here?"

"Don't know." Henry shook his head. "It certainly is possible."

"How's Lawton?"

"Okay, I guess." Henry unbuttoned his cuffs and began to roll up one sleeve. "He pretty much shuts down when I try to talk to him—I can't tell how he really feels—I'm not sure he even knows. I just dropped him off at a friend's house for supper." Henry stood up to move physically away from any discussion about Issie. He picked up a jar of marinated shrimp on the counter and turned to Eliza. "Did you make this?"

"Would I impress you if I said yes?"

"Completely."

"Okay, then assume the best."

"Indeed I will, but first"—Henry hid the jar behind his back—"a truth check—what, besides shrimp, is in this jar?"

"Olive oil, vinegar, onions, celery, capers, and bay leaves."

Henry brought the jar close to his face and examined the contents. "Correct. Did you make only one?"

"No, there're more in the fridge. I just took one out—it was going to be my dinner."

"Then I came just in time." Henry opened the refrigerator door and leaned down. "Excellent, five more jars of shrimp, lettuce, tomatoes, an unopened bottle of white wine, we have everything we need. How about a picnic outside?"

"May be a bit humid and buggy."

"Then kitchen table it is." Henry rolled up his other sleeve and began to wash his hands. "I'll make the salad." He looked at the last pile of papers Eliza was clearing off the table. "So have you definitely decided to pursue Dave?"

"I'm thinking about it. That's what all this is," she said and raised the stack of books and papers in her arms. "I'm trying to read all I can about Edgefield pottery. So far though, I've only found a few articles that mention Dave. But I did find one article on buttermilk in the *Edgefield Advertiser* that mentions him."

"Buttermilk?"

"Buttermilk. I'll read it to you if I can find it. It's here somewhere." Eliza shuffled through her pile of papers. "Here it is." She waved a manila folder in the air. "It's dated April 1, 1863. Simple title of 'Buttermilk'—See," she said and turned the copy to Henry. She began to read, "'One day in years gone by we happened to meet Dave Pottery whom many readers will remember as the grandiloquent old darkey once connected with a paper known as the *Edgefield Hive* in the outskirts of his beloved hamlet. Observing an intelligent twinkle in his eye, we accosted him in one of his own set speeches, "Well, Uncle Dave, how does your corporosity seem to sagitate?" "First rate, young master, from top to toe—I just had a magnanimous bowl-full of dat delicious old beverage buttermilk." '"

"So he was quite a character?"

"Whether he was or wasn't, I don't know, but I suspect Dave might have been playing the role of the 'grandiloquent old darkey' to make life easier for himself."

"So what do you think you will end up doing?"

"I spoke to Helen Halsey, and she said the Gibbes and Charleston Museum would consider a jointly funded exhibit on Dave. They have one pot and have just been given a second. She didn't say from where, but I wonder if it's not the pot that Lucas said Charles Lowndes had donated to the Gibbes."

Henry shrugged his shoulders. "Could be."

"Anyway, Helen said she's always wanted to have an exhibition of Dave pots but needed more information and someone to write a monograph that could serve as an exhibition catalogue. She asked me to write a proposal, and she said she would speak to Matthew Cuthbert."

"That sounds great." Henry looked in the refrigerator again and got a lemon.

"What else do you need?"

"Mustard, onion, vinegar, and olive oil."

"I'll get them, they're in the pantry."

Eliza returned with her arms full and set the jars and onion down on the counter. "I can't remember if I told you this, but Peter Marshall called Mrs. Vanderhorst and agreed to take the picture on consignment at eighty thousand with a twenty percent commission or buy it at forty-eight."

"I didn't know you had come to a definitive view on her portrait," he said.

"I haven't, but I don't think I ever will. The shape and size of the eyes are different enough to nag me. But it's tough because I know of examples of contemporary artists modifying their style for brief periods, and I know, too, that if we examined their work two hundred years later, we might not be convinced the work was by the same hand. Mrs. Vanderhorst asked me what I would do, and I told her I would take the commission arrangement. Even though her portrait cannot be attributed decisively to Henrietta Johnston, I think, given the quality of the picture and the rarity of Johnstons, it would sell. It seems that having original Charleston art is important to the people who come down from the North and buy these historic houses. But I don't know what Mrs. Vanderhorst will do."

"Forty-eight to sixty-four thousand is a clever spread. Perfectly calibrated between certainty on one side and uncertainty on the other with just enough upside. I guess it will depend on how quickly she needs the money."

"You're probably right." Eliza laid two linen place mats and two wineglasses on the table.

Eliza drained the marinated shrimp and put them in a bowl on the table, and Henry opened the bottle of wine, and they sat down to supper. Henry described the situation at the paper. "I'm going to have to spend the first part of each week in New Orleans. *The New Orleans Gazette* is proving to be more difficult to turn around than I had thought. The major problem is the advertisers and the senior editors. The advertisers are taking advantage of the change of ownership to try to squeeze margins. And the senior editors are upset that they were not offered an equity interest in the paper as part of the sale. As a result, they are threatening to quit. It doesn't help that the new owner is Yale educated and thirty-two."

"God, Henry, do you think you can fix it?"

"I have to. But these problems with the advertisers and editors are not going to get fixed unless I spend a lot of time down there, and every day that this situation goes unresolved, it's costing us a lot. The sooner we settle these issues, the sooner the paper stops losing money. The paper's acquisition costs are going to be more than we estimated, but I still think the paper can be turned around by this time next October."

Before he left, Henry said, "We need to talk about what we are going to do now that Lawton is back."

"I know, but it's okay. I miss not being with you, but everything seems so fragile for him. And you're so busy with the paper in New Orleans. Lawton needs as much of your time as you can give him when you're here."

"I guess you're right, but once we get all this behind us, we should talk about us—about our life together."

# CHAPTER TWENTY

THE HEAT AND HUMIDITY OF AUGUST CONTINUED TO stretch through September. While Henry traveled to New Orleans each week, Lawton stayed with his grandmother. Henry told Eliza that he had agreed with Issie that she could collect Lawton from school on Tuesdays and Thursdays and take him to tennis practices. He reported back that for now that seemed more than enough for her. On two occasions Issie had forgotten Lawton and the school had called Mrs. Heyward. Eliza kept her work in front of her and made progress on her research on Dave. Because Dave was a slave, facts were scarce. There were no records of his birth and death, but there was a consensus among the academic community that he had been born sometime around 1800 and died sometime around 1870. As a slave, he had been sold or traded six or seven times, but even when records were found, nothing was conclusive. The 1850 U.S. Federal Slave Census only mentioned slaves by gender, age, and color—not by name. When Dave was freed after the Civil War, he

most likely took the surname of Drake after one of his early owners, but even that information could not be confirmed. Dave had
worked over a forty-year period and had made hundreds of pots.
Eliza had located twenty-six pieces with inscribed couplets, six
more than she had originally understood had existed. From what
she could tell, there was a seventeen-year gap from 1840 to 1857
when he wrote nothing on the pots he made except, occasionally,
his first name.

As she was researching Dave, Eliza had begun to think about
pursuing her doctorate. The rhythm of life in Charleston had
given her time to consider a topic first suggested by her adviser at
the Courtauld, the paintings in Tennessee Williams's plays. The
image of the Charleston house painted by both Hopper and Ruellan that had intrigued her at Peter Marshall's gallery had served
as a prompt for her to remember that Williams also had a connection to Hopper. He had mentioned Hopper's painting *House
by the Railroad* in his description of a scene in his early one-act
"This Property Is Condemned." The more Eliza thought about it,
the more she became convinced that Williams's lyrical sense com-
bined with his visual imagination gave his plays a power that was
rare. She wrote her adviser about her idea, and he wrote back that
indeed he thought she was onto something and would be happy to
assist in any way. By giving her the opportunity to write an article
on Williams and Bonnard, he had been leading her to choose a
topic that would make use of her master's in both English and art
history. She remembered him saying, "No one has written on this
topic. Yet." He had said *yet* as if he were dropping a heavy pile of
books on the floor. He had even added that if he were forty years
younger, he would give serious consideration to this topic. Williams's standing as a playwright was growing, and yet, so far, no
scholar had explored the power of his visual imagination. Eliza
thought her monograph on Dave would be finished by the end

of the year, and then she could turn to the subject of paintings entangled in Williams's work.

By the beginning of October, the cool crisp air of autumn had begun to tempt the days. Everything began to feel secure and solid again. Henry continued his weekly trips to New Orleans. Issie remained in Charleston and kept to the schedule that she had agreed with Henry. Henry told Eliza that he was relieved that Issie had not pushed for more time with Lawton or lobbied to have him stay with her. Eliza worked long hours during the weekdays and waited for him to return each weekend. At the end of October, Henry told Eliza that the negotiations were getting down to the wire, and he was going to have to spend the next two weeks in New Orleans. On the day he left, he called her from the airport. "I forgot to help Lawton choose a poem for his school's Poetry Day. He has to pick a poem by Wednesday. Can you help him with it?"

Eliza said she would be happy to help. She didn't want to read too much into Henry's request, but she knew Henry would have already checked with Lawton and that this was what he wanted.

"Are you any closer to deciding what kind of dog you would like?" Eliza asked Lawton when he came over after school. "Are Belgian Griffons or Polynesian Pipsqueaks still in the running?" She had finally gotten a smile. "My guess is it's between a Lab and a golden retriever."

"How did you know?"

"It's what I would choose between if I could have a dog. How will you make your decision?"

"I don't know. What would you do?"

"Me? Hmm, I think I would trust that the right dog will come my way and leave it at that." Eliza asked him about a few unusual dogs she had seen around town—a tan dog that looked like a Weimaraner, a huge white dog that was as large as a Great Dane, a tiny caramel fluffy one that looked like a fox. He identified them as, most likely, a Viszla, a Pyrenees Mountain dog, and a Pomeranian, and filled her in on their temperaments and history.

"So your dad tells me you have to choose a poem to recite by memory." Eliza showed him her father's library. "We have a whole section over here for poetry," she said. "We should be able to find a poem for you. You know, I had to do something very similar at Ashley Hall. I memorized 'The Wreck of the Hesperus,' and I think I still remember the first verse."

Lawton looked at Eliza and waited.

"Okay, let's see, 'It was the schooner Hesperus / That sailed the wintry sea; / And the skipper had taken his little daughter / To bear him company.' That's all I can remember."

"What happened to them?"

"It's very sad. The ship is destroyed by a hurricane, and everyone, including the captain and his young daughter, dies." Eliza shuddered. "So do you have any idea what you might like to do? Hopefully not something so sad. "

Lawton shook his head.

"Well, why don't we start by looking at a few volumes of poetry." Eliza got up and looked across the spine of books. "Do you know who Archibald Rutledge was?" She looked over her shoulder at Lawton, who shook his head. "He was the first poet laureate of South Carolina. He was from McClellanville and wrote about hunting and fishing in the Lowcountry." Eliza pulled down *Under the Pines* and flipped through it and read, " 'I stood beneath those sounding purple spires / As down the pathway of her solemn light, the moon descended.' Hmmm, what do you think? Sort of old-fashioned."

Lawton nodded in agreement. Eliza returned the slim volume and continued searching. "How about something by DuBose Heyward? A very distant ancestor of yours. He wrote *Porgy* and he also wrote *The Country Bunny*. Have you read that? About the mother bunny who dreams of becoming one of the Easter bunnies but is laughed at by all the other bunnies."

"You mean *The Country Bunny and the Little Golden Shoes*?" Lawton asked.

"Yes, exactly, that's the one."

"We had to read it in second grade."

"Did you like it?"

"It was okay."

"So shall we see if Mr. Heyward has a suitable poem," she asked as she opened *Carolina Chansons* and ran her finger down the list of poems in the table of contents. "How about one on pirates? Let's see," she said and turned to the correct page. " 'I stood once where these rows of deep piazzas / Frown on the harbor from their columned pride.'" Eliza closed the thin volume. "Not quite the ticket. I think we can do better, don't you?"

Lawton nodded and smiled.

"Here, *The Best Loved Poems of the American People*. I bet we can find something in this. Come sit next to me." She patted the seat of the sofa as she sat down. "If I remember correctly," Eliza said, opening the book, "this book is organized by subject. Let's turn to the contents and see if any categories interest you." She shared the open book with Lawton. "The first is 'Love and Friendship.'" Lawton twisted his mouth into a knot to keep from smiling and shook his head no. "Inspiration." A lift of shoulders. "Lawton, I need your help—I'm not finding anything titled, "Dogs, Screech Owls, and the Battle of Thermopylae."

"I know about the Battle of Thermopylae."

"I'm sure you do, but we have to find a poem."

"My dad said there's a famous poem about baseball he thought I would like."

"Then let's see if there's one on baseball." Eliza ran her finger quickly down the list. "Here's one, 'Casey at the Bat.'"

"That's the one. That's the one my dad told me about." Lawton bounced up and down on the sofa.

"Let's have a look, page two eighty-two by Ernest Lawrence Thayer." Eliza turned to the poem. "It looks pretty long, Lawton, let's see, thirteen verses of four lines is how many lines?"

"Fifty-four, no, fifty-two."

"Right. What do you think about that many lines? When is Poetry Day?"

"November fifteenth."

"Okay, so we need a battle plan. You have a little more than two and a half weeks to memorize fifty-two lines, so if you could memorize four each day, two on the walk to school, two on the walk back, you should be more than fine, what do you think?"

Lawton turned his mouth down and smiled. "I think I can do it."

"I've got some note cards in the kitchen. You can number them and write two lines on the front and two on the back, and you can take a card each day." Together they sat at the kitchen table. Eliza dictated, and Lawton wrote the four lines of each stanza on the front and back of each card. "You write just like your father. He must have taught you. You also have your father's laugh." Eliza could tell that Lawton was pleased that she had recognized these correspondences. When the thirteenth card was completed, Eliza filled two glasses with ginger ale and ice, and they toasted the end of the task.

"IT'S A LONG POEM," ELIZA TOLD HENRY WHEN HE CALLED that night. "But he seems to want to do it. We wrote the lines out on note cards so he can memorize four a day on his way to and from school. So everything here is under control. How are things where you are?"

"Being an optimist, I will say so-so."

"It's that bad?"

"Fifty-something-year-old men who have spent their entire careers at this paper are not interested in anything an owner not much older than their sons has to say. So we'll see. I should be able to get back late Thursday evening. Want to spend Halloween together?"

"Do I have to wear a costume?"

"Nope."

"Okay, then yes. But who's going to take Lawton trick-or-treating?"

"The Logans have invited him over for the weekend starting Thursday. There's no school on Friday. Lawton is in heaven with all those boys—plus they have three springer spaniels. So it works out perfectly. Issie wanted to take him, but he didn't want to go with her, so this avoids Issie getting upset. Plus I get to spend the weekend with you. And the Mortons invited us to a party Saturday night to celebrate their moving into the Sword Gate House. What do you think?"

"I thought they were planning to do a lot of work before they moved in?"

"They did, and it's done, they had a massive team working on it. I could go either way, I just should respond by tomorrow. We haven't been out in a while. Might be a nice change from our suppers at your kitchen table—which, by the way, I love—and, if we go, I was hoping you'd wear something decidedly non-Southern."

As they arrived at the Sword Gate House, they met Cal Edwards leaving. He pronounced that the party was in "full throttle." Two waiters, dressed as Colonial soldiers, stood positioned on either side of the entrance and offered arriving guests glasses of champagne. The brick walkway to the house was lit with candles in glass hurricane lanterns. "Good Lord," Henry said when he spotted the string quartet, also in period clothing, stationed at the far end of the first-floor piazza. As they approached the house, he said, "Joe used to sit right over there." He lifted his chin toward the musicians. "Every day. Feels strange for him not to be here."

"I remember him handing out candy for Halloween. He never said anything. We were always sort of scared of him."

"I guess he was Charleston's version of Boo Radley. I don't think I ever saw him beyond the boundaries of this garden," Henry said, looking around the perimeter. Every time I rode my bike by I would shout 'Hi, Joe' and wave. He was always there. And he would always raise his hand in an Indian salute."

"Do you know what has happened to him?" Eliza asked.

"Ross gave him a job and, with no help—I might add—from Historic Charleston, found a small apartment for him at the Sergeant Jasper."

As they entered the house, Nina Morton, in an off-the-shoulder cocktail dress, was descending a grand double staircase with Lydia Alston, Louisa Eveleigh, and Virginia Middleton. "Let's, for the moment, avoid that posse," Henry said and guided Eliza through the crowded entryway into the dining room. They ran into Randolph Porter, who was exchanging his empty glass of champagne for a full one.

"Oh, Eliza dear, you are just the person I want to see. There is something—"

Henry interrupted, "You know, maybe I should have a word with Louisa, she looked as if she might be up to something I should know about. I'll be right back."

"She is here." Randolph bounced on the balls of his feet.

"Where?" Eliza asked and looked behind her.

"Oh, not in here, dear, in the study."

"Who?" Eliza asked, fearful he would say Issie.

"Kit's portrait, the one you worked on."

"Oh God, sorry," Eliza said, relieved. "I thought you meant someone at this party."

"Follow me."

Eliza followed Randolph across the large room brimming with guests to a smaller room paneled in dark wood. "There she is." He pointed to the portrait, hung above a small walnut veneered desk. "I think that lovely Queen Anne desk was Kit's, too," Randolph said, with a serving of disapproval.

Eliza could feel Randolph waiting with expectation, but she caught herself from speaking. Nothing good would come of saying anything. She was surprised Mrs. Vanderhorst had not told her that she had sold the portrait. More than ever, Eliza wished that she had been able to discover the identity of this young woman. On seeing her again, Eliza was struck with how young and hopeful she appeared. This young woman's safe passage through generations of one family was over. Eliza knew it was silly to think about inanimate objects in such a way, but somehow she felt as if this young woman had been abandoned.

"Found you," Henry returned.

"Look," Eliza said. "It's Mrs. Vanderhorst's portrait."

Henry looked quizzically at Eliza. She shrugged to indicate she didn't want him to ask anything with Randolph present. They were pushed closer to the portrait as a few more people squeezed into the room.

"God, is it crowded in here. Want to go outside?" Henry said.

"I'm off in search of more of those mini lobster rolls. Apparently flown down this morning from Maine." Randolph contorted his face into a mixture of enthusiasm and disdain. "Oh, I do say, the garden is quite something. And the swimming pool, oh my, I've never seen anything like it." Randolph waved his cocktail napkin as he turned to leave.

"I knew nothing about it," Eliza said when Randolph was swallowed by the crowd. "I would have thought Mrs. Vanderhorst would have told me what she had decided."

"I am surprised she didn't tell you, too. What do you make of that?"

"I don't know. I just hope she got a fair price. Do you think I should ask her?"

Henry paused before he spoke. "No, Eliza, I would leave it. I'm sure it's not a pleasant subject for her. And you know nothing in this town stays quiet for very long. If there's too much talk about the portrait, then the Mortons might change their mind and ask Peter to take it back, and that could be the worst outcome for Mrs. Vanderhorst."

"I guess you're right." There was nothing more to say. "So what was Louisa up to?" Eliza asked.

"Exactly what I feared. She was planning something for the paper, but my worries were preempted by Nina who had already suggested that the paper do a 'feature'—her words not mine—on their restoration—and, by the way, from the looks of what the Mortons did to this house, *restoration* is the wrong word. They should have called it a 'replacement.' I haven't come across one thing that has been restored. An article on an eighteenth-century replacement—it definitely will be a first for the paper."

"It's funny you say that. I only remember this house from when we used to come here trick-or-treating, but I don't remember that grand double staircase."

"That's because it wasn't there. There was a very modest staircase in the area where the study is. You couldn't see it from the front hallway." Henry took Eliza's empty glass and gave it to a

waiter as he passed by. "What do you say we go outside? There's a
door to the garden down the back hall," he said, "assuming it's still
there."

"God, this is nicer," Eliza said once they were outside. "It was so
noisy in there."

"My sources"—Henry looked down at Eliza and raised his
eyebrows—"tell me Mr. Morton put lead in all of the walls to keep
out the noise of birds. Apparently Ralph is a light sleeper, and early
morning bird calls wake him up. Or, at least, that's what he told the
contractor."

"Ross Barnwell?"

"Ross Barnwell." Henry nodded. "Other sources tell me lead is
installed in walls to keep people from listening to phone calls. I had
discounted these reports, but now that we are outside, you'd never
know there's a party going on, and yet when we were inside, the
noise was brutal."

"Clearly all those sound waves were bouncing off the lead,"
Eliza offered in her most scientific tone.

They both laughed. "Oh God, Eliza, do you ever wonder what
we're doing living down here?"

"Every day," she said and rubbed her arms.

"Cold? Here take my jacket."

They walked toward a series of elaborately planted garden
rooms arranged along a north-south axis. An oyster shell path led
through the parterre beds of the first room to statues of the four
seasons.

"Wait, I want to look at something," Eliza said. Henry watched
as she walked slowly around each statue. "These are really good,"
she said as she touched the stone and leaned closer to the figure of
Winter. "They're marble. I think these are the ones that sold last
April at auction in London. They were from an important house in
Norfolk, and there was an uproar about their leaving England. The

export license came this close," she said, pinching her thumb and forefinger together, "to being denied. I remember reading that the buyer was rumored to be American. So here they are. That's wild. I'm feeling a little bit better knowing Mrs. Vanderhorst's portrait is in such good company."

Henry and Eliza continued on to the second garden room—a rose garden with a teahouse, and then the third—a lemon garden that opened onto a long pool surrounded by putting-green-perfect grass.

Eliza reached down to touch the coping of the pool's border. "It's tabby," she said, referring to the mixture of lime, shells, and sand that had been used as a type of stucco in the eighteenth and nineteenth century in Charleston. "I've never seen tabby used this way, it's lovely." She stood back up. "I wonder who designed this garden."

"I think I heard someone from Belgium."

"Belgium?"

They sat down on a wrought-iron garden bench.

"You know, when I was doing all that research for Mrs. Vanderhorst at the Historical Society, I came across these garden plats— many of them dated back to the early 1800s—and they were sophisticated and very French. I don't know if many people are aware they exist. I mentioned them to my mother, who's been in the Garden Club for over thirty years, and she didn't know about them. The garden designs of Loutrel Briggs in the 1920s and 1930s are about as far back as anyone goes. A number of the Charleston gardens could be restored to their original eighteenth- or nineteenth-century design. I'm sure there was one for this garden."

"Too late," Henry said as he looked around. "Much too late." Henry turned back to Eliza. "Any more on Dave?"

"Not really. I guess I've come to think that everything there is to know is in his work. Everything else is speculation. I've read a number of articles that mention him, and the dots that get connected have more to do with the writer than with Dave. Very few documents are cited, and there is little or no supporting evidence. For example, there is a gap of seventeen years from 1840 to 1857 when no pots with poems have been found. Dave had several owners during this period. From what's been published, it's pretty much believed that the different owners prevented him from writing verse. The idea has merit—there had been a slave uprising in Augusta in 1841, and South Carolina had a law that prohibited free slaves from teaching free or slave children to read or write. But there are some pots during this period signed Dave. So was it just verse he wasn't allowed to write? Pots are still being discovered and identified. So what if a pot turns up with verse dated in that period, then that theory is discredited. Even if one doesn't turn up, all we can accurately say is that one hasn't turned up, not that one was never made. These scholars may be right, but at this point I think they are making educated guesses."

"Do the actual verses give any clues?" Henry asked.

"You mean about the gap? Hard to say. Of the twenty-six known pots with couplets, seven were made in the period 1834 to 1840, and their verse tends to be light and somewhat oblique, like 'Ladies and gentlemens shoes, sell all you can and nothing you'll lose,' or 'Another trick is worst than this, Dearest Miss spare me a kiss.' But after the seventeen-year silence—"

"Alleged," Henry interrupted.

"Exactly, alleged silence." Eliza smiled. "The remaining nineteen are, not surprisingly I guess, more serious. Six have bibilical references such as, 'I saw a leopard and a lion's face then I felt the need of grace.' But if one or two early pots surface with biblical references, then that observation is wrong, too. I wish I knew how Dave learned to read and write. Then I might be able to make some comments on his verse. The *Edgefield Hive* was owned and run by one of his owners, and there is some speculation that Dave was taught to read and write so that he could set type, which is not a crazy theory, but it is, from what I can tell, only based on that article I read you on buttermilk. The exact words were that he was 'once connected' to the *Edgefield Hive*. 'Once connected' could mean a number of things."

"Does the Edgefield Library have any records?"

"There wasn't a library back then, so I have no way of knowing what people were reading. Children were taught with a primer, and I am in the middle of figuring out what primer they would have used. The Bible and the newspaper were the other two sources. I need to get up to Edgefield. The Historic Society has some photographs, but their collection has been in storage while they do renovations. After Thanksgiving, it should be available. I'm just waiting for that. Also, there's a potter currently working who makes large pots with the same alkaline glazes used by Dave, so hopefully, he can help me with a description on the actual craftsmanship of these pots especially . . ." Eliza stopped speaking when the sound of the party interrupted her. She finished her sentence, "the large ones."

Henry raised his hand. "Open door—someone is leaving the party."

"You don't really think the Mortons put lead in the walls, do you?" Eliza asked.

Henry shrugged his shoulders. "I don't know." He shook his head and smiled. "What do you say we get out of here?"

As they stood up to leave, they saw Charlie and Ginny Walker walking toward them.

"Where are all the pool attendants?" Charlie looked around him and held the palm of his left hand open to the sky, as if feeling for rain. "I suppose they must have run out of eighteenth-century costumes. Before we leave I'll have to speak to Nina to—"

"Stop." Ginny interrupted her husband. She turned back to

Henry and Eliza. "Good champagne always does this to him." Charlie raised his empty champagne flute in mock surrender. "Okay, but I can guarantee if the pool attendants were here, they would have trays weighted with champagne flutes, and we all would be just a tad bit happier, and by the way, Eliza, that's a great dress."

Henry leaned back and winked at Eliza.

"This pool is really beautiful, isn't it?" Eliza said to Ginny.

"You know"—Charlie put his arm around Henry's shoulders—"this pool is giving me inspiration. Laddy is coming back in December, and we could have a sixteenth-year reunion of our swimming pool adventure. They did away with the pool at The Fort Sumter when the hotel was converted to apartments, so we could use this one as our starting point."

"Maybe, but I doubt, as owner and editor of *The Charleston Courier*, I could resist the headline—even if I were in it—'Prominent Physician, Award-Winning Architect, and Local Editor Caught—'"

"What are you talking about?" Eliza pulled Henry back toward her. She turned to Ginny, "What are they talking about?"

"I have no idea."

Eliza tugged at Henry's arm. "Charlie, I'm sensing you're a bad influence, I'm taking him away from you."

Charlie laughed and raised his glass. "The girl has good taste and good judgment. Think about it."

Henry turned and waved good-bye.

Charlie cupped his hands and called after Henry, "I'm going to take your silence as a positive response."

Henry put his arm around Eliza's shoulders.

"So do you want to tell me about the swimming pool adventure?" She leaned into him.

"Not particularly." He looked down at her. "And just for the record, let it be known that I deny you nothing."

"Duly noted."

"Did you ever know Laddy and Chisholm Baker?"

"Not really, I knew who they were, but they were older . . ."

"That's right. Laddy's a year older than I am, and Chisholm's four. When we were growing up, we all worshipped Chisholm. He was the epitome of cool. Laddy and Chisholm's parents were never around, I don't know why— Anyway, Laddy and Chisholm lived with their grandmother on Water Street, but Chisholm pretty much raised Laddy. And Chisholm was tall, a great athlete, and a very good artist, and he always had beautiful girlfriends. And we all idolized him and did whatever he told us to do. The Thanksgiving of his first year at college, he came home and told us about this amazing short story he had read about a man, one night, swimming in all the pools in his town. It was his way of saying good-bye to his town and his life. And because Chisholm told us this was the coolest way in the world to say good-bye to everyone, we all completely agreed with him. And then he organized our own swimming pool adventure."

"But what or who were you saying good-bye to?"

"Nothing, no one, but it didn't matter, it was beside the point. We came over in the evening, mapped out our route, and all agreed to meet at White Point Gardens at midnight to set off. The pool at The Fort Sumter was the start. We climbed over the fence, swam the length of the pool, and then got out and ran down to the Bowmans on Murray Boulevard, followed by the Warings next door. There was one other on Murray Boulevard on the corner of Limehouse, I think. Back around to South Battery, the Izards on the corner of Rutledge Avenue, the William Gibbes house at 64 South Battery, and so on."

They turned onto South Battery and Henry pointed in the directions of the houses he had just mentioned. "It took us several hours, which was the point because Chisholm wanted Laddy out of the house because his girlfriend, the beautiful Mabel Geohagan, was visiting. Needless to say, he did not come with us."

"So where are the Baker boys now?"

"Chisholm married Mabel and, believe it or not, is an Episcopalian minister in Richmond—we all were certain he was going to be a famous writer or film director—and Laddy is an architect in Charlottesville. He got married a couple years ago to a girl who also is an architect. If Charlie is telling the truth about Laddy coming back, we should get together with him. You would like him."

When they crossed Meeting Street, Henry pointed north. "We swam in the Bennetts' pool at 7 Meeting and the McCradys' at 35, but I don't think there were any more pools on Meeting."

"It must have been cold."

"It was freezing."

"So did you make it back without getting caught."

"We didn't get caught, but around two or three A.M., the swimming pool idea began to lose its appeal, and I think we slouched back to Water Street before we completed the adventure."

They turned up Church Street. "Enough of the past," Henry said.


"HENRY, CAN YOU UNDO THE CATCH ON MY DRESS?" ELIZA lifted her hair up.

"It's difficult," Henry said and bent close and squinted to see if he were moving the catch in the right direction. "There."

"Thanks."

"God, I'm happy to be back here with you." Henry fell back on the bed as if falling back into a swimming pool. "Meanwhile back at 32 Legare Street, Mrs. Middleton is making a mental inventory of all the Charleston pieces the Mortons have acquired so . . ."

Eliza sat on the bed next to Henry and put two fingers on his lips. "I think I can take this away—so she can report back to her bridge club her memorized inventory of each room for those who did not receive an invitation to the party. There will be a lot of 'tsk tsking' as it becomes clear that the Mortons are on their way to assembling an important collection of Charleston decorative arts—furniture, paintings, silver. A few members of the bridge club will make themselves feel better by noting that nothing has been inherited. And when the eleven members of the Charleston Symphony Board assemble next week in the ballroom of the Nathaniel Russell House, the short, plump chairwoman of the board, never without her signature double strand of large South Sea pearls, will call the meeting to order and open for discussion the replacement of one of the board members who has passed away. A frail man in a seersucker suit and bow tie will suggest the new couple whose party he has just attended. The head of the Garden Club will object because they have put a large pool— 'beautiful but inappropriate'—in the middle of the garden. The frail man will adjust his bow tie—how am I doing?"

"By all means, carry on."

"And"—Eliza laughed through her words—"the frail man who has just adjusted his bow tie will remind his fellow board members that the symphony runs on an annual deficit and their goal is to increase the endowment enough to balance the budget each year. He will say with great gravity, 'It may mean inviting a certain type we would not otherwise consider.' From years and years of practicing law, he has learned to compromise. 'Yes, but it was a Loutrel Briggs garden,' the head of the Garden Club will be compelled to add." Eliza pushed off her bed to finish undressing. She removed her earrings and placed them in a box on her dressing table. "The chairwoman will finger her double strand of South Sea pearls and call for more ideas, but no one will be able to come up with anyone else with such financial promise. Feeling the polarization the topic is causing, the chairwoman will suggest postponing the topic until next month. She will shift directions and ask for suggestions on the theme of the Autumn Ball. And even though Mrs. Middleton only lives three blocks away, the chairwoman will be sure to give her a ride home in order to continue discussing the Mortons. She will say things she could not say at the meeting. Mrs. Middleton will agree, and then she will ask the chairwoman if she saw the Poinsett girl with that wild Henry Heyward at the Mortons' party, and she will wonder out loud what Pamela's daughter is doing with him. Again."

Henry stopped unbuttoning his shirt. "And the answer is?"

Eliza leaned against the wall with her hands behind her back. "Because she loves him."

# CHAPTER TWENTY-ONE

H ENRY RETURNED TO NEW ORLEANS SUNDAY NIGHT, AND Eliza returned to her work on Dave. Helen Halsey had been able to secure ten of the twenty-six pots for an exhibit in May, and Eliza was almost ready to start writing her essay. She had come to the conclusion that to find any more information would require a huge amount of time and an even greater amount of luck.

Eliza dropped by 14 Legare to meet with Lawton several times after school to look over his homework and to check on how he was progressing with his memorization of "Casey at the Bat." Each time she stayed behind to have tea with Mrs. Heyward. They mainly chatted about Lawton, but Eliza could tell that Mrs. Heyward was pulling for her and Henry.

The day before the recital, Henry called from New Orleans. "I was hoping to make it back tonight so I could go to Lawton's poetry recital tomorrow, but I can't get away before tomorrow night. Any chance you could go? It's not a big deal. Everyone recites their poem, and the top ten from the class go on to compete in front of the entire school next week."

"I'd love to go, but what about your mother or Issie?" Eliza asked. Henry's absence had made it easier for her to get closer to Lawton. She had enjoyed helping him pick out the poem and memorize it, and it appeared he had felt something of the same.

"Lawton said they could only invite one person. Apparently his teacher wants an audience for them to practice in front of, but they have limited space. If he makes it into the next round, then he can invite everyone—if he wants to—but he's still uncomfortable including Issie in anything that involves other children. He is okay with her walking him home from school, but he insists on meeting her a block from the school on the corner of Queen and Logan."

WHEN ELIZA ARRIVED AT THE LOWER SCHOOL LIBRARY A few minutes before the start, there were only a few seats left—one in the middle of the front row and two in the back. As she slipped to the back, she waved hello to India Logan, Sam's mother. A few minutes later the fourth grade students, arranged alphabetically by name, arrived in single file. Lawton was in the middle, and Sam was right behind him. The thirty-seven students took their places in four rows of folding chairs. Eliza looked at her watch. She wondered if she would have to stay for everyone to finish. She had an appointment at the Gibbes in an hour. Helen had arranged for the pots from the collections of the Charleston Museum and the State Museum to be brought to the Gibbes and made available with the two from their own collection. Helen had also secured the loan of three important pots from private collections. Maybe after Lawton recited his poem she could slip out.

When Lawton's turn came, he stood up, and Eliza could tell he was nervous. She was at the end of the row, and she pulled her seat out a little into the aisle so he could see her. Lawton looked down at the floor and began, "'It looked extremely rocky for the Mudville nine that day. The score stood two to four, with but an inning left to play.'" Lawton's voice was shaky, and he was rushing too much. She wanted to tell him to breathe between lines, but by the second stanza he had settled into the rhythm of the poem and looked up and spoke more slowly. By the sixth stanza he seemed to be enjoying what he was reciting. "'There was ease in Casey's manner as he stepped into his place.'" Lawton took a step forward and mimed being ready to bat, a gesture they had practiced together. His classmates and audience were listening with eager attention for his next lines. "'There was pride in Casey's bearing and a smile on Casey's face; And when responding to the cheers he lightly doffed his hat.'" But as Lawton was miming doffing an imaginary cap, all eyes had turned to the disturbance in the open doorway.

Issie stood and was mouthing the question "Is this the fourth grade?" Lawton's teacher, who was sitting off to the side opposite the doorway, waved her in. Issie wore an outfit similar to the one Eliza had seen her in at Peter Marshall's gallery. Her bracelets jangled as she darted to the empty seat in the middle of the front row. Colorful feathers dangled from each ear.

All that Eliza could hear was the whispering of the children seated behind Lawton. Lawton repeated his last recited line, "And when responding to the cheers he lightly doffed his hat three times." But he could not find a way forward. He was lost. Eliza looked for Lawton's teacher. She did not have a copy of his poem and could not help him with a prompt. After his third try of failing to remember the next line, his teacher finally spoke, "Lawton if you need to take a break, we can go on to the next student, and you can come back later." Lawton shook his head, and he brushed the tears from his face as if swatting mosquitoes. He started to repeat the line a fourth time. Eliza caught his attention as she moved her chair close to the front row. She silently said the next two lines with him. "'No stranger in the crowd could doubt 'twas Casey at the bat. Ten thousand eyes were on him as he rubbed his hands with dirt.'" Together they moved forward. Tears were rolling fast down Lawton's cheeks, but he did not take his eyes off Eliza as he stumbled across the seven remaining stanzas. When he finished, the audience clapped and the tension, that had held the room still, disintegrated into relief. Lawton sat back down in the middle row, and Eliza could see his shoulders moving up and down with uneven breaths. He wiped his face several times with the back of his jacket sleeve.

Issie stayed for Sam to recite his poem and when the next student was shuffling through the row of seats, she darted out of the room. Eliza stayed for the entire recital. She couldn't leave without saying something to Lawton. When it was over, she went up to him and put her hand on his shoulder. "You got rattled, but you did a great job recovering. You picked a hard poem." He shrugged and shook his head. She wanted to put her arms around him, but she knew that would only make things worse. She patted him on his back and smiled at his teacher, who gave her a look of sympathy.

Outside the school, Eliza walked past a small group of mothers who had stopped to chat. She was relieved she did not know any of them. She was almost an hour late for her appointment at the Gibbes. She checked her watch again, as if by looking a second time, she would regain minutes. Lawton had practiced so hard. She hated seeing him so upset, and yet there was nothing more she could do. Eliza wished she could bring him to Henry, but Henry was far away. How did Issie even know about the recital today? Had Henry told her? Eliza doubted that. He wouldn't have asked her to come if he had known that Issie was planning to attend. As she walked north on Archdale, past the Unitarian Church, she checked that she had everything she needed in her satchel. She turned east on Clifford where she had chained her bicycle to the wrought-iron fence of St. John's. And then it became clear how the morning had assembled itself. If Lawton had been practicing his lines on the afternoons that Issie had walked him home from school, she could have learned about the recital. And Lawton may have been vague about the time of the recital so that Issie would be sure to miss it. In fact, it was certainly possible that Lawton had, on purpose, told her the wrong time. Eliza was lining up the numbers on her bicycle lock when she heard her name called. Across the street a woman got out of a dark blue coupe. It was Issie.

"Eliza," Issie called again.

Eliza straightened her back. Issie ran quickly across the street and then slowed down as she came nearer.

"I just wanted to thank you for what you did in there." Issie crossed her arms and gripped her elbows to keep her hands from shaking.

Eliza shook her head. This was not what she expected Issie to say. "I didn't do anything, I wish I could have. He just got rattled. His poem was probably too long."

"No, you got him through, you got him through it. He looked at you. I saw how he looked at you. I didn't mean to come late. He told me the recital was at eleven, so I thought I would come early to find a place in the back. And instead I get there forty-five minutes after it's started." Issie rubbed the inside of her left wrist. Eliza noticed a small tattoo in the shape of a delicate feather.

"It's not a big deal. I wouldn't worry about it." Eliza placed her satchel in her bicycle basket.

"Eliza, please. I'm trying to thank you. I know you hate me but . . ."

"I don't."

"Eliza, you must."

"No. I don't. What happened was between me and Henry." Eliza wrapped her bicycle chain around the seat and closed the lock. She looked back up at Issie. "But I don't think we have anything to say to each other."

Issie took a step forward. "Everyone in that room knows I'm the reason Lawton got upset. It's hard to come back here and feel as if everyone, but especially your own son, doesn't want you around."

"Your relationship with Lawton has nothing to do with me. I have to go, I'm late for a meeting." Eliza wanted no part in any conversation with Issie, especially one about Lawton.

"It has everything to do with you."

"What are you talking about?" Eliza felt as if she had just walked into a brick wall.

"You're making it difficult for me to get close to my son."

"Issie, I just helped Lawton pick out a poem. That's all."

"But he wanted you to come, not me."

"That's not my fault. But you just can't show up after all this time and expect him to act as if he has known you all his life, you can't expect him to open his arms wide for a mother who didn't want him."

"That's not the way it was, that's not fair."

"Sorry. I shouldn't have said that. You're right. It's not fair. But nothing about any of this is fair. Lawton is trying to come to grips with everything—but he's only nine years old. I guess what I am trying to say is you can't force it—the it—whatever the it is—has got to come from him."

Eliza started to get on her bicycle, but she felt off balance. If Issie said anything back to her, she did not hear it. She walked her bicycle down the street, wishing she could run and not stop until she had worn out everything inside of her body. She didn't dare look behind her. It was hard enough to avoid the jagged edges of the past without Issie creating more.

Eliza had known that sooner or later she would come in contact with Issie, and she had practiced the range of possibilities—

from acting as if nothing had happened to acting as if everything had happened. And she always thought she would be somewhere in between the two extremes. She had not realized she was going to say what she did until she heard her words. How could anyone allow themselves to break a child's heart?

When Eliza arrived at the Gibbes, Helen was waiting for her. "Helen, I'm so sorry I'm late."

"Don't worry, I have to run out, but I'll check in when I get back. We've put them—all ten—in the conference room on the second floor. They're magnificent. I think you'll be very pleased. Oh, and we have arranged for a photographer to come at two."

As Eliza climbed the stairs, she realized that Issie was not the person she had conjured up in her mind all those years. The woman who had stood in front of her on the street was no longer the reckless beauty who could take anything she wanted with no regard for the consequences. She was still beautiful, but there was something broken and desperate about her. Was it possible that what had happened between Issie and Henry had damaged Issie more than anyone? Eliza thought back to all of the conversations she and Henry had had where he told her how irrational Issie was being, but maybe it was Issie's own way of fighting back to a place she had once belonged. Here she was, in her early thirties, feeling miserable that her son did not want her around. What had happened—not being wanted by Henry and being sent away by her family—had broken Issie up. Henry had been right when he had said she was fragile. Even so, Issie had thanked her for what she had done for Lawton. But when Eliza had tried to resist getting pulled into an emotional conversation, Issie had lashed out. Eliza had felt Issie's desperation, but she had also felt something else. She didn't know if it were courage or selfishness or some strange combination of the two.

Ten pots were assembled in the boardroom—two from the

Gibbes, three from the Charleston Museum, two from the State Museum, and three from private collectors. The pots had been made to store oils and grains and meats and were thick and sturdy with wide rolled mouths and ear-shaped handles. With the exception of one, they were all over twenty inches tall with wide circumferences and glazes in variations of olive green, oatmeal beige, and brown. Despite or perhaps because of their utilitarian purpose, there was a beauty in their strength and singularity. Eliza sat down in one of the chairs to collect herself. She had seen assembled works of artists many times before, but she had never felt such a need to be quiet. The making of these massive storage pots would have required a substantial physical power, but now these pots were all that was left. She was reminded of an American poet's description of Morandi's late drawings as being, in their "wonder and singularity, lifelines to the unseen." She closed her eyes and ran her hand over the cursive writing incised on the neck of the pots before they were glazed. The edges of the clay had been pushed up and in some cases had not been smoothed down and had the roughness of a scar. This was what was left of a life, she thought. Sturdy pots that had been made for service and yet the maker had also made them beautiful.

Maybe Jamie had been partly right—there was no point in looking for what once was or might have been because you would never be able to find it. It only made sense to look for what was lost if you were prepared to find something unexpected. Maybe that was what she had been trying to say to Issie. She shouldn't come back looking for and expecting to find a son. Any possibility of that had disappeared when she had left nine years ago.

Of the ten assembled pots, only two were dated before 1840, the remaining eight dated from the period that began in 1857. Eliza considered the research she had done. After Captain Stoney had donated the pot to the Charleston Museum, its director had traveled in 1930 to Edgefield to interview its residents about Dave. In one of the transcripts, an elderly former slave remembered Dave. "He used to belong to old man Drake . . . and it was at that time that he had his leg cut off. They say he got drunk and layed on the railroad track." Eliza could find no other reference to Dave having lost his leg.

In another document detailing Harvey Drake's property in 1830, Dave was listed along with another slave, Lydia, and her children. A few years later Harvey Drake died, and his estate was settled. On the sale inventory was listed, "1 Negro Woman Lydia and two children sold to L. Drake for $600.00" and "1 Negro man named Dave to Drake and Gibbs for $400.00." As part of the westward expansion, Lydia's owner moved to Louisiana and took her and her children with them. Dave's owner also moved westward, but Dave remained in Edgefield, where he changed owners several more times. The accounts Eliza read asserted that the reason Dave did not travel westward with his owner was because he was too valuable as a potter in Edgefield. Most scholars assumed Lydia was Dave's wife. Eliza could find no documentation to support these assumptions, but it did provide a romantic and poignant story.

In 1858 Dave wrote, "I wonder where is all my relations, friendship to all and every nation." His next known pot was inscribed, "Making this verse: I had all thoughts, lads and gentleman never out walks." And six months later, "The sun, the moon and—the stars. In the west there are plenty of bears." Eliza looked at these three pots next to one another. The lines did suggest a narrative that was plausible—about Dave's missing family and certainly his thoughts about the West—but unless she uncovered more evidence, it was not robust enough for her to write about. One conflicting piece of newly discovered information could shatter any such fragilely constructed theory.

Eliza moved on to the remaining pots. The next four were massive, too. The lines all related to verses from Acts and Revelations. On the last pot Dave was known to have made, he wrote, "I made this jar all of cross, If you don't repent you will be lost." It was dated 1864 and was smaller than the others, a clue that perhaps he was getting weaker with age. The large pots required skill and a physicality he may no longer have possessed.

Eliza ran her hands over the smooth glazed surfaces of each pot, as if to discover a sense of resilience and offer of consolation. So many people were broken by life—not by what they did, but by what others did to them. And yet they carried on. Dave's sense of humanity had survived in the lines that he had written. Eliza understood why Lawton was acting the way he was. He was protecting himself. He was suspicious that Issie would disappear again. Maybe the right thing for Lawton was for Issie to stay. Was Eliza tempting Fate to even think that? She wanted the world to settle down and be calm for him. She knew what was better for her, but what was better for Lawton?

For the next hour, Eliza carefully examined the pots and made extensive notes on each one. She hadn't given up on Cleve's bowl. The color and texture of its glaze and the shape of its rim were similar enough to the pots to warrant a side-by-side comparison. As she was jotting down a thought to herself about possibly including the last lines of Wallace Stevens's poem "The Planet on the Table"— lines about something bearing some lineament or character of the planet of which they were part—as an epigraph for the monograph on Dave, Helen stuck her head in the conference room. "I'm back. They're amazing, aren't they? I just wanted to check with you how you were getting along. You'll be pleased to know that I saved you from Peter Marshall. He has a pot—I think it's the one that has been for sale for ages in the paper. He was very excited to hear that you were working on a monograph on Dave. He wanted you to come by and authenticate his pot. I think he already has the Mortons lined up for it. The glaze and rim gave it away—it wasn't even close. I'm not even sure it's Edgefield. Oh, and the private collectors of these pieces," she said, referring to the pots assembled in the room, "have agreed to your including photographs of their pots, our lawyer is reviewing the permission forms you will need to send to them."

# CHAPTER TWENTY-TWO

Lawton said it didn't go so well," Henry said when he called her that evening.

"Oh God, Henry, it was painful. In the middle of his poem, Issie rushed in and sat down in the front row, and Lawton got rattled. He couldn't remember his lines. He tried to hold everything together, but he couldn't. He managed to finish his poem, but when he sat down, he was very upset."

"Issie was there? Lawton didn't tell me that. He seemed disappointed he didn't make it into the next round, but he seemed okay. How did Issie even know about it?"

"Issie said Lawton told her, but he told her it started at eleven not ten."

"I doubt that, he said he could only invite one person, and he wanted you to come."

"Maybe she learned about it when she walked him home from school, when he was memorizing his lines. Issie left soon after Lawton finished, and then when I left, she was waiting outside, she wanted to speak to me."

"Outside the school?"

"Yes, on Chisolm Street by St. John's."

"What did she want?"

"She began by thanking me for helping Lawton through his poem. I was sitting in the back row, and when he lost his place, I moved to the front and started silently saying the words with him."

"Is that all she had to say?"

"No, she was upset that Lawton didn't want her around."

"What did you say to that?"

"I told her that it had nothing to do with me, that I only helped him with a poem, and then she became agitated and said it had everything to do with me, that I was the one making it difficult for her to get close to Lawton. It felt like the conversation could explode at any second. I told her I had to go and didn't really give her a chance to say anything else. But then later when I was looking at the Dave pieces, I began thinking she was hoping I would tell her that she should stay. And maybe I should have. She has just lost her father, and even if they didn't have a good relationship, maybe that makes it worse. And she comes back here to see her son who doesn't want to see her, and you don't want to see her, and she has to spend her time going through her grandmother's property in order to sell it. She's pretty alone."

"You shouldn't think that. She's emotionally very erratic, and she does what she wants. She feels things acutely when it comes to herself, but she's reckless with everyone else. The sooner she leaves the better—really. Lawton doesn't need her in his life. She will twist his heart in ways you or I could not imagine. I'm sorry you had to go through that. I guess something like this was bound to happen. My guess is she will calm down, and everything will go back to the way it was. I still think she'll split at some point but probably not for a while."

Eliza wanted to ask Henry if Issie had always had a small feather tattooed on the inside of her left wrist, but she didn't. Instead she asked, "How are things going there?"

"If everything stays on track we should have everything signed by Tuesday, Wednesday at the latest. I don't think anyone wants to go into the Thanksgiving holiday with things unresolved. It would be a disaster for the paper if that were to happen."

Eliza collected her disappointment around her before she spoke. "So I guess that means you can't come home this weekend?"

"No, we're working through the weekend. I can't risk leaving. Hopefully this all will be over Tuesday, and I can come home."

"I forgot to mention my mother called a few days ago to invite us to Middleburg for Thanksgiving. I told her I thought I could come, but I doubted you would be able to make it."

"Actually, no, that would be great, my mother has decided to fly out to Wyoming Saturday to see her brother. Lawton has a full week off from school next week, and we both thought it would be good for him to go. He's invited Sam Logan, so they will have a good time pretending to be ranch hands. I'm all yours."

"But isn't that going to be difficult with Issie?"

"No. She and her cousins are meeting in Boston to discuss their grandmother's estate. So to Middleburg—are we driving or flying?"

"I was thinking driving but—"

"A road trip. That'll be good, I don't think we've ever gone on a road trip together. By the way, Eliza, your mother isn't going to give us separate bedrooms?"

"She might."

# CHAPTER TWENTY-THREE

Aᴿᴇ ʏᴏᴜ ᴘʟᴇᴀsᴇᴅ?" Eʟɪᴢᴀ ᴀsᴋᴇᴅ ᴡʜᴇɴ Hᴇɴʀʏ ᴄᴀʟʟᴇᴅ Tuesday afternoon and said that they had signed the agreement.

"Mainly just relieved it's over. The terms were not what we wanted, but we can live with them, and I think we pushed them as far as we could. We just couldn't delay any longer. Anyway, it's over, now everyone can get back to work. I'm heading to the airport, hoping to get the four thirty flight. If I miss it, then there is one at five fifty, but it doesn't get in until after eleven."

"Do you have the key I gave you?"

"I'm pretty sure I left it in my Jeep at the airport. I'll call you if it's not there."

"Eʟɪᴢᴀ." Hᴇɴʀʏ ɢᴇɴᴛʟʏ sʜᴏᴏᴋ ʜᴇʀ sʜᴏᴜʟᴅᴇʀ. Hᴇ ᴛᴏᴏᴋ her book, *Summer and Smoke,* and marked her place and put it on the table. He leaned down. "Eliza."

She shook her head. "You're back," she said and put her arms around his neck. "What time is it?"

"Quarter to twelve."

"Was your flight late?"

"A little." Henry's voice was quiet. He sat down on the sofa next to her. He reached down and picked up a map from the floor. "So I guess we really are driving to Middleburg tomorrow. Does your mother care what time we arrive?"

"Umm, if possible," Eliza said, still a little disoriented by sleep, "she would like us to get there by dinner."

"It's about a nine-hour drive, isn't it?"

"It is, if we take 95," Eliza said, "but we could swing west through the Blue Ridge Mountains. It would be a nicer drive, but it would add at least an hour."

"Let's see," Henry traced the routes with his index finger.

Eliza ran her fingertips lightly over the top of his hand down to the end of his fingers. "When I was working at the Jasper Marlowe Gallery in London, a young Italian artist came in with his slides. He had painted hands on such a large scale that they looked like landscapes. He said he had been inspired by Benoit Mandelbrot's theory of fractal geometry. I thought his paintings were beautiful, but Jasper wasn't sure he could sell them. I wonder what happened to him." Eliza turned Henry's hand over and traced the creases in his palm and the creases across each finger. "Have you ever had your palm read?"

Henry shook his head. "Have you?"

"No, never."

"So let's change that. Here, give me your hand. This may be the one thing you don't know about me—I'm very good at palm readings. Here, let's see. Interesting. You have an interesting journey."

"Henry, come on, you're making fun of me." She tried to pull her hand back, but he held on and pulled her closer.

"I'm not. I'm really not. Look you have a line here that forks into a V. So you could have gone this way—more to the east, that was London—but instead the stronger line is the one that points south."

"Henry, that's north."

"Not if you turn this way." He lifted her up and shifted positions with her and took her hand again. "And you are going to fall in love with a man named Henry Heyward—see, you can almost make out a double H here. He is going to be so charming that you're not going to be able to resist him, you will try—but you will fail—see how this line stops—that signifies the end of your resistance."

"Okay, okay"—she laughed and pulled her hand away—"you're only describing what has already occurred. I see you're not going to take me seriously."

"Eliza, I am." He held her face in his hands. "Look at me. I could not be more serious."

ON THE MORNING OF THE DAY BEFORE THANKSGIVING, THE air was fresh and cool, and the sky was a hard blue.

Henry reached over to the bedside table and checked his watch. "Twenty to ten, we probably should get up."

"Five more minutes," Eliza said and pulled the covers back over her shoulders.

"Okay, but I'm off to the shower."

Henry returned and sat down on the bed next to her. "Ten to ten. If we want to have any hope of making Middleburg in time for dinner"—he ran his hand down her back and smoothed away the drops of water that had dripped from his hair—"you need to get up."

"You smell like lavender."

"That's because I used your soap." Henry leaned over to put on socks.

Eliza turned toward Henry and observed what he was doing. "Socks? New look?"

"No, backup plan."

"Backup plan? For what?"

"Stealth tactics." He waved a sock in the air. "In case your mother gives us separate bedrooms."

Henry stood up to finish dressing, but then steadied himself on the chest next to the bed. He braced himself with his two arms and stepped away to put his head down. "God, I feel really dizzy."

"Are you okay?"

"I don't know."

Eliza helped him to the edge of the bed.

"I can't breathe."

"What can I do?"

"Call Charlie. Get him over here."


CHARLIE INSTRUCTED ELIZA TO GIVE HENRY HALF AN ASPI-rin and have him lie down. "I'll be right over." When Charlie arrived, he called an ambulance and told Henry to stay lying down, not to get up. Eliza drove with Charlie to the hospital. He explained that it was hard to know what the problem was until tests were done.

Charlie and Eliza found Henry in a curtained-off area of the emergency room. Painkillers and sedatives were being administered through an IV. A nurse was taping multiple ends of EKG wires to his chest and back. Eliza could tell that Henry was still in a lot of pain.

A few hours later Charlie and the cardiovascular surgeon, Dr. Allison, arrived to speak to Henry. They had reviewed all of the tests. Dr. Allison did his best to explain to Eliza the rare heart condition Henry had inherited from his father. Certain muscles in

Henry's heart had thickened and made it hard for his heart to pump effectively.

"It's a rare form of hypertrophic cardiomyopathy that does not always respond to medication. Henry, you need to undergo a septal myectomy." Dr. Allison then proceeded to explain the complex procedure.

"Do I have any other options?" Henry asked.

Doctor Allison lowered his glasses. "I really don't think so, Henry."

Henry looked at Charlie, who confirmed Dr. Allison's judgment. "Dr. Allison is right, Henry."

"Do you have any more questions?" Dr. Allison asked.

"No, I don't think so."

"Okay, then, we'll get things going as fast as we can." Dr. Allison left the room.

"You sure this is the only way?" Henry asked Charlie.

"Yes, Henry, the drug you've been taking hasn't worked like we had hoped. I'll be there the whole time," Charlie said. "I need to go change." He gave Henry a pat on the shoulder. "See you in a bit."

Eliza sat sidesaddle on the bed. "How are you feeling?"

"Not great," he said.

Eliza tried not to watch the waves of lines across the screen.

Henry winced and looked up at the ceiling.

"Are you in pain?" she asked.

"A bit," he said, but she knew he wasn't telling the truth. "Just hurts to talk. You talk, I like to hear your voice."

"Okay," she said and squeezed his hand. "I remember the first time I met you. We were all down at Fenwick Hall for a summer party, and everyone had gone to where Stender Bennett and a few others where shooting skeet in one of the back fields. Stender had somehow acquired the revolving base of a Kentucky Fried Chicken sign, which he had mounted on a two-wheel trailer, and he had rigged up a skeet machine so that clay pigeons were slung over a three-hundred-and-sixty-degree radius. Weezie and I walked down to the dock to get away from what seemed like a very dangerous activity. You and Charlie were going off in a canoe to repair a dike. Do you remember that?"

"I do."

Eliza had watched Henry get out of the canoe and walk across the top of the dike, arms out to the side, balancing one foot at a time on the top of the narrow boards that had been slotted between four square end posts placed eight feet across. And Eliza remembered being scared for him, she didn't know what would have happened to him if the top board had wobbled and his foot had slipped and he had lost his balance and had fallen into the hole where all the water was rushing. She watched him walk across the top of the planks and then jump down on the opposite side and begin working with a board that had gotten jammed.

Eliza didn't tell him how afraid she had been for him. "I remember thinking it was pretty great that you knew how to fix a dike. None of the other boys from Charleston knew how to do that."

"Summers with Cleve." Henry clenched his jaw and squeezed his eyes shut.

"Can I do anything?"

He shook his head. "It helps," he said, "your talking."

"I also remember the first time you asked me out, a week later. You came to Weezie's and my rescue on a rainy summer afternoon. It was high tide, and the low places on Lockwood Boulevard were underwater. Weezie and I were in Billy's yellow Volkswagen Beetle, and when we went around the curve, the car stalled and wouldn't start again. We were trying to get it started when you stopped to help us."

"I recognized Billy's yellow Beetle."

"And you gave us a ride home. You dropped Weezie off first.

You said you'd come in from the country to go to a coming-out party that night—I can't remember whose—and I said I was going, too, and when you dropped me off, you suggested I ditch my date and come with you."

"I remember that," Henry spoke in short breaths.

"But I wouldn't do it because it wasn't the proper thing to do. But then at the party you took being proper to an extreme and barely talked to me."

Henry closed his eyes and shook his head. "I wasn't being proper."

"You weren't?"

"I was playing hard to get."

"You were?"

Henry nodded his head. "As I remember, it worked pretty well." He clenched his jaw.

As Eliza spoke, she noticed her distorted reflection in the silver convex railing of the bed. She found it hard to keep her thoughts going forward. It was as if something had shattered, and words and images were spilling everywhere. She was unable to comprehend anything except that Henry was in the hospital, and he did not seem okay.

Eliza could find nothing more to say, and they sat for a few minutes listening to the hospital sounds in the hallway—a food trolley rattling past, a visitor asking a nurse for directions, a doctor giving a resident instructions as they walked briskly down the hall.

The drugs administered through the IV had begun to take the edge off Henry's pain and make him groggy. "So tell me, Eliza, have you always been in love with me?"

"Perhaps."

"Oh no." Henry tried to raise up on his elbows.

She touched his shoulder. "Lie back down and rest."

"You are missing your lines again, and there's that word again.

You were supposed to say, 'Yes, of course, I have always loved you.' When I get out of here, we really need to practice your responses to my perfect setups."

A nurse entered and said that Dr. Allison was ready for Henry. She began to move things out of the way to roll the bed forward.

"Eliza, come to think of it, you never told me what you wanted to steal from Anne's house." The nurse's eyes widened. Henry winked.

"We were interrupted, weren't we?" Eliza played along.

"Louisa arrived with Charles Stevens before you could answer me."

"Yeah," she stretched the word out into two long syllables.

"So?"

"Umm."

"Eliza, there you go, missing your cue again. The correct answer is Henry. And come to think of it, you never gave me the present you said you had for me in your duffel bag. The one I almost destroyed my shoulder with."

Eliza was tempted to tell him about the copy of her notes on the Magritte that she had bound for him, the one in which she had written his name in the margins whenever her adviser had left the room. At the time, she hadn't even been aware of what she was doing. But she didn't. "I'll bring it to you tomorrow."

"Eliza, Charlie's going to be with me the whole time."

"I know," she said.

The nurse left to find an orderly to help her move the bed.

"You know, Eliza, I've been thinking that a winter wedding might suit you. It would be so unsouthern, say—mid-January but no later than February. Does that appeal to you?"

The nurse barreled in with a large heavy-set man in green scrubs following behind her. "Okay, we're ready," she said in an overly cheerful tone. She asked Eliza to step away from the bed.

The orderly pulled up the side railings until they clicked in place.

"There's no way I can kneel at the present moment."

Eliza leaned down and kissed Henry. "I'll be waiting right here for you."


ELIZA WATCHED THE DARKNESS COME. SHE WAS COLD IN the hospital room and couldn't find a comfortable way to sit in the chair. She would not let herself think too long about what Henry had said. When his words came close to her, she felt that if she listened too much to them, they would disappear, and she feared they would never come back. Eliza remembered being in the chapel at Simon and Caroline's wedding and hearing that soft laugh—like the slowed-down sputter of a lawn mower and, without thinking, looking back over her shoulder for Henry. At some point in the night a nurse came in and told her that the surgery was going longer than expected but that Dr. Allison would come and speak with her when it was over. The nurse returned with a blanket. As Eliza waited through the night and early morning, she missed hearing the bells of St. Michael's strike the hours. On her fingers she counted all of the churches on the Charleston peninsula south of Calhoun. Fifteen. She traveled each street to double-check herself—on Meeting Street—First Scots Presbyterian, St. Michael's, the Circular Congregation; on Church Street—First Baptist, the French Huguenot, St. Philip's; on Archdale—St. Luke's Lutheran and St. John's Unitarian; on Hasell—St. Johannes Lutheran and St. Mary's Roman Catholic Church; on Broad—the Cathedral of St. John the Baptist; on Anson—St. Stephen's Episcopal; on Wentworth—Grace Episcopal Church and the Redeemer Presbyterian; and on Pitt—the Bethel United Methodist. Eliza roamed the streets again to make certain she had not left any out. She wondered how the Master of the Moon was doing. When Henry was better she wanted to go and try to find him. The evenings were cold now, and she wanted to make certain he had a warm place to sleep. She thought about Charlie's two little boys chasing fireflies and the simple joy they got from trying to capture beautiful things. She tried to think of things that didn't make her sad, but over the course of those long hours she felt a slow gravity pull her down away from everything.

The morning was well on its way when Dr. Allison appeared. Charlie stood two feet behind him. Something had shifted. Eliza remembered only two things. She remembered the space between the moment she saw Dr. Allison and knew what he was going to say to her and the moment he actually did say it. The space was solid, a large invisible block that stopped everything in the room. And she remembered his shoes. He wore white rubber clogs.

# CHAPTER TWENTY-FOUR

Eliza felt that if she concentrated hard enough she would be able to discover where Henry was. She believed she could find him again. He would be in his beaten-up Jeep coasting along, arm hooked outside the window, sleeves rolled up, tanned face, blue eyes, calling her name, and she would be with him again.

Eliza drove down to Folly Beach. She felt as if she were looking for something she had lost, something she had misplaced, that if she kept looking she would find it again. She felt certain she could find Henry. She knew where to look. If she just opened one more door, turned one more corner, he would be there. She walked to the water's edge and watched the curved shadows of worn-out waves. He was somewhere out there in a boat, mainsail line in one hand, rudder in the other, and jib line held between his teeth, and he would be tipping his boat on its side to go as fast as he could.

Eliza went to the back of the island. She was certain she would find him fishing in the salt marshes. She was certain as she turned the corner she would see him standing waist deep in the water and casting across the marshes. She would call to him. As she ran down the narrow, uneven path through the scrub pines and brambles, she became more convinced the closer she got.

His battered tennis shoes, stiffened by the salt, were in the same place he had kicked them off. She knew if she looked underneath them she might find a trace of Henry, some clue that he was still somewhere. They felt heavy in her hands. But she could find nothing. She went inside and found herself moving a blue and white plate that had been left on the kitchen table.

She drove down to Oakhurst. She parked outside the locked gates and walked around the brick piers through the woods. She walked down the oak allée to the house. She knew she would hear his camera click, and she would hear him call to her, and she would turn and see him emerging from the woods. He would wave, and everything would be just as they had left them.

The sun cast stretched-out shadows of the live oak trees across the lawn and burned the expanse of rice fields across the river. She walked down to the edge of the Edisto and watched the tide take the river away. She would hear Henry telling her about the river, about the tides, and the fish, and the nest of baby egrets he had just discovered.

A GREAT BLUE HERON HUNTING MINNOWS IN THE MARSH launched itself in the air with a slow graceful lift of wings and arced low and then high across the river.

ELIZA COULD ALMOST SEE HIM AT TIMES, SEE HIS SMILE, hear his laugh, feel his touch, almost, almost. . . . She had always believed that somehow she would know where he was. But now all she felt was the space that he had once taken up, as if the air that had been pushed back and shaped around him—still remained. That was all she felt. But with time that would disappear, too. For someone who had been so alive, to be so completely gone, to vanish, and to leave no trace of where he had gone.

SHE WOULD NEVER SEE HIM AGAIN. SHE WOULD NEVER HEAR him tell her she was missing her lines. She would never be able to give him the manuscript with his name written in the margins. There was no chance of her ever catching a glimpse of him or running into him or hearing the slowed-down sputter of his laugh or feeling his hand on her wrist. Never.

# CHAPTER TWENTY-FIVE

O N THE MORNING OF THE DAY AFTER HENRY'S FUNERAL, a gray geometric tanker appeared on the horizon and throbbed a steady beat. An orange sun rose above Castle Pinckney and disappeared behind gray clouds. Joe Childs walked down three flights of stairs at the Sergeant Jasper and waited on the corner of Broad and Ashley for the bus to take him to work. At the Confederate Home, Kit Vanderhorst moved a potted tea olive out of the direct sunlight and sat back in her chair to wait for the day to pass.

In the late afternoon, Eliza went to see Mrs. Heyward. She embraced Eliza and asked her to sit next to her on the sofa. She held Eliza's hand. "I just think of him at Oakhurst. He was always disappearing down there. He loved it down there. So I just tell myself that he is at Oakhurst." As she spoke, Mrs. Heyward looked at the ceiling to keep the tears from spilling. "I'm just so grateful that he had you. He always adored you, you know." She took a deep breath before she continued. "The Heyward men have not been blessed with strong hearts. No one ever thought that it would affect him now, but Henry did have to take drugs every day. It's too early to know yet, but Lawton may have to be careful, too."

"How is he?" Eliza asked.

"He is very, very sad. I know you know." Mrs. Heyward squeezed Eliza's hand. "You were not much older than Lawton when you lost your father. But Lawton has a lot of love and support in Charleston, and, of course, he will always have me. You may not know this, but he is very fond of you. He often tells me about conversations the two of you have had. You have always understood him."

Rascal trotted into the room and looked up at Eliza and waited for her to pet him before lying down at Mrs. Heyward's feet.

"He's a very sweet little boy. I remember how proud he was to tell me about the baby screech owl he and Henry rescued."

Mrs. Heyward smiled and blinked hard. There was nowhere left to go with words.

Rascal got up and began growling at the fireplace.

"Rascal." Mrs. Heyward clapped her hands softly. Her tone was more of a plea than a command. "I think there must be a nest of baby birds in the chimney, but it is the wrong time of year. But I do think that is what he's hearing."

Mrs. Heyward turned back to Eliza and shook her head, "And that Issie. She left right after Henry's funeral. I knew she wouldn't stay long. I didn't see her at St. Michael's. She left me a note and said she had to go back to Boston to take care of some things and would let me know when she would be coming back. But I don't expect to hear from her anytime soon."

"She left?" Eliza asked. "Did she say good-bye to Lawton?"

Mrs. Heyward shook her head. "She is just a child, that girl . . ."

"Where is Lawton?"

"He's in the carriage house. He's been there since the funeral.

I can't get him to leave. He fell asleep there last night, and I had to get Isaiah to carry him to his bedroom upstairs, but it's too much for Isaiah. I can't ask him again." She looked out the window. "And this rain, I just feel if he could get outside, he would feel so much better. It's stopped now, but they say it's going to start again tonight and last all week."

"Can I go see him?"

ELIZA LISTENED TO THE SOUND OF HER FEET ON THE OYSTER shells. She remembered that first night when she had come back from London and stayed with Henry. Everything had been dark, and the sound of their footsteps on the crushed brittle shells had seemed so loud and so familiar and yet so foreign, as if they were crossing into a world they had just discovered. Eliza opened the door to the carriage house and called up to Lawton. She looked out to the garden before she climbed the stairs.

"Lawton? Lawton?" she called again, but she also knew that saying his name made her feel safe as she crossed through Henry's bedroom. She did not allow herself to look anywhere but straight ahead.

Lawton was crumpled on the floor of his bedroom with a shoe box of black and gray and white Lego pieces beside him. "Oh, Lawton," she said, "there you are." He cradled a half-built ship in his hands. He didn't look up.

Eliza pulled up a low stool from the corner of the room and sat down next to him. "Can I see that?" He didn't respond. "Lawton, I know your heart is breaking. And I know it doesn't feel as if you will ever be able to put it back together." Lawton didn't look at her but instead kept staring at his pieces of Lego. He rocked his foot back and forth, as if warding off grief.

Eliza leaned forward and put her hand on his shoulder. "I know something of what you are feeling. When I was about your age, I lost my father, too."

Lawton stopped rotating his foot from side to side and continued staring at his half-made ship.

"My father was driving back home late one night from Augusta, Georgia. He was driving down Ashley River Road, and his car crashed into one of those large live oaks that line the road, and he was killed. And no one could tell us—my mother and me—why. He could have fallen asleep, or a deer could have run across the road, and he swerved to avoid hitting it. We will never know, but what we do know is that he was on the last mile of Ashley River Road before it intersects with Bees Ferry. Just one more mile and he would have been safe. And I remember someone coming to tell my mother, and I remember thinking, no they have it all wrong, he will be home soon, and when I came to understand that my father would never come home again, I felt as if someone had pushed me in a tight box that I couldn't escape from, and I felt as if I were suffocating. I hated everything around me. And then one day Anne de Liesseline came to see me—she and my father had been great childhood friends, and she took my hands, just like this." Eliza leaned forward and took Lawton's hands in hers. "Anne turned my hand over and said, 'Look at that.' I didn't know what she was talking about, and she said, 'Look, you have your father's hands.' I looked at my hands, and I saw that she was right. And she told me to go look in the mirror, and she said, 'You have your father's cornflower blue eyes, and you might not be able to see it right now, but you also have your father's smile. When you look in the mirror, you'll always see him. And when you're by yourself, you'll always be with him because he's so much a part of you.' And, Lawton, it's the same with you, but even more so. Doesn't everyone always say you look just like your father?"

Lawton shrugged his shoulders.

"I want to show you something, I'll be right back." Eliza stood up to get the photograph of Lawton playing with a toy car from the chest of drawers next to Henry's bed. She kept her eyes on the floor in an attempt to dodge the emptiness of Henry's room.

Eliza sat back down next to Lawton. "See this photograph of you playing with a car? I want to show you something."

She turned the frame over and opened the back. Lawton pushed up off the floor and stood next to Eliza to watch what she was doing. She lifted another photograph from behind the plate. It was another image of a small boy playing with a toy car on a table. She handed Lawton the photograph.

"Do you know who that is?"

"Me?"

"No, it's your father. Turn it over." They read in silence, "Henry, age two, April 1961." Eliza put her arm around Lawton. "Not only do you look just like him, but you have his laugh. Before I met you, I thought your father was the only one in the world who sounded like a lawn mower slowing down until I heard you laugh. You know, Lawton, when I am with you, I feel as if Henry is right here. I can hear him telling you to jump for the sun."

Sobs like indifferent waves knocked Lawton into her arms, and she comforted him—afraid that if she let go he would drift beyond reach. Wilted with grief and exhaustion, he finally gave up his anger and his fear and collapsed into her arms.

"Would you like it if I stayed here with you tonight?" She smoothed his bangs away from his eyes. "Do you want me to ask your grandmother if it's okay?"

AND AS ELIZA WATCHED OVER LAWTON ALL NIGHT IN THE armchair by his bed, she listened to the sound of the gentle rain on the clay tiled roof of the carriage house. And that night, as she wrapped herself in the sound of the rain and in the sound of Lawton's slow and steady breathing, she knew that she would stay until Lawton no longer needed her. And through the hours of that early morning, she tried to unravel all that had happened until finally she understood that reasons and road maps could not be found. And she understood, too, that Charleston had not finished with her, and she knew that it might never be.

For Eliza's discussion of Henrietta Johnston, I have relied primarily on Margaret Simon Middleton's biography, *Henrietta Johnston of Charles Town, South Carolina: America's First Pastellist* (University of South Carolina Press, 1966), as well as the 1991 exhibition catalogue *Henrietta Johnston: who greatly helped . . . by drawing pictures* (Museum of Decorative Arts, 1991).

For information on the slave potter Dave and on the tradition of Southern stoneware, I have drawn on *I Made This Jar: The Life and Works of the Enslaved African-American Potter, Dave,* edited by Jill Beute Koverman (University of South Carolina Press, 1998); *Crossroads of Clay: The Southern Alkaline-Glazed Stoneware Tradition,* edited by Catherine Wilson (McKissick Museum, 1990); and *Great & Noble Jar: Traditional Stoneware of South Carolina* by Cinda K. Baldwin (University of Georgia Press, 1993).

For Eliza's discussion of Dave, I have relied primarily on Jill Beute Koverman's essay "Searching for Messages in Clay: What Do We Really Know About the Poetic Potter, Dave?" in *I Made This Jar.* The passage quoted on page 245 is sourced by Koverman from the *Edgefield Advertiser,* April 1, 1863, volume XXVIII, no. 13., p. 2; the passage quoted on page 261 is sourced by Koverman from the Charleston Museum Archives, "Notes made on trip to Seigler's Pottery, near Eureka, S. C. October 4, 1930"; and the passage quoted on pages 277–8 is sourced by Koverman from the South Carolina Department of Archives and History, Columbia, SC, Edgefield County Probate Records, Estate of Harvey Drake, Box 9, Package 304, microfilm roll #ED8.

The couplets attributed to Dave are taken from Koverman's list of all known (at the time of publication) verses composed by Dave and inscribed on his pots, in her essay "Dave's Verse as Social Response," in *I Made This Jar.*

The passage quoted on pages 172–3 is taken from Joseph Brodsky's collection of essays, *On Grief and Reason* (Farrar, Straus & Giroux, 1997).